RAFAEL JEROME

A NOVEL
by

Tobias Maxwell

REVIEW COPY

Rafael Jerome

Copyright © 2023 Tobias Maxwell. All rights reserved. No part of this book may be reproduced or retransmitted in any form or by any means without the written permission of the publisher.

Published by Wheatmark®
2030 East Speedway Boulevard, Suite 106
Tucson, Arizona 85719 USA
www.wheatmark.com

ISBN: 979-8-88747-007-8
LCCN: 2022914913

Bulk ordering discounts are available through Wheatmark, Inc. For more information, email orders@wheatmark.com or call 1-888-934-0888.

Direct author inquiries to:
TOBIAS.MAXWELL.AUTHOR@GMAIL.COM

Cover Illustration by Johnny Wales, website:
www.johnny-wales.com

Cover design by Rebecca Quinn

This is a work of fiction. Names, characters, places and incidents are either the product of the author's imagination or are used fictitiously, and any resemblance to actual persons, living or dead, business establishments, events or locales is entirely coincidental.

ALSO BY TOBIAS MAXWELL

NOVELS
Thomas
The Sex and Dope Show Saga
And Baby Makes Two
The Month after September
2165 Hillside

MEMOIRS
1973: Early Applause
1977: The Year of Leaving Monsieur
Naked Ink: Diary of a Smalltown Boy, vols. 1 & 2
1983: The Unknown Season

POETRY
Homogium

*For Betty Garrett, ever gracious.
And for David Mallon,
who introduced us.*

CONTENTS

PART I
Paris, Summer 1997
1

PART II
Ottawa, Winter 1997
153

PART III
Calgary, Summer 1998
187

PART IV
Santa Barbara, Winter 1998
271

But the purest refrain will haunt us again
And he has that with me
When we've nothing to bring
I sing for the man in the wings.
>   —*Alison Moyet/Pete Glenister,*
>   *"The Man in the Wings"*

PART I

PARIS, SUMMER 1997

ONE

The seventh arrondissement felt quite safe as Jeremy's taxi dropped him off at his hotel shortly after midnight. Neither the deserted street nor the unseasonable fog could detract from the quaintness, though he was reminded quickly enough as to why the accommodations had been so cheap upon settling into his room. A glance at the carpet showed it had seen better days—just shy of mildew from the aroma. The toilet and shower inside a closet made you tuck in your elbows for fear of scraping skin. The sink next to the tiny table desk beside the window looked forlorn as if to say, "Why here?" Even in the dark of night, Jeremy could see the outlines of interior balconies and alcoves from neighboring buildings. The behind-the-curtain Paris that was rarely shown on modern postcards. When the noise of copulating neighbors commenced, right next to where his head lay—both at night and once again in the morning—it signaled much more than paper-thin walls. It had the implicit, painful hallmark that he was all alone in the city of love. Had this been a mistake?

After his late-night arrival, Jeremy was primed to take in all the sights he could that first day. He was eating a stale granola bar, seated on his single bed, the feel of a broken bedspring against his butt, when he was startled by the sight of a naked man walking along an outside parapet not twenty feet away from him. The swarthy, raven-haired man reached for a towel laid against a railing. Jeremy watched as the stranger dried himself, smiled back at his admirer when his peripheral instincts told him he had a peeping tom. Jeremy looked away, not wanting to be *that* man.

On the street, the smell and sounds of Paris were intoxicating. After the bland no-man's-land of Los Angeles, the Haussmann architecture and the patisseries were inviting. He stopped at a second bakery on the same block, unable to control the urge to stuff himself.

"Bonjour." The attendant was dressed in black slacks, a crisp white shirt, and a red-wine apron.

Flawless, Jeremy thought, as were the confections. He pointed to a pastry, then another and a third.

"Autre chose?"

"Non, c'est tout." Jeremy's French was fine for Canada, but his vocabulary would surely be challenged on this trip. He presented her with the francs he hoped were enough, took his change, and walked outside. The street was narrow, but cars zipped along at what he thought were ridiculous speeds. The mille-feuille tasted of creamy custard and butter with just the right amount of sweetness from the glazed topping. The gooey layers made a terrible mess, and the solitary, thin napkin he had been given was scant relief. He licked his fingers and finally gave in to an old Kleenex from his jeans pocket to finish the task of tidying up. With his two other sweets tucked away in a plastic lunch bag in his backpack, he headed to Notre Dame.

He was not a religious man, but as he crossed the Pont Saint-Michel onto the Île de la Cité, the spires of the cathedral in the distance resonated with his love of history; this sense of majesty with the weight of centuries called out. The horde of tourists milling about, though, congregated in groupings, was less compelling. His hope of going in and walking around without too much fuss seemed dashed. He hated standing in queues for almost anything, but he especially drew the line at religious buildings. It took away from the sacredness, he thought, and Disneyfied the prospect of finding solace in the absence of any faith.

At kilometer zero, standing in Parvis Notre-Dame, the lines of gawkers across the way was discouraging. "Damn it." He was on the verge of leaving and choosing another site—a museum perhaps—when he saw a gentleman smiling at him. The man, in his sixties, judging from the gray of his hair and the textured lines to his skin, had an amused look. Jeremy returned the smile, unsure if he was being picked up.

"Not lost, are you?"

"Me? Lost? No. I'm exactly where I wanted to be. Give or take."

"Give or take? Okay. I'll bite. Why the 'damn it?'"

Only an American would be this forward. "I hate lines."

"And …"

"And," Jeremy said, pointing in the direction of the cathedral. "I was hoping to go inside without having to wait for all of … them ahead of me."

"Is that all?" The gentleman walked over. "I'm Gary."

"Jeremy. Hi." The handshake lasted longer than Jeremy would have preferred. Definitely a pickup vibe, if he had to guess.

"Your first time?"

"Here? Or Paris in general?"

"Both …?"

"Don't know why I made that distinction." Jeremy hated admitting his maiden status. "Yeah. My first time for both." He had always imagined him and Justin coming here for an anniversary or a birthday. A celebration of their years together. They had certainly talked about it on more than one occasion. Now, Jeremy was doing the trip solo at the ripe old age of forty-two. Even the year, 1997, reeked of nothingness. Everything about this trip had been an afterthought. When his plans to travel back to Canada for a visit were cancelled, he had contemplated going to London.

"You've been to the UK already. Twice. Go somewhere else," David, his work colleague, had advised him.

"Yeah, you're right."

"Do Paris. It's not bad in July. Except for the crowds."

"I don't want to go there on my own."

"Why not?" responded David, a math teacher at his high school who was very straight, nonsexual—if his self-reporting over the years was accurate.

"No, David. Paris is for lovers. It's …"

"Maybe you'll find a lover there. It could happen."

That was on Jeremy's mind as soon as Gary let go of his palm. He didn't think of himself as ageist, but his time with Justin, eight years his junior, had predisposed him to a particular mindset. He reproached his bias as soon as he realized how he was judging Gary.

"All those lines are for tours," said Gary. "We can go in. Wanna follow me?"

Gary put his camera back into the case he carried around his neck and they set off like a follow-the-leader had been declared. They entered from the side closest to the Seine and proceeded down the middle of the structure. "Have you ever been to the Vatican?"

"Yeah. Years ago. Why?" Jeremy asked.

"Well. There's no real opulence here. This really is the people's cathedral."

"Is that from Hugo?"

Gary laughed. "No. From me. A lapsed Jew from California."

"Where in California?"

"Santa Barbara. Why?"

"I'm from LA."

"A native?"

"No. No. Long story." They continued down the nave towards the altar at the far end under the magnificent painted apse, whose circular dome appeared to float up there in the morning light. The men leaned back to take in the full visual effect.

Gary removed his camera from its case and pocketed the lens cover. He got down on one knee then stood up and balanced against the wooden pew to steady his aim. He snapped a few shots.

"Enough light?" Jeremy asked. "You didn't use a flash."

"No. I'm using a 400 ISO film." Gary could see the man was unfamiliar with the term. "It's made for this sort of lighting. I knew I'd be doing indoor shooting today." With that, he moved away to catch other angles of the stained-glass windows. Jeremy followed in silence. He watched as Gary angled and contorted, going up and down, leaning in and out, to take shot after shot.

"Are you a professional photographer?"

"Do I give off that vibe?"

"Kind of. Yeah."

Gary smiled, pleased by the observation. "No. I'm not. But I like to shoot a lot of film. Can I take your photo?"

Gary's phrasing of the ask reminded Jeremy again of their handshake. Was this a planned tactic all along? Did Gary pick up guys this way? "Here?" Jeremy asked, thinking the location an unlikely one for a decent photograph.

Gary arranged him slightly. He took Jeremy by the shoulder and gently changed his position so that the light favored the left side of his face. "Just like that. Don't move."

Jeremy did as he was told. As the shutter opened and closed, the sun outside anchored into the rose-tinted window, highlighting the interior of the church like angels were on call. "One more. Just. Like. That." Gary clicked a couple of times, the whir of the camera the only thing between them that seemed to breathe.

Jeremy was aware of being observed. Fully. Carefully. Imagined how he must have looked from the viewfinder. Self-conscious. Put upon not so much by Gary as by the moment, the light, the intricacies between a stranger, a camera, and standing on terra firma in a foreign country. He thought of his pastries. "I'm hungry. Can we go outside? I have goodies in my backpack."

They crossed over to benches by a strip of grass overlooking the Seine. The sun was full on and the July heat had begun to bring on humidity, where before they had entered the cathedral less than an hour prior, the July morning had still been welcoming and fresh. Jeremy showed him his selections. "Which would you like?" Gary chose the chocolate croissant and Jeremy settled for the marzipan confectionery. They ate in silence. "So, are you here alone too?"

Gary's mouth was full. He swallowed from his water bottle and nodded. "I'm okay with that." The man studied the why that was on Jeremy's face. "You?"

Jeremy couldn't ascertain if Gary meant it or not. Was that all part of disarming him gradually? Make him vulnerable to his sway? "I *should* be okay with that. But apparently I'm not."

"A broken heart?" Gary asked.

"Oh yeah. You might say that."

"Recent?"

"Not recent enough to be healthy." He sighed, audible enough to be pathetic. "It's Paris. I always thought …"

"You and a billion others!" Gary punched him amiably on the upper arm. "You, dear friend. Need a compadre. To make Paris more palatable."

"I do?"

"No strings attached—I might add."

Jeremy wondered if he was that obvious in his lack of interest in the man. He felt guilty suddenly, at a loss for words to backtrack. "How well do you know Paris?" he said, as though querying a tour guide to haggle on pricing.

"Like the back of my hand. I came here as a child. My mother loved this city. We had an apartment in the seventh arrondissement. That was before Dad left us. Before all the money ran out."

The emphasis on wealth, dramatizing the fixture of it, made Gary's story fascinating to Jeremy. "My hotel is in the seventh. But it doesn't sound like the type of apartment you had."

"Grungy, is it?"

"I haven't been bitten by bugs … yet. But there's always tomorrow."

"Ugh!" Gary stood up. He gave Jeremy his elbow. "Where would you like to go next?"

"Umm … Let's see." Jeremy had a slew of options on his to-see list. The idea of being escorted about town, like Dorothy along the Yellow Brick Road, changed the feel of Paris and the City of Light turned on exponentially. "Surprise me," he said. "I want to see everything the city has to offer."

TWO

The next morning's shower proved as tricky as it looked. The hot water was tepid, the soap bar rather filmy.

"You get what you pay for," Gary had said when he dropped Jeremy off at the hotel at two a.m. He had whispered it as he ushered him into the lobby, aware that the night clerk was listening in. "You're going to be okay getting up those stairs?" Too much scotch had made walking unmanageable for both men.

"I'll be *fine*," Jeremy blubbered, trying to get his bearings. Staying over at Gary's hotel had been out of the question without it ever being articulated. They had walked over there for a nightcap after their day of sightseeing. Gary's accommodations may not have been a palace, but his hotel did have the word in its name. The suite, three rooms in all, had brought home to Jeremy that they were on different trips, at very different junctures in their lives. "You shouldn't keep the taxi waiting, Gary."

As Jeremy dried off and slipped into clean boxers, he took a gambit at checking out the view. Would his naked stranger reappear for an encore? His head throbbed from the excess of alcohol that still trailed in his veins. The previous day had gone off like some fête in a foreign picture. They had walked miles, doing museums—Les Invalides, Rodin, Quai d'Orsay. They had strolled Les Champs-Élysées up to the Arc de Triomphe. Their conversations had mingled so that each now knew snippets of each other's backstories—Jeremy, the expat Canadian transplanted to Los Angeles; Gary, who had lived abroad and traveled extensively before moving to Santa Barbara to live with Samuel. Neither was impressed with Picasso. Both had a fascination with Bruegel.

The men had agreed to regroup for a late breakfast. Their rendezvous for ten-thirty sharp was in the lobby where they had parted. "Bonjour, madame." Jeremy handed in his key to the day clerk, a dowdy woman with a weight problem whose scowl registered contempt.

"Bon," she said, not particularly happy with her lot.

He could smell the espresso coffee brewing in the alcove where she sat; hear the sounds of a radio station with men arguing about an election— if Jeremy was deciphering the French correctly.

"Slept well?" Gary inquired.

"Like a charm."

"No lovebirds making out?"

"If they did, I was too smashed to hear."

Out on the street, the weather was as remarkable as the

day before. Jeremy inhaled the sun's rays as he took in the beauty. "How perfect is this," he exclaimed, gesturing with his arms and hands as though the proprietor of this bright universe.

Their plans that day were for a quieter pace. The Pantheon, browsing Rue Mouffetard, and a few gardens in the area. "We'll do the Jardin du Luxembourg first."

"Lead on." Jeremy was conscious that his presence had changed Gary's entire trip agenda. "I really appreciate you doing all of this."

Gary tried to dismiss any of his reservations. "Do I look like I'm being inconvenienced?"

"I can't tell. I don't know you well enough, do I?"

His fellow Californian had a point. Gary took him by the crook of the elbow, very Parisian, old-style. "Mon cher frère … Trust me. I'm an open book when it comes to my feelings. I don't cover them up well." They had reached a location Gary thought worth exploring. "This is a curiosity. Do you believe in miracles?"

"Miracles?"

"You know, Catholic apparitions?"

"Like the Virgin Mary?" Jeremy was stumped at where this was going.

"Bingo."

"No. Not at all."

"Well, this place has an interesting history."

With that, they went into a passageway.

Jeremy saw the French for Chapel of Our Lady of the Miraculous Medal on a sign. "What is this place?"

Gary indicated the bas-reliefs against the wall and let

Jeremy study them as he went further down towards the statue of a saint.

Jeremy skimmed the material. This was not like Notre Dame. The modernity here held little fascination for him. He reached Gary and pulled at his shirt. "I want to leave."

"What? Don't you want to see inside?"

Jeremy was perplexed. What Jew would want to come *here*, a temple of Catholicism with all the make-believe of miracles that Jeremy could not abide? He shrugged in acquiescence and followed his guide. The chapel was not that large so that the fifty or so people gathered there gave the impression of being crowded. Nothing like the cavalcade drawn to Notre Dame with the awe of architecture and its pedigree; here was a skein of devotees, with not a skeptic in sight. He watched as Gary watched others. He was sure his camera would be put into action, but the device never came into play. The men walked around, gazed at what there was to see, then walked back out onto the street.

"I'm confused."

"You are? What about?"

"You're Jewish," Jeremy said, whetting his appetite for a debate. "You don't buy that stuff, do you?"

"Miracles?"

"Yeah."

"You don't know much about Judaism."

Jeremy's ambivalence was growing by the minute. He thought he knew enough about the religion to know that a location like that, dedicated to the Virgin Mary and her intercessions, would not be a high Jewish priority.

"We *created* miracles. It's in our DNA." When Jeremy

looked too incredulous for words, Gary hummed a tune from *Fiddler on the Roof*.

"Really? You're going with Broadway to prove your point?"

Gary gave him a mischievous smile. He loved where this was going. They were at the perimeter of the Luxembourg Gardens. "Voilà. A miracle," he said, pointing to the greenery amidst the cultural chaos of Paris. They crossed over and sat down on chairs just out of reach from the shade of trees. "We should have picked up sandwiches. Any baked goodies in that backpack of yours?"

"I wish." Jeremy kept his eyes on Gary, wanting more answers. "If me, an ex-Catholic, abhors what I saw back there … What can I say? I'm surprised you even knew about that place."

"I told you. Mother and I ventured everywhere. She knew about that church from somewhere. Someone. I wouldn't put it past her that she prayed to the Virgin Mary herself."

"She was Jewish, right?"

"The Virgin Mary or Mother?" Jeremy had a deadpan reaction. "Trick question. Both were." When Jeremy's expression didn't change, Gary added, "You're really stuck on that, aren't you?"

Jeremy wondered if this might be their first disagreement. Religion. It fit. "I'm sorry. I don't mean to sound …" He didn't want to use the word anti-Semitic; he didn't feel he had crossed that line. But perhaps he had? Ignorance was often that blissful, he supposed. "It wasn't meant in the negative."

"I'm the one who misjudged. I just assumed your

Catholic background. The French-Canadian culture. Maybe I'm the one being ignorant here." He'd said it before realizing the implication, that Jeremy might have been obtuse. "I didn't mean it that way. Honest."

Their impasse lingered in the July morning air. The twittering of birds and the kids screaming and laughing over a game on the lawn, some yards away, were all welcome distractions.

"For the record," Jeremy said, sensing a relegation to a stereotype. "My family wasn't very big on religion. When Mom died at fifty-five …"

"I'm sorry to hear that."

"Lung cancer. It was very fast," he said, reluctant to go into that sorrow. "As I recall, there was a five-minute discussion on whether any mass or Catholic ritual would be observed. Dad said, 'Not over my dead body.' That was that. They had lost their faith years before. No explanation that I ever heard of."

"You weren't baptized?"

"Yeah. Yeah. In 1955, they were still connected to the church. But not as much as you might think."

Gary looked at his Rolex. "It's early but I'm starving. There's tons of places to eat if we go that way. We can come back here right after."

The bistro they found was behind the palace across the street from the gardens. "Mother was very religious in a non-Jewish sort of way," Gary said midway through their entrees. Both men seemed relieved that the topic of religion was back on for discussion. That unfinished business never boded well for new friendships. He tasted the veggie compote next to his quiche. "This is delicious."

"What do you mean?"

"It's sweet *and* tart …"

"Not the food," Jeremy said. He saw how Gary smiled. "Oh …"

"We went to temple. We did Jewish holidays, but Mom was fascinated by all things religious. For her, religions were like a boreal forest. Worth investigating. She took me everywhere to see what there was."

"The whole smorgasbord?"

"The whole enchilada. Buddhism. Sufism."

"Not Islam?"

"Oh yeah. No stones unturned for Rebekah Silverman."

"Wow. I'm impressed." Jeremy lifted up his glass and they toasted. "She believed in miracles then?"

Gary weighed how he wanted to depict his mother's quirks. "Carl Sagan once said, 'Extraordinary claims require extraordinary evidence.' Mom didn't see it that way."

"And you …?"

"I don't believe in miracles, per se. No. But I'm not bothered by someone who does."

"That explains back there." Jeremy could see Gary's attraction to the chapel now, the familial bent that made it more rational. His own family baggage was cut from a different cloth. "To be honest … I had a visceral response to all of that. I just wanted to scream."

"Wow. Really?" Their desserts arrived and Gary took a bite of his cake. "Oh, this is heavenly. Wanna taste?" They exchanged forkfuls of their desserts. "Damn, this is good."

"Safe to say we both have a sweet tooth?" Jeremy's plate was already clean.

"Oh yeah. Got that from Mother as well."

"Can I ask what your mom died of, Gary? If it's not too painful …"

"Some obscure liver disease. Blood based. We found it so late in the game. She didn't go as fast as your mom seemed to go. About a year … She never stopped hoping for a miracle though. Kept an open mind till the day she died. God rest her soul."

"How old was she when she passed away?"

Gary counted backwards, as though it had been many years now. "She died in 1980. Seventy-four? Yeah. Seventy-four. How can I forget, it was just three days after her birthday. She was sick as a dog but insisted on a big cake." He laughed. "*Who* does that in hospice!" He chugged the last of his pilsner. "She was a hoot."

"Sounds like it." Jeremy looked over at the display for desserts. "Should we get something to go?"

"Why not. When in Paris, right?"

THREE

"The Pantheon in Rome is much smaller." Jeremy's observation went unchallenged. "I wonder why that is?"

"The French have a thing for hero worshiping."

"They do?" Jeremy considered the Reign of Terror, how mercurial the French could be, apt to self-destruct given half the chance. Hero one day. Enemy of the people the next. To the guillotine and all that.

"Haven't you seen old film footage of them falling all over themselves after someone famous dies here?"

Jeremy wasn't sure who exactly Gary was referring to. He thought of excitable Italians he had met on his one trip to Italy. All the caricatures of hysterical Italians in the movies. "Don't all countries tend to do that with their famous countrymen when they die?"

Gary appeared to be digesting the point. He took in the massive weight of the columns, the Foucault pendulum.

The Pantheon in Rome *did* pale in comparison. "Rome's Pantheon is much, much older too, right?"

"I guess. I just remember the hole in the ceiling. I was very fascinated with that feature."

"The oculus." Gary took out his camera. "Was it raining when you visited?" He took a photo of the painted ceiling.

"No. Sunny. I recall because the building felt somber compared to the brightness outside. Nothing like this." He could tell Gary was going to take a photo of him. An adaptive spontaneity kicked in and he posed without being asked. How many pictures had Gary taken of him now? He had stopped counting. How odd that a stranger would have all of this history of his trip to Paris in his archives. He made a mental note to ask for copies—one of the other upsides of having met Gary on his first day in town.

"Did you know that when it rains, the water just falls into the center of that building? Right down on the floor. They just wipe it up."

"Really? No. That can't be. Wasn't there a screen or some type of glass up there?" But even as he asked, Jeremy remembered a pigeon, possibly more than one, flying around the interior of the Italian mausoleum. "No, you're right. It is open."

They were in front of the tombs of Hugo, Dumas, and Zola by now. "How inspiring is *this*?" Gary took a quick shot with a fisheye lens he retrieved from his camera bag. "It doesn't get better than this."

"What year did you go to Rome?" Gary asked. They were headed to Rue Mouffetard for a change of pace.

"Ten years ago, maybe ..." Jeremy tried to do the calculus in his head. "It was Justin's semester abroad. His third year of law school. Spring semester. 1988." Saying the date out loud brought pangs of melancholy that embarrassed him. Five years had seemed to do so little to settle any of the acrimony from their breakup.

Gary stopped Jeremy with a tug on his polo shirt. "He was studying abroad? Law?"

Jeremy could see this impressed Gary. "Yup."

"His Italian was *that* good?"

"No. It wasn't in Italy. He did his semester in Aix-en-Provence. Not far from Marseille. His French wasn't bad—thanks to my tutoring. He was practically on the Riviera for four months."

"Ouch!"

"You're telling me." Jeremy indicated a patisserie and they went in and ordered. In between bites, Jeremy explained. "Now you know why I'm so fucking depressed being here."

"Didn't you want to see where he was studying?" Jeremy's tears took Gary by total surprise. "I'm sorry ... I don't ... I didn't mean to upset."

"Upset! Oh, we're way past upset." Jeremy hadn't had a good cry over his broken heart in a while. The salty flow down his cheeks felt liberating. He didn't care that it was in public, in front of someone he hardly knew. "I needed to do this." He dabbed at his eyes with a Kleenex. "I've been wanting to cry for days. Weeks even. Being here in France ..."

Gary scooped him into his arms. "Buddy ..."

Jeremy let himself be held. He felt wanted and safe momentarily. As though the crashing return that often accompanied emotional breakdowns might be lessened with the touch. Even if in incremental degrees. He could see the caption under his photo, *Loser!*, sensed it time and again when the loss of Justin came over him, leaving that ugly ball of turmoil in his stomach. He got a grip on himself. "Thanks," he said, pulling away from the consoling embrace. He pointed to a bench and they sat. "How far is Rue Mouffetard?"

"Forget about that."

"No. I want to see it."

"It's just a couple more blocks. It can wait." Gary finished the tartelette and craved a coffee after the doughy sweet. "That's why you answered the way you did yesterday when I asked you if this was your first time here?"

"You're lucky I didn't do *this*." He indicated his entire comportment. "You'd have run away fast then, right?"

"I don't know …"

That Gary could compromise like that made Jeremy hesitate. What kind of codependent did he have here, he thought. "I didn't suspect anything in '88. Justin had never been to Rome. Nor me. It wasn't like he was here in Paris. That might have changed things. We thought … No. No, *he* convinced me that Rome would be a better destination for the one week I had for spring break at school."

"Okay … Makes sense."

Jeremy could tell Gary was unconvinced. "Well … Now, after all that went down between us. The break-up. How it happened. I suspect there was more to his rationale …"

"He was cheating on you? Didn't want you to meet the guy?"

"You've been around the block too?"

Gary didn't need to pause to answer. "First of all. It's basic Gay Relationships 101, Jeremy. Not that it doesn't sting." His words were not comforting. "I lucked out. My Sam was older than me. Very conservative. Didn't cheat. Sorry … Me, on the other hand …" The expression from the furrowed brows suggested promiscuity on Gary's part.

"Justin and me. We had an open relationship. Sort of. At least, we never promised exclusivity. But early on like that. I thought we satisfied each other."

"Well, the boy *was* in the south of France." Gary couldn't tell if he was on solid ground. "Away from his lover for four whole months."

"I know!" As if Jeremy hadn't told himself that repeatedly as he had planned this impromptu trip to Paris. "But *I* didn't stray. I stayed celibate. I wrote to him every week. A postcard from every location in and around LA to remind him of home. Of me!"

"Oh, you poor dear." Gary stood up, having decided sightseeing was what they both needed. "On y va?" He offered him his hand and Jeremy reached for it. "He was your first?"

"Well, not my *first* boyfriend. But my first. My only real love. How pathetic is that?"

"How long since you broke up?"

"You're going to think I'm a loser."

"Maybe …"

"Fucker!" The men tousled. Gary, bigger and taller, had the advantage. He tugged a lock of chestnut brown hair. "Ow," Jeremy yelled.

Gary quickly kissed the back of his pate. "There. Better?"

They had arrived at Place de la Contrescarpe where the famous Parisian street began and where throngs gravitated. "We broke up back in '92. It's five years already." Jeremy saw a shop that looked appealing and led them inside. "Are any of these antiques legit?"

Gary inspected a dozen items on a counter. "Some. Not

many." He put the copper pot back down after seeing the price. "Not for what they're charging. Tourist trap."

Back out on Mouffetard, the sun had begun its westerly trajectory. "Where to?"

Gary considered where they were and the hour. "The market's quite far from here. With all this foot traffic … a good forty-five-minute walk? It's up to you."

"I'm game."

They window-shopped and checked inside stores as they ambled. It was past seven when they settled down for a supper off the beaten path, a Greek restaurant with live music. Their wine had arrived and a toast seemed in order. "To Gary."

"To me?"

"Yeah. You've been such a good sport."

The message between the lines was plain for both to read. Jeremy was not interested in anything more than friendship here, and Gary understood so he repeated the toast. "To Gary," he said, "a good sport." His feigned British accent, meant to amuse, fell flat. They tapped glasses and sipped. Unperturbed, Gary prodded. "I could be *so* much more than that." He thought of speaking French, hoping that might induce a seductive mood to their exchange then reconsidered. "So, why haven't you moved on? You're attractive. You have those soulful eyes. You've got a decent job. You're funny. Well, when you're not crying that is."

"Gary, if I had that answer …" He left it unfinished because he could recite the answer by rote. He had a broken heart that could not be mended. Justin had ruined it for others.

"You've tried?"

Had he? Had he really attempted to move on? Jeremy was sure that he had. "I think I have." He had dated. Gone on awkward blind dates. Hung out at gay functions. Danced at clubs.

"Convince me."

Jeremy knew intuitively where Gary was leading with his dare. The *it* had to be spoken aloud. "Listen, Gary. You're a really, really nice guy."

"Ooh, I think I liked it better when I was a good sport."

"I can't explain it."

"You just did." Gary tossed back the remainder of his burgundy in one gulp. He signaled for their waiter to bring more wine. "You ready for another?" Jeremy nodded and Gary put up two fingers for their waiter to see.

When their drinks had arrived and the mood had relaxed some, Jeremy faced the gauntlet. "I've not met anyone that's intrigued me enough to want to pursue things past a few dates."

"A *few* dates?"

"Maybe I went out with one or two for longer. But not much more."

"You've had sex with others since …"

"Yeah. Yeah."

Gary was relieved. This was salvageable, he thought. He took a slice of pita bread and spread the tapenade. He chewed the salty mess and swallowed. "Do you think you're comparing the guys to Justin?"

"Probably. How can you not? Isn't that what makes moving on so damn tricky?"

Gary bobbed his head side to side, and saw how Jeremy

was reacting to this. "If I thought of replacing Sam with anyone, I'd never be able to date a soul."

"He died when again? I don't think you said."

"In '95."

"Oh shit. That's just two years ago."

His tone implied mourning still, a state of mind that Gary rejected altogether. "It feels like an eternity."

The weight of Gary's comment sunk in for both but from totally different perspectives. Gary realized that the time frame had been a period of moving on for him. That Sam was already in the past; buried but not forgotten. That his heart was open to all the possibilities hearts could lend themselves to. Not so for Jeremy who considered his five years since losing Justin as years of ambivalence, an eternity for entirely opposite reasons. Not enough time had elapsed to make sense of the loss. Not having let go, he was unable to let anyone else into his life for fear of having to move on from something he was incapable of facing: being rejected and deserted by the one man he loved.

"It's just two years …" Jeremy said, his voice trailing.

"Sam died of complications from AIDS. The meds stopped working. It's not like we didn't know the possibility was there. He'd been living with that reality ever since AZT hit the market." The musicians had assembled on the raised platform at the back of the restaurant. Gary could tell a party was about to get started. "You like Greek music?"

"Yeah. I think so."

Gary thought of getting a bottle of ouzo. He was in the mood for some excitement; and he accepted grudgingly that

Jeremy was not interested in him for sex, only companionship. Did he dare go out on a limb and get them drunk again? When their waiter arrived with their entrees, he ordered doubles. "When in Paris, right?"

FOUR

"You packed an umbrella?" Gary asked, standing under the awning of the Cinémathèque Française. The museum had seemed a suitable destination for their first rainy day, a slightly more intellectual pursuit than simply escaping to the movies.

"I just paid a fortune for this." He held the contraption up to show the fancy wooden handle to justify his expenditure. "It'll be my Paris souvenir. Let's hope it lasts."

"You could have taken a taxi. I could have picked you up with my cab now that I think of it."

"We were in no condition last night to make those plans."

Jeremy's glance was hard to gauge as Gary surmised resentment. "We overdid the ouzo. Yes. My fault entirely."

"You didn't force it down my gullet."

"No …"

"But you *were* persistent."

"I was." Gary's hangover had left him with a banging

headache so that the quiet of the Cinémathèque along with the darkness were an anticipated blessing. It was only once inside, when he saw how hot it was, stuffy with little air, that he regretted the day's itinerary. "How are your legs?"

Jeremy grabbed at both of his thighs mimicking a sumo wrestler about to engage. "Sore as hell." He dipped and made a circular motion with his arms to his sides. "What's the name of that dance again?"

"I can't recall. Circle dance will suffice."

"Well, we circle danced the shit out of it last night." He saw one of the tourists nearby look their way. Jeremy smiled, mouthed "sorry," and got a knowing response in return.

"That we did." Gary noticed the prohibition of cameras inside the premises and went to the lockers. "Do you want to put the backpack in here too?"

Jeremy had also seen the sign. "No choice, right?"

"Yeah. It's been years since I came here. It used to be in a different location."

With only docent-guided tours through the museum, the extensive exhibits—even for two eager film buffs—proved long. Their stamina, weakened by the drain of hangovers, made the men abandon ship after two hours. Outside, the rain was coming down in sheets.

"Shit, this is bad," Jeremy said. "Where to, maestro?"

"Don't panic …"

"Well, of course, that's an invitation to panic. What?"

"Why don't we cab it back to my hotel. The restaurant there is fabulous. My treat."

"And …?" Jeremy asked, aware that there was a proviso about to shed some light.

"And …" Gary laughed. Jeremy had a way about him, a

mild paranoia that was appealing in small doses. "I need to just crash for forty winks. Some shut-eye. No hanky-panky. You can watch TV, read a magazine …"

Gary's proposal was not untoward in the least. "My legs could use the break too."

"Great. You can even take the bed. I'll take the couch. That way …"

"That way, you'll be cheated out of the luxury mattress you paid for. I'll take the couch. I'm fine with that."

The ride was quiet in spite of the downpour outside, with Parisians running to their destinations with and without umbrellas; the heat that came with the humidity in July that mixed with the exhaust of all the traffic and muffled the beeping of horns; and the taxi radio that played a soothing violin sonata. Gary and Jeremy didn't speak a word. As though they were being driven to a destination that held an aura neither could stave off.

At the hotel, in the lobby, they went by the menu for the restaurant. "Am I dressed okay for this place?" Jeremy asked, seeing the exorbitant prices.

Gary examined his attire. "It doesn't ask for tie and jacket."

"And you can't lend me anything. None of your clothes will fit me, right?"

Jeremy had a point. "We'll look and see. You can always buy a jacket in there." He indicated a men's shop down the corridor. "I'd love to buy you something."

"Are you that loaded?"

"Now you're being uncouth."

The rebuke came suddenly and Jeremy was unsure of himself for a second. "I'm sorry."

Gary laughed. "That's what Sam would have said to you. No doubt about it." He put his arm around Jeremy's shoulders. "Listen. It so happens that Samuel Bronfman left me with a small fortune. Along with all the assets from the antique business and a house people say is more of a mansion. I'm *very* comfortable. Buying you a nice shirt. A jacket. A tie. Cufflinks. Whatever. It would be a treat. I don't do this a lot. Trust me."

They were in the wood-paneled elevator, the stillness almost spell-binding. The doors opened and they walked along the corridor to his suite when Jeremy remembered his umbrella. "Shit. I left my umbrella in the cab."

Inside, Gary went to fetch bottled water from a refrigerator. "Want some?"

"I'm dying. Yes."

The men sat at the sofa and drank two glasses a piece. "I have to pee." Gary rose and went to the restroom.

The door, left slightly ajar, meant that Jeremy could hear the tinkle of liquid on liquid. The interrupted stream of urine—bursts followed by dribbles— made him nervous, but why? He had been there two days prior. Nothing had transpired then. Did he doubt his own lack of willpower, conscious of how weak he was or how needy he could be? The flushing noise brought him back to the present.

"There's nothing better than a strong piss when you're hungover and tired." Gary undid his belt along with the button at the waist. His fly was still unzipped. "Should I set the alarm?"

"I'm tired," Jeremy said, unsure. "But I don't think you need to do that. I'll wake up soon enough."

"Do you snore?"

"Me? Uh, maybe. Sometimes."

"I snore. So be warned." The man went into the other room and closed the door.

As Jeremy lay his head on a throw pillow, he was amazed at how comfortable the settee was. He laughed at how dreadful his hotel room was in comparison; he thought of the first night with that couple fucking their brains out. The sound of both man and woman had been clear as day. Their moans had not been English or French moans. Their language had been of Scandinavian origins. He had not seen either but he envisioned all their blondness and their blue eyes. It's what prompted his dream … their invitation to join them. Out in the hallway, Jeremy had found himself naked and wondered why, when he knocked on their door to see if they had a towel he could borrow.

The girl—for that was how young she was, no more than eighteen—said something in her native tongue and Jeremy repeated it. Fluent in whatever language it was they were all speaking now. The boy took him by the hand and gestured to lie down on the bed. The couple began to caress Jeremy's legs, his chest. The girl kissed him on the forehead and played with his tresses, commented on the texture, the curliness that was more wave than curls. All this, Jeremy understood. He replied that he had always wanted straight, blond hair. Like Justin's hair, he said.

The mere mention of Justin caused the girl to stop cold. She seemed angry at hearing the name. "Why? Why talk about Justin *now*?" she said. Jeremy could see she was hurt and wondered how she could possibly know who Justin was and asked as much. The boy took Jeremy by the arm and jerked him off the mattress, ranted and swore, told Jeremy to apologize. All arousal was gone; neither man had erections anymore. The girl was crying and Jeremy had no sense of how to extricate himself from this entire mix-up. He tried to caress the girl's belly, hoping to make amends when the boy gripped his scrotum and squeezed.

"Ahh …!"

"Jeremy. Jeremy, wake up. Wake up." His eyes opened to the darkness in the room.

"What …" He could see the sky outside was dusky. "What happened? What time is it?"

"We really crashed out. That ouzo stings. I'd forgotten how much."

Jeremy sat up. "I must have … Went out like a light." He rubbed his forehead and felt the moisture around his mouth. The dried spittle in the corners.

"You had a doozy of a nightmare."

"I did?" Gary nodded. "Did I scream?"

"Oh yeah. Talked and talked. I should have taken notes." The men realized at once that Gary was in his jockeys. Self-consciousness came over them. "Let me put some pants on." He left the room and came back in a bathrobe instead. "Listen. Why don't we do room service? The restaurant by now will be crowded with evening guests. Dress code might be an issue."

"You just don't want to buy me new clothes."

Gary, amused by the teasing, answered, "That too." He looked for the room service menu. "What do you say?"

"Can I take a shower? I smell. I must have really sweated out here."

"There's another bathrobe hanging in the closet by the door. Be my guest." Jeremy stood. "What did you dream about, by the way?"

Jeremy paused trying to recall. His boxers were sticking to him so he knew lust had likely been involved. He didn't want to admit to any wet dream but that was all he could think of when the vision of the blond couple came back to him. "I don't want to turn you on …"

"Oh, darling. Too late for that, I'm afraid."

Gary's retort only added to Jeremy's concerns. "Let's just say there was a threesome …"

"*Really* …?"

"You've never had a threesome?"

"I have."

"Well, ironically. I haven't. This was my first."

"Do tell."

"There's nothing to tell," he began, then remembered why it had all turned ugly. "Justin fucked it all up."

"I'm beginning to really not like your ex." Gary had gone to get the bathrobe and gave it to Jeremy. "What did he do to ruin the threesome?"

Jeremy pulled off his polo shirt and donned the robe. He slipped out of his jeans and put them on the back of the side chair. "He didn't. I did. I brought him up. That's when all hell broke loose."

"Did you come?"

"Did I come …?"

"Yeah. In your dream."

"If I did, I … I don't remember." He wasn't about to confess the condition of his underwear to Gary, not when they were already in a more compromising situation than Jeremy preferred.

"Oh well, dream sex is better than no sex, I suppose. I rarely ever have those anymore. Not at sixty-six."

"I usually don't. Not that I ever recollect." He tightened the sash, ill at ease with the subject. "It's that couple next to me that first night."

"The fuck bunnies?"

"That would be them. They came a knockin'." Jeremy laughed at his joke, saddened, possibly disappointed at the outcome of the fantasy. "Do you want to order while I'm in the shower?"

"Sure." He handed Jeremy the menu. They made a list and Jeremy went off, hoping to scrub himself of all the Justin memories he could find.

FIVE

The meal had been sublime—spicy ceviche shrimp appetizers, entrees of veal marsala with roasted balsamic vegetables on the side. The champagne, a Crystal '88 vintage, a misguided attempt to tame the remaining hangover effects each nursed from the previous night's binge. They were taking a break before moving to their desserts and coffee.

"This robe is wonderfully soft." Jeremy loosened the sash that was too tight now that he had eaten. He had left his boxers to dry in the bathroom, along with his polo shirt to air out the armpit perspiration. He could see his jeans on the couch behind where Gary was seated across from him at the table. "I'm usually not a fan of terry cloth. Too bunchy and too warm."

"You can keep it. To make up for the shirt and tie I never bought you." The reference to earlier that evening brought a smile to his dinner partner.

"Won't they notice it's gone?"

"They'll put it on the bill. It's done all the time." Gary could see he was unaware of that protocol. The lull in conversation made Gary think of the nightmare. "Did people ever comment on you and Justin, your names? How well they went together?"

The non sequitur caught Jeremy off-guard. "Uh … Yeah. Jeremy and Justin. Often enough."

"And your own name's pretty alliterative too. What was up with that?"

Jeremy was used to jibes about his name. "My grandmother. She was from France. She suggested it."

Gary was intrigued. "How so?" he asked, curious as to why a grandparent would play such a pivotal role. "Unless you're about to tell me you're landed gentry …"

"First of all. Jerome isn't French. You know that, right?"

"Should I?"

"My grandfather, Dad's dad, immigrated from England. Met my grandmother right off the boat in Montreal." That explained nothing. Jeremy could see that. "According to my mom, it was grand-mère Alice who loved the name Jérémie. We could never prove it but the rumor was that that had been the name of a lover back in France. Or a great admirer, at the very least."

"You've got a lot of history with this country, don't you?"

"Not really. No, not much. My grandmother was the last of her line. She was an only child. Her mom died giving birth. Every one of her family—that we know of—died. The two wars. The 1918 pandemic."

"Is your name Jeremy or Jérémie on your birth certificate?"

"That's where it gets complicated. I have both. Mom and Dad went with the Anglo version. No accents on my birth certificate. Jeremy Jerome. Quite English. But for the baptismal certificate they caved in and made it French for Alice."

"That's strange. She had all that power?"

"I know. And yet, she was the sweetest lady. Never a harsh word. Though she did make sure we learned some French at school."

"Was she your godmother? Is that why she controlled the bash?"

"No. Not at all. She and my grandfather were my older brother's godparents."

"You have brothers?"

"One. Older. Matt. And a sister. Paulette."

"They're up in Canada?"

"Yeah."

"And your dad?"

"Passed away. A heart attack."

"He's *dead*?"

Jeremy thought the rise of the voice—upturned and strained on the question mark—quite peculiar, as though Gary had had a stake in that outcome. "Why did you say it that way?"

"That way?"

"I don't know. It sounded weird."

"It did?" Gary got up and went to the window. The Paris lights from his hotel view were picturesque. Camera-ready, if he had been in the mood to memorialize it. "When did he die?"

Jeremy knew that Gary would make more out of this then was warranted. "1992."

"Wasn't that the same year you and Ju …"

"Yes. It was."

"Which came first? Your dad dying or the breakup?"

"Same month."

"Jesus. Did Justin have no heart? Who *does* that!"

"It's not like anything was planned. Dad died suddenly. A massive heart attack at work. Just like his father. Justin had already met Stuart and made his plans to leave to be with him in Manhattan. He was basically all moved out when Dad died."

"And he didn't stick around? Help you out with your grief?"

"No. Not really." Jeremy's recollection came to life momentarily. "But it's not like he and Dad were close or anything."

"They'd met, right?"

"Oh yeah. We'd go up to Canada once a year. He met them at least … five times? Yeah, five. I don't think we went up there together until our second year. We did Christmas the first time he came up with me."

"So, he got to meet your mother?"

"Yeah. Once or twice. But he and Dad were chummier, now that I think of it." The hurt at Justin not being around for the funeral and all that came from putting the family house on the market, the getting rid of family possessions, was another thing stuck in his craw. The Justin list of indefensible actions taken and not taken by his ex was *long* indeed.

"The baggage we carry, right?" Gary came back to sit down. He took the desserts from the side cart that room service had brought up and poured each a cup of coffee. The aroma filled the room quickly. "Smell that." He sniffed the dark of the roasted beans. "Cream, right?"

"Yes, please." They ate and sipped.

"Did your parents ever come down to LA to visit?"

Jeremy almost choked on the coffee that came very close to spewing out of his nose. "No. Never." He cleared his throat.

"What's so funny?" Gary gobbled up the last of his tiramisu unable to resist the sugar cravings.

"Mom was petrified of flying. I mean, scared shitless."

"Did she have a bad experience?"

Jeremy shook his head and laughed.

"She *never* flew?"

"She hated traveling. She was a homebody. A bit like Dad."

Gary's mood changed again. He had that look that Jeremy had picked up on minutes prior.

"They never went anywhere on holidays?"

"We had a cottage. A nice cabin up in the Laurentians. Summers were spent there." Jeremy poured himself another cup of coffee. Black, this time, to get the full-bodied flavor. "They went to Florida by car. Twice, I think." He fetched the data from his memory bank. "Twice. Both times with an aunt and uncle of mine. Mom's brother. They'd rented a condo or some kind of apartment. Daytona Beach sounds familiar."

"And …?"

"I think that was it. They enjoyed it but not enough to do more than that."

"So, Europe was out of the question? No cruises?"

"I think a cruise *was* on their to-do list. But Mom died. And Dad would never. Not on his own."

"Really?"

"You say that, Gary, very strangely. I don't … I can't explain it. You have a tone. It's been there twice. No, three times now. Like you knew the man."

"I did? I do …?"

"Listen, Gary. My dad. He was an enigma all our lives. He worked hard. He was faithful to my mother. He never raised his fists to us. Paid for our schooling. And we *weren't* rich at all. One tiny step above working class. But he was a very introverted man. Mom and he. They were happy together. But I don't think they fulfilled each other. They had us. They were dedicated parents. Made sure we did something with our lives." Jeremy recognized that he was rationalizing what needed none. "My dad and I. We weren't close."

"Do you know why?"

The psychological tinge, as though an examination under way, was too heavy for Jeremy. "Oh God, we're doing therapy now?"

"No, not therapy. Just chatting. We all got to here somehow, right? I'm sure you've been wondering how fucked up I am from my early childhood with my mother." Before Jeremy could disagree, Gary had a finger pointed at his face as if to say, "Don't deny it." The man shrugged. "I'll tell you all about Mother if you tell me all about your dad. How's that?"

"Rafael Jerome by Jeremy Jerome." Jeremy parodied doing a class presentation against his better judgement. "Dad and me were like two peas in a pod. First of all. We looked a lot alike. Especially as I got older."

"Not when you were younger?"

"Yes, I suppose so. But I didn't see it. But now, when I look in the mirror, I can see it more clearly as I age."

"But you're a chatty Cathy. Didn't you say your dad was a quiet man?"

"Yes, I'm more excitable than him. But we had the same internal energy. I'm more hyper than him because my lifestyle permitted it. He came from a different generation." *Your generation* was on the tip of Jeremy's tongue where he left it.

"Was he okay about you being gay?"

"Yeah. Sort of. I mean we didn't talk about it much. It happened on occasion."

"When did you come out to them?"

"In college. It was the thing to do. Mid-seventies? Both of my parents were okay with it but the issue was rarely discussed afterwards. They knew. They didn't ask much." Jeremy wanted more coffee, but not keen on being up all night from the caffeine, he poured himself a half flute of champagne instead. "Want some?" Gary nodded so he emptied the remainder in Gary's glass. "Dad and me. It's hard to explain."

"Did he always live in the same town?"

"We lived just outside of Ottawa. That's where my grandparents landed. Dad was a low-level civil servant. Same job for most of his life."

"He never went to college?"

"Uh …" Jeremy had to think about how to describe the events as he knew them. "Dad didn't finish high school. He went out west to work on an uncle or a cousin's farm. My mom's side of the family. Not his, I think."

"He wanted to be a farmer?"

Jeremy finished the champagne and was craving something stronger. He glanced at the minibar. "Any liqueurs?"

"Yeah. Help yourself. Bring me a Drambuie."

They settled back at the table with their *pousse-café* in hand. "I don't think he ever wanted to be a farmer."

"So why go out west to do that?"

"I … I always suspected that he and Mom were at an impasse."

"Could be. He was young. If he wasn't going off to college, marriage would have been the next step for him, right? Maybe he didn't want to …"

"All I know is that he went out to Alberta. A farm near Calgary. And …"

Jeremy paused and it seemed, to Gary, predicated on something grander than simple career indecision on his father's part.

"Like I said. There was a family connection out in the prairies. Me and my siblings, we don't quite know what happened. Nothing bad or anything." Jeremy was frustrated because he didn't have a clear explanation himself; part of the family mystique that never got answered fully. "A family altercation is all we kids ever assumed. Big enough that that part of the family is a mystery to us. I couldn't even give you names. I'd have to do some searching to get those. How's *that* for bizarre?" He sipped his B&B liqueur, savoring the thick sweet burning the alcohol produced against his tongue. The glass was half empty when Jeremy noted Gary's demeanor, how it had altered. He had not described anything distasteful so he asked, "Something wrong?"

Gary rose at the question, lifted by its substantialness.

He stood at the window for some time sipping his drink. He had been contemplating how this next scene, how the situation they were in would play itself out. "I know about your relations in Alberta."

The admission, rife with innuendo, made Jeremy want to get up but his feet had turned to clay. Like they were remnant appendages from an evolutionary phase that had made them redundant, that served no more purpose than the coccyx once humans no longer had need for tails.

"I don't understand," Jeremy said.

SIX

Los Angeles in 1949 was so different than it is today. It's unimaginable how changed a city could be. Though, I suppose, that could be said of any major metropolitan the world over. Time that changes, that transforms all? Santa Monica was a small town then, with a sense of community that was about to be lost to progress once Interstate 10 stormed through the city within the next decade, marking the end of the road for those crisscrossing the country on the famed Route 66 from Chicago to Hollywood and Vine.

In those days, I was either alone with a book or with my two best friends. Jethro Beauregard—this was before a certain '60s sitcom had forever ruined the name. Back in '49, Jethro was a catch. A heartthrob on the Santa Monica High School football team who had come from old money, once upon a time. Rounding out our trio was Herbie Landau, who would go on to brief prominence before dying young. Too soon to make much of the early promises his academic prowess had suggested.

That early August, as the weather continued to shine a brilliant 73°F, with ocean breezes that caressed and lingered, we were clueless as to what life had on offer for us. We had made plans to meet at Muscle Beach not far from the Santa Monica Pier, hang out, and swim before catching a movie at the Criterion on Third Street—*Mr. Belvedere Goes to College.* The pick had been a fitting option since we were all leaving soon for far-flung collegiate locales of our own. Herbie to Columbia and me to Stanford. Only Jethro was headed nearer to home with a football scholarship to USC, though his parents had hoped he might have changed his mind and gone to an Ivy League school back east, which had also courted his talents on the field, so as to reclaim some of the prestige his family was forever yearning. That day, we were doing what eighteen-year-olds with enough money did during their summers before going off to college, before the disbanding that moving on from high school brought to friendships that, hitherto, seemed would have lasted a lifetime.

Mother had dropped me off at Ocean and Pico, running late for some appointment back in Brentwood. I had strolled, killing time. Checked out surfboards on Main Street. I was a block from the boardwalk when I saw Rafael sitting by himself on the curb. He appeared preoccupied. Not exactly a bum, but he had seen better days; road-weary as though he had traveled far to get here. When he saw me staring his way, he turned defensively. "You gotta problem?"

I was so taken aback, I walked by him hurriedly not wanting any complications, got a whiff of his body odor, and suddenly felt pity for the guy. He *had* to be homeless, I thought. I was yards from the boardwalk when I thought of turning around. When I did, he was standing up. I didn't know if he was crazy, on the verge of assaulting, but I held my ground as he approached.

"I'm sorry," he said.

I could see now that we were about the same age. He was maybe five feet ten inches to my six feet. His dark hair, which curled slightly so that it gave him waves along his temples, was scruffy, just shy of matted. It was clear he could do with a shower. "It's okay." I waited before I added, "You hungry?" Rafael looked embarrassed before he admitted as much. "I have money," I said. "Come on. There's a burger stand around the corner."

We walked in silence before he said, "I smell. Sorry."

I laughed. "Yeah. You do." I remembered the showers on the beach. "You know you can clean up on the beach. They have facilities to get the salt and sand off after you swim." I showed him my towel. "You can borrow this if you want." I handed it to him. "I'm Gary, by the way."

"Rafael," he said, offering to shake hands, which we did.

"The archangel. Not a bad way to start life."

Rafael eked out a smile. "I could use an angel myself right about now."

I bowed and said, "At your service."

He gulped down his burger and fries as though he hadn't eaten in days, which I suspected was the case. He never said and I didn't ask. "I'm meeting up with friends. Not far from here. I'm going to walk you to where the showers are. You can come and meet up with us after you're done."

"Okay …"

His answer seemed hesitant and I wondered if I might have been saying goodbye to my beach towel when he said, "I'm from Canada."

"A long way from home."

"Damn right."

"Did you hitchhike?" I asked. As if I needed to have *that* confirmed. He resembled a junior hobo now that I'd been standing by his side for a spell.

"I sure did."

We headed onto the sand. His shoes, boots really, were heavy and I could tell how cumbersome they were. "Why don't you take those off? Walk barefoot in the sand." Then I realized how filthy he might actually be. "It's up to you. You don't have to."

His sheepish grin let me know I'd intuited correctly. Outside the men's room, I pointed to where the showers were, then grasped that he wouldn't have a bathing suit. "Here. Put this on inside the restroom. Come out with your gear and shower off. Then you can go back in, dry off and come out. I'll wait. My buddies aren't going anywhere. We've planned the afternoon hanging out here."

Rafael followed my advice. He went in and came out with his bundle in hand. "Here. You wanta hold these. They smell."

He was certainly right about that. I saw how baggy my swimming trunks were on him. He was thinner than me. Not rail thin but he could have benefited from a couple more pounds. There was muscle definition in his chest and abs but he *was* gaunt. "Why don't you put your underwear under the water too and rinse them out." I scrounged and found the boxers. And his socks and shirt. "Here. They'll all dry out soon enough in this weather. We're just staying on the beach."

He stood under the cold shower and didn't seem too bothered. I could tell he was relieved to have that luxury. He grinned as he saw me grinning in kind. After he had finished his shower, soaked his clothes, and turned them inside out, he handed me the wet items. "Here. You can wring them out while I go back in."

"Do I look like your maid?" I was so used to kidding with Jethro and Herbie, I forgot how my tone could be misconstrued.

"I … I'm sorry. I wasn't thinking," Rafael blurted. "I wanted to not have you be late. That's all."

I waved as if to say, "My fault entirely," but he'd already taken back the dripping apparel and was walking away. "Rafael, I was joking. Honest to goodness. No offense taken at all. You were being considerate. I appreciate it. Here. Let me. Come on." I stepped towards him and put out my hand. He gave me the garments and walked back into the men's room with his pack and my towel. I hadn't been squeezing and wringing for more than a minute when I heard a commotion from the restroom. The shouting sounded like it was Rafael so I ran inside. I could see Rafael in a state. He was standing all alone in the corner and two men—one burly and tattooed, the other younger and quite striking were by the urinals. "What's going on here?" I asked.

The tattooed guy glared at me about ready to fight. I had a mind to get in his face but something about the entire construct, where all three were standing in relation to each other, made me revise my approach. "Rafael. You coming?"

He wasn't half dried and his boots were still on the cement

floor when he snatched them, lifted up his pants without any underwear and came out with me. "What was *that* all about?" I asked. I could see Rafael was shaken.

"Queers."

The word sputtered and landed squarely at my feet. I was flabbergasted without recourse. "What?"

Rafael had taken his bag and scrounged a pair of dry socks that had holes in them. He sat down and put them on and slipped into his boots. "It's nothin'." He stood and looked around to get what I assumed were his bearings.

"You're new here? Your first time in LA?"

"Got in late last night. I just walked and walked. I ran out of cash a few days ago. I was worried the cops around here might pick me up for vagrancy."

I whistled, never having had to go hungry. I was dying to get his story and hated that we had to meet up with Jethro and Herbie. Easygoing as they were, my bringing a total stranger, a Canadian drifter no less, on one of our final outings before the end of summer, might not fly as easily as I had hoped. I glanced at my watch. There was still another twenty minutes to kill. "You know what you need?" Rafael gave me the same cautious look he had when he had spotted me back on the street. What was *that* all about?

"Yeah. I'm listening."

I wanted to be tactful but I had no time. "You need some sneakers. Maybe some shorts."

"I have shorts. Cut-offs. In my bag."

"You do? Why didn't you put those on instead of your jeans? It's warm here if you haven't noticed."

"They're grungy. I didn't get a chance at washing any of my clothes when I left."

"And why's that?" I was being nosy now. Plain and simple.

"I left in a hurry. I was going to do it along the way on the road. Some washing. It just never happened."

"Well, Rafael. You're in luck." I took out my wallet. "I'm loaded." I caught Rafael eyeing my wad of dough. "You're not a thief, are you?"

"No!" he said, then added, "Are *you*?"

He was genuinely hurt; and his comeback was understandable. I could see that too. "Glad to hear it," was all I could think of replying. I put my palm on his shoulder. "Let's go shopping." The Sears on Colorado was too far, so I settled for Mickey's on Ocean Avenue. A half-hour later, Rafael came out of the store with me a different man. His Bermuda shorts were worn over a rayon Lastex swimsuit, and his sneakers were too new to be cool but a whole lot better than his army surplus boots.

We strolled down the boardwalk to Muscle Beach. Jethro was swinging on the exercise rings, making a show of his prowess as he exaggerated each exchange. When he got to the end, Herbie was waiting, holding their bottles of pop. I waved as we approached. "Hey, guys. This here is Rafael." I looked to Rafael for his last name.

"Jerome."

"Jerome's your last name? Are you Jewish?" Herbie asked.

"No. Not that I know of."

"Trust me, you'd know."

"That's Herbie Landau. Jewish. And the muscleman is Jethro. Beauregard. Not Jewish."

"T'es Français?" Rafael asked him.

I loved hearing French spoken. "No, Rafael," I said on behalf of Jethro. "He's not."

"You speak French, Gary?"

"He thinks he does," Herbie punted. "Four years of high school French doesn't make you bilingual."

"I used to speak it well as a child in Paris."

"Here we go with the Little Lord Fauntleroy routine." Jethro jabbed me in the stomach to make his point.

"I was just explaining …"

"My family is from the South," Jethro interrupted. "We spoke French. A long time ago, that is."

"And had a plantation too, no doubt," Herbie teased.

"No doubt about it," Jethro taunted. "Long gone."

"Where in the south?"

"Louisiana. You ever been?"

"No. This is my first trip to the United States."

His using the name of our country like that sounded foreign to us. I could tell my buddies were curious as hell where I'd met up with this fellow. "Rafael got in last night. Hitchhiked all the way from …" I realized how little I knew about any of his background.

"Calgary. I hitched all the way from Calgary."

"You a cowboy?" Jethro asked.

"A French cowboy." Herbie said it like he had made a discovery rather than an observation. "I never would have guessed that one."

"No. No cowboy. And I'm not from there. I'm from Ottawa. You heard of Ottawa?"

"That's the capital, right?" Jethro asked. He guzzled the last of his pop and flung the bottle all the way into the trash can to a round of applause from those around us. He bowed, loving the attention.

"Yeah. Like your Washington."

"Who's your president now?"

Rafael looked at me and we both grinned at Jethro's ignorance. "We don't have presidents. A prime minister."

"Oh, yeah. Forgot."

"Louis St. Laurent is in power, right?" I asked Rafael. He nodded, happy to see that I knew that.

"A Frenchie prime minister? Is everybody French in Canada?"

"No, Jethro," Herbie answered. "Just back east. Quebec, right?" Rafael agreed. "I went with my family to Montreal when I was a kid. We have a cousin up there. Very friendly people, Canadians. I liked the city."

This connection gave Rafael some comfort. The slant of his shoulders told me he was loosening up. His whole facial expression thawed. What had transpired in the restroom on the beach seemed to be left behind. "I have family there too. We go there every summer."

"How far is it from Ottawa?"

"About two and a half hours by train."

"Who's up for the high bars?" Jethro walked away knowing he would have an admiring audience once he began his routine. We followed him to the apparatus.

"What brings you out here?" Herbie asked. I watched closely, wondering what Rafael would share.

"Oh …" He wavered, and I couldn't tell if he was coming up with a story or a version of the truth. "I just needed to see the world a bit."

"Uh huh." Herbie could no more contemplate taking that type of risk than asking Shelly Lapeer to the senior prom.

Which he hadn't done. We glanced at each other, impressed. "So, you just stuck out your thumb and ... took off?"

"Kind of."

With no more information than that, Herbie and I were left to imagine the worst. The coolest. The craziest.

"Well, you got guts. I'll give you that, buster."

Rafael appeared to like Herbie's compliment. Till then, he had been more mystery than much else. This shift was a good sign.

By now, Jethro was in full form. He had mastered the high bar routines by observing the more athletic musclemen on the beach. He may have worked on his technique in gym class back at school, but it was here that he had been given all the best tips. Standing straight up in the air, rigid arms in a handstand, his toes pointing to the sky, he was perfection atop that high bar. You would never have guessed such agility from a quarterback. Poised to swing back down and around once, twice, before dismounting, he was a delight to watch. The ladies, and likely some of the guys too, drooled at the sight. I know I did.

When Jethro, who had sat next to me in French class back in the ninth grade, had asked for my help, he had barely completed the first of his growth spurts. Had he been even half of what he was to become by his senior year, would he have ever bothered with the likes of me? With Herbie? That he wasn't Jewish—as goyishe as one could be, Herbie was fond of saying—made us an oddball of a trio.

Back in September at the start of the school year, Jethro had paired up with Charlene Bennett. Cheerleader, glee club singer, and all-around perfect girl specimen. They had gone to first base by Christmas break; made it to second base by the drunken night of senior prom. When that evening's shenanigans were brought to light, Charlene's parents had put their foot down. They had read her the riot act.

"No ruffian football player is going to ruin *my* daughter's chances at a decent life," Mr. Bennett had declared over the phone to the consternation of Jethro's father, who then repeated the threat verbatim to his son.

The parental moratorium had lasted until early July when a concocted encounter on the pier rekindled hope for Jethro. They had been inseparable last weekend when we had celebrated my eighteenth birthday at the Fireside Room in the Santa Ynez Inn up in the Palisades.

Herbie, on the other hand, was a very different kettle of fish. He had pined for Shelly Lapeer ever since she had transferred from Beverly Hills High School in the tenth grade—a move that had been necessitated when her father had died under mysterious circumstances at the MGM studios—feeding rumors that ran the gamut, which we all talked about behind her back but never with Herbie once we saw how the gossip hurt him. Lapeer's name had appeared on screen credits with the likes of Bob Hope, Hedy Lamarr, Clark Gable, and a slew of other famous names too long to list. When Shelly had walked into our algebra class right after Passover in '47, Herbie had melted. I had never seen that happen before. The smartest of us, he went weak-kneed and stuttered in her company. He had strategized on asking Shelly out for over a year. Practiced and rehearsed with us on how he could break the ice to have a reasonable chance with a girl who was totally out of his league. In the end, Alexander Craig had swept her off her feet by the middle of our junior year and got engaged the day after Senior Prom, leaving poor Herbie to wonder about all the what-ifs that high school boys dwelled on when their lack of courage or chutzpah was exposed when it came to the fairer sex.

By the summer of '49, I, too, had managed to mature and develop. I may not have been movie star material, but after my geeky phase in middle school I had evolved and some might have described me as attractive. Not handsome like Jethro; I didn't have the musculature that came from sports, but I swam avidly. I was lean if not mean. Even Herbie had become quite dapper in his own, Jewish intellectual style. We had all come of age as we turned eighteen during our senior year, desperate to sow our wild oats.

Though, for me, life was more complicated. Herbie and Jethro suspected my secret and kept it safe. We never discussed it. Never delved into what couldn't be delved into openly. I was *finicky* was our code word for me and girls. I was a late bloomer. I was shy and not into sex the way most boys were. Luckily for me, they didn't care. Less competition in their eyes, I suppose. Jethro, as captain of the football team who played baseball and soccer, didn't give a damn what anyone thought about who he hung out with. I had been his savior for French in the ninth grade. Herbie had rescued his ass with crib sheets for science in the tenth and eleventh grades. We had helped him when math became more complex than he cared for. The guy was far from stupid, but when it came to the academic part of academia, he didn't apply himself much, preferring to fall back on his physical talents. We joked that together we could rule the world. Alone, not so much.

When Jethro aced his landing off the apparatus without

even a bobble, the applause was instantaneous. "You're good," Rafael told him.

Jethro could be surprisingly humble at times. He made a hand signal to say, "Ah, get on with you," and that was that. The admiration from the ladies in the crowd was a different matter altogether. He craved that as much as the other athletes who trained and made their presence known on Muscle Beach. "Is Malcom here?" Herbie asked.

"Haven't seen him," Jethro said, looking around again in case he had missed him before. "You ever heard of Malcom Brenner, Rafael?"

I would have been astonished if our Canadian guest had.

"No," he said, "is he famous?"

"He was Mr. Muscle Beach this year. He's a gas. A former anchor clanker. He's usually around. We know him."

"You, Jethro. You know him," Herbie intervened. "He doesn't know me and Gary from a hole in the ground."

"He does too. He sees you're with me."

"Oh. Yeah." Herbie replied. "I guess he does," sarcasm dripping oodles.

"Who's up for a swim?" Jethro asked. "You got a swimsuit, Frenchie?"

I cringed at the nickname he'd just ascribed to Rafael but my new acquaintance didn't seem bothered so I let it slide.

"Yeah. I do."

"Are you a good swimmer?"

"Pretty good. Never swam in the ocean though."

"You're in for a treat."

We ran towards the surf and lay our towels and our gear down.

"Is it safe to leave our stuff here?" Rafael asked.

Since I knew how broke he was, I wondered if he was worried about my stash. "Usually. But I got a lot of greenbacks from Mom today."

"Ya did …" Jethro said. "What for?"

"A long story."

"Do tell," Herbie inquired.

"Listen, why don't you three go in. Show Rafael the ropes. Make sure he gets the feel of the undertow. Rip currents. The whole deal."

"Yeah, yeah. He's safe with us, Mother."

Jethro pulled Rafael by his side and Herbie joined them. I put on my damp swim trunks—the ones Rafael had showered with— under the camouflage of my towel and watched as all three went diving into the Pacific Ocean.

The sun at two-thirty p.m. was absolutely splendid. The August version of Paradise for Santa Monica and surfers. For a Monday, the beach was crowded, but nothing like the weekend traffic we had just seen. On Friday night, after leaving the Fireside Room—too expensive and boring for us—with Charlene at Jethro's side, the four of us had done the rides and stuffed ourselves with cotton candy, with Herbie and I making ourselves scarce toward the latter part of the evening. We had huddled with the masses as we gave the couple time to rekindle and work out what they might say to Charlene's parents in order to give Jethro a second chance. His going off to the University of Southern California while Charlene attended UCLA seemed a match made in heaven to us.

The guys came running back a short while later. "How was it?"

"Unbelievable." Rafael's entire being was more innervated. "Never would have guessed how powerful the ocean could be."

His enthusiasm was infectious. "Glad you liked it." I stood up and put my sunglasses down. "Want to swim some more?"

"Hell yeah."

We ran and jumped into the surf, the sandy saltwater pelting our skin. "You're a great swimmer," I told him.

"We swim a lot during the summer." He ducked and came back up. "Have to make up for the long winters stuck indoors. But it's rivers, mostly, back home." Rafael was treading the waves. "Nothing like this." Rafael dove back under like he might have been a dolphin. The gloomy man I had met sitting by the sidewalk, three hours before, had vanished. The altogether happy soul before me caused my heart to flutter. I recognized that sensation well. We played tag for a bit, then jumped off each other's shoulders trying to get some height against the pounding waves.

"I'm bushed," he yelled at one point. I could see he had swallowed some water.

"You all right?" He headed for shore so I followed.

"For a newbie, you did well, Frenchie." Jethro threw him his towel.

"Are you okay with that nickname?" I asked him.

Rafael laughed. "Hell, I don't care. I'm French, aren't I?"

"Well, technically, French-Canadian, no?" Herbie stated, always a stickler for precision.

"You have nicknames back up in Canada too, don't you?" When Rafael nodded, Jethro said, "Don't bust my chops, Gary!" I knew better than to comment. For a second, I thought Rafael might come to my defense but he remained quiet, aware, I believed, of my discomfort. "You got a girl back up in Canada?" asked Jethro.

"I do. I did."

"Well, which is it?"

Rafael hesitated again. "It's complicated."

"Always is with dames." Jethro affected an air like he'd been around the block, which he hadn't. Other than Charlene, his girl experience was quite limited. A few trial-and-errors in grades ten and eleven; a couple of hot girls he made mistakes with by trying to go too fast.

"What's her name?" Herbie asked, sincerely interested, his own regrets at losing Shelly Lapeer to Alexander Craig triggering a concern for Rafael's dilemma.

"Lucille. Lucille Leclerc."

"What happened?" I asked, now that Herbie had begun to pry.

"She didn't want me to go out west to work on the farm for the summer."

"Farming? I thought you were a cowboy."

"I said I wasn't, right?"

"Oh yeah. My goof. Forgot."

"I don't know what I want to do with my life. I didn't know then. Don't really know now."

"You finished high school? How old are you?"

"I was supposed to graduate in June. I'm eighteen. But my grades weren't great. I needed to redo two classes in summer school but opted out."

"No college then …?"

"No." Rafael's answer surprised all three of us. We didn't understand that.

"How come?"

"Uh. Where I come from, we don't … I'm not college material. I needed to work. Make some money."

We suddenly realized how lucky we all were, that the background Rafael came from was not ours.

"Lucille wanted me to stay and get a job at a factory. She had a connection. Her uncle's a foreman at the plant. But I wasn't ready … if that's the right word." He looked around at the ocean, at the stretches of sandy beaches as though he had just spied something quite miraculous about the world and all that it could offer him. It was in the twinkle of his eyes and he appeared to tear up. "I know she wants to settle down, get married. Have babies. The whole nine yards."

Herbie, Jethro, and I whistled in unison, shocked at how real his fate was. Our different tones of incredulity made him laugh. He giggled aloud. "She's quite pretty. It wouldn't be the end of the world. It's just …"

"You're too young to settle down," Jethro said as definitively as he could, like a man of the world. "That's why you escaped. Came here. Right?"

The suggestion bounced past Rafael and he didn't answer momentarily. I saw the way he watched me, knew how I had found him. Lost and abandoned on a curb. That was *not* the man Jethro was proposing he was, though something about escaping did seem to ring true. His eyes implied as much.

"Yeah. Sure. Why not?"

Jethro patted him on the back. "Well, hot diggity dog, you came to the right place. How long you planning on staying?"

I had to intervene. "He's only here for a few days."

"Where are you staying?" Herbie asked.

"I don't know as yet …"

"With me, of course."

"Oh …" Jethro and Herbie exclaimed together.

"Where'd you park your car, Jethro?" I wanted us to get a move on before Rafael could be put on the spot some more.

"Up by the pier."

"Why don't we drive up to Third Street? Check the show time for the movie. We'll grab some food up there." I could see Rafael waver. I signaled with my eyes that it was all right but his discomfort was plain to see.

SEVEN

"So, you paying for this guy?" Herbie asked at the urinals.

We had driven to the Brentwood Country Mart to show Rafael the latest the locale had to offer. I was at the sink washing my hands and I grimaced. "That obvious?"

Herbie nodded as he zipped up.

"Do you think Jethro picked up on it?" I asked.

"Maybe. I suppose so."

I could see Herbie had that "what gives?" expression on his face. How did I explain away *this* phenomenon?

"You know I'm not an eager beaver ..." When Herbie didn't disavow the fact, I argued, "What?"

"Ya kinda are, Gary. You can get excited over ... stuff."

"Stuff? Like what?"

He went into a litany I didn't like.

"Okay. Maybe. On occasion." So, that's what I went

with to explain away my adopting a street bum. A French-Canadian urchin who was broke and starving who I felt sorry for.

"You don't know him from Adam. You gonna let him stay over at your house? What's your mom going to say?"

I hadn't quite devised my story until now. "I was hoping you could play a small part in that."

"What!"

"I could tell Mother that *you* met Rafael at the pier. You introduced us. It'll be less suspicious."

"But just as crazy."

"Come on, Herbie. Just this once …"

"And how did that lead to him staying over with you, not with me?"

"That you guys keep kosher?" Even my witticism wouldn't fly. Not today. Not for something like this. "We could say he was robbed. He's too embarrassed to call back home. His family's poor."

"Your mother's not going to like that part."

"Which part?"

"The poor part. Come on, Gary. Your mother looks down on *my* family. And we're Jewish. Some poor French-Canadian schlub? I don't think so."

"He's not a schlub."

"Okay. Goy. Any better?"

He had a point. "She's not beyond doing a mitzvah now and again."

"Yeah, I suppose." Herbie's hands were clean and dry by now. "So, what's the story going to be?"

"For Mother or for Jethro?" I could see how complicated this was becoming. "Shit!"

"All Jethro needs to know is that Rafael was robbed and he's short on cash," Herbie said, wise beyond his years. "Waiting for his parents to wire him some. I can handle Jethro; I'll pull him aside when we go out. For your mom …? You can play the sob sister angle. Tell her I found him on the boardwalk. Felt sorry."

"A good thing I've got all that cash."

"About that …?"

"You won't believe this, Herbie. She took me to the bank this morning. Right then and there, she confessed that the old man left me cash for college. She'd been keeping it in a separate account. All this time."

"No shit?"

"She wanted me to go with Jethro and you to look at cars today."

"No shit!"

When we reconvened at the patio tables, Jethro announced, "Charlene's coming to the movies with us."

"She is?" I said.

"Yeah. Just got off the ameche. She's free."

"You called her house? You weren't afraid her mom would recognize your voice?"

Jethro indicated Rafael. He grabbed him and pulled him up like he was a newfound hero, ruffled his hair. "He was on the nose. Polite. Her mother bought it. Hook, line and sinker. I *love* this guy!"

I was taken aback by this latest tangle. I cued Herbie who asked Jethro if he wanted to check out comics at the drugstore. As soon as they were gone, I broached our plan with Rafael. He seemed uncomfortable again. "If it's the money …"

"It is. I want to pay you back."

"Natch. You can send me the money when you get back home." I could see he was bandying the decision. "Look, so this won't be too awkward, I'm going to give you a bit of cash now. This way," I put two tens and a twenty on the table, "when you have to pay for stuff, it'll look like you had a bit of money all along."

"Won't that be confusing for Jethro?"

"Don't worry about Jethro. With Charlene around, he won't be paying you any attention."

The four of us drove to Hastings Chevrolet on Euclid. "Don't let them know your wallet's loaded with clams," Jethro announced. "They won't let us off the lot. We'll just say we're browsing."

"What if Gary finds a deal?" Herbie asked.

"You don't want to buy anything today. We can come back tomorrow. Make them wait," he said, as though he had bought more than only one car in his life.

"Is that how your dad did it?" I asked him.

"No. Dad did it all wrong. A rookie really. No. The guys at the beach told me how it's done. Trust me. My dad could have saved himself some lettuce."

When we parked and were standing on the lot, I was surprised at how old the salesmen were. I had thought this was a younger man's game.

"Can I help you fellows?" The man in a three-piece suit approached and shook Jethro's hand. His dark shirt and tie were the only things that said hipster instead of geezer.

"Yes, sir. My pal here," he pointed at me, "is about to buy his first car."

"You've come to the right location." The man took me by the shoulder. "Scott Smith." He shook my hand quite vigorously.

"Gary. Silverman," I said, set back on my heels immediately. I hadn't felt under such pressure since cousin Saydie had insisted to my mother that I *had* to have a Bar Mitzvah.

"You're thinking of buying new or used?"

"He hasn't made up his mind." Jethro said it like he had been my business advisor for years. "He's got time. He's not leaving for Stanford for a few more weeks."

"Stanford. Such a promising future." The edginess in Smith's voice increased and I couldn't tell if he imagined me a legacy student from a long-line of Stanford alumni men. Saw me with a silver spoon from birth and a rich daddy's money to spend. He would have been half-right yet totally mistaken in his assumptions. "A used car," I said, quickly dispelling him of his high hopes. "A '46 coupe. Maybe the '47 Fleetmaster sports coupe. Depends on the price."

Scott Smith was undeterred. "I wouldn't be doing my job if I didn't try to tempt you just a little bit." He took me by my elbow, like we were on a date, practically scooped me up towards a beauty. "This is our '49 Deluxe Fleetline model."

All four of us whistled. "What do you think?" Smith smiled like a boastful father with his month-old baby. Jethro was salivating at the lines and size of the beast that *were* something to behold.

"You want to take her out for a spin? You have to with this beaut." He was talking to me, but I could tell he had decided that Jethro was the leader of our pack.

"Yeah," said Jethro. "You wanna drive, Gary, or let me?" he asked, knowing I wasn't into cars the way he was.

"It's my money …" I said, adding suspense to what I already knew was my answer.

"Yeah …" Jethro said, deflated, about to give in when he saw me smile. "Hot diggity dog." He grabbed the keys from Scott, who opened the door to let Rafael and Herbie get into the back seat.

"You have to sit up front," Scott told me. "Get the feel of the ride." He slid into the back seat next to Rafael who was out of his milieu, scrunched in between.

"The paint job's beautiful," I said, admiring the cream-colored interiors.

"Monaco Blue Metallic," Smith bragged. "Same for the wheels. The stripe is silver."

I marveled at the leather and cloth interiors. More buttons to play with than I had ever seen in a vehicle before. "What are these for?"

"Push button door handles. It's never been done. All new this year."

We came back to the car lot a full ten minutes later, having driven down to the beach and back, filled to the brim with the dreams that every eighteen-year-old mustered. But barring another windfall, my budget wouldn't allow me this luxury.

"So how much?" Jethro asked, aware that he would be bursting the bubble once that was answered.

"Why don't we go inside? We can talk more quietly."

"Listen, Scott. We're not buying today," Jethro said, throwing more cold water on Scott's prospects for a sale. "Just ballpark it for us. That way, we'll know if it's a new model or a used one that's in the making. My friend, Gary, here. He's got a lot on his plate. Getting ready for university and all."

"Fourteen ninety-two and you drive it off the lot today."

All that money, I thought. I had the amount *and some* between my wallet and my new bank account, but it was for a car *and* my books *and* my first year's tuition costs. Room *and* board. "We'll think about it," I said.

"I can show you some more."

"I like the '46 coupe convertible over there. How much for that?"

"I'd have to look that one up. Ya like her?"

"A lot. Tell you what, Scott. We're in a hurry. We have a movie date."

"What are you seeing?"

"*Mr. Belvedere Goes to College*. It's at the Criterion."

"I took the wife to see it last month. It's still playing?"

"It better be." I signaled for the others to go. "I'll be back tomorrow. More than likely. I'll want to take that '46 out for a spin."

"I'll be here. I'll put that one aside until five p.m. tomorrow."

We were back in Jethro's Ford convertible coupe, top down, the warm early evening air in our faces, going down towards Third Street and the Criterion when Herbie, in the passenger side seat, spotted Charlene coming out of Grayson's Ladies Ready to Wear store. "Heh, isn't that Charlene?" he said.

We all looked to the side as Jethro tapped his horn and came to a stop. Her gaze fixed on us and she ran to the curb. "Jethro." No one could doubt how happy she was to see him. "Hi fellas." She waved and paid close attention to the stranger among us. "You must be Rafael." She put the few boxes in her other arm and waved to her companion. "Judy. Here." That's when we all saw Judy Mosley coming up behind her. She had double the merchandise and was decked out to seduce. "This is …"

Before Charlene could point Rafael out, Judy bent into the car, her bosoms hidden behind expensive linen, pressed against the lowered window on the passenger seat side. She presented her hand. "Enchanté."

"Does everybody here speak that lingo?" Jethro said. "Geez Louise."

It was no exaggeration that Rafael was taken by Judy's flirtatiousness. Any hot-blooded male would have. The girl was nothing if not vivacious with all the right curves. Lips like red, soft cushions that could only produce hunger in men. Envy in females. He took her hand and with no other recourse, he pecked it and flashed a smile I hadn't seen on him yet. Enraptured described it best.

Pleased with herself, she pulled her ringed fingers away and declared, "A gentleman. Finally."

Not about to be upstaged, Jethro took the bull by the horns. "Here, Charlene. Put your stuff in the car. You too, Judy. We'll go park this jalopy and come back."

Hearing Jethro refer to his brand new '49 Ford Club Coupe as a jalopy made me laugh. He might have wanted to race it like a jalopy, but this was a premium, custom convertible his father had paid serious cash for.

"You don't need all of us to do that," Herbie offered and jumped out of the vehicle like he was auditioning for some title on Muscle Beach. I had never seen him this spry. He passed me the remainder of the packages and I stacked them between me and Rafael.

"That it?" I said. I could see Judy's eyes had not left Rafael for even a second. We drove off and I leaned into him. "Be careful. She's khaki whacky, if you catch my drift." That got Jethro laughing.

"Leave him alone, Gary. He might just get him some tonight."

"What is that, khaki whacky?"

"You don't have that expression up in Canada?" Jethro was backing into a parking spot.

"Not in my neck of the woods."

"It means she's wild. Boy crazy." He put the car in park and turned to Rafael. "And something tells me she's hot for your French baguette." He slapped Rafael's knee like they had been buddies forever. With no inkling if the rumors about Judy's escapades were actually true, her reputation was still the talk of the school whenever she showed up wearing too much jewelry. A new perfume. "She's quite the cookie. Got kicked out of a Catholic boarding school." Jethro wolf whistled. "You son of a gun. You just got here and you're going to get to third base if you play your cards right." He put the top up and had me stack the packages in the trunk.

Outside the Criterion, people were gathering, lining up for the evening show. Jethro had already escorted Charlene by the arm when Judy waltzed up to Rafael. "Vous me permettez?" She took him by the arm and he willingly went with her. I watched as he bought their tickets with the money I had given him.

"That must suck," Herbie whispered to me. "Seeing as how *she's* loaded."

"Shut up." Herbie had already guessed that my interest in our new friend was more than altruistic, that was plain to see. Inside the lobby, Jethro and Charlene were deciding on treats when I suggested, "Shouldn't we get our seats? The place is going to fill up."

"What do you want? I'll get it for you, Gary." Jethro had his wallet out. "You and Herbie can grab a row. Not too close. It's not like Betty Grable's on the screen."

Charlene took it upon herself to punch him in the upper arm. Good for you, I thought.

Herbie and I walked down the right aisle. With rows of twelve seats in the middle section, the giant palace had more room than any Monday night crowd would ever fill. "You choose," I told Herbie. We went down about fifteen rows from the front, a few feet going up the raked slope. I nodded when he looked back for confirmation. "So, who's going to sit next to whom?" I asked.

Herbie laughed. I had seen how he had perked up when Judy approached the car. She was no Shelly Lapeer, but she did come from similar backgrounds—movie studio executive dad and a society mom. More importantly for her status, her father was still alive, still producing at Paramount. If her famous pedigree carried the stigma of scandal, we were not aware of it.

"You'll hate yourself if you sit next to her and she's all googly-eyed for Rafael," I said, not wanting at all to be cruel.

"And what about you? You gonna sit next to him?"

"Plus ça change …"

We were both at a stalemate, had never been this honest about my condition. I felt his pangs for the ineffable loss of Shelly Lapeer and he felt what for my …? What to call what it was that I had for Rafael? A crush? It worked for me.

The two of us were at our seats standing, waiting, with four empty seats between us, eager to see how the lineup would pan out. Herbie was the closest to them as they entered the aisle. Rafael, holding hands now with Judy, sidled past him and sat next to me. "You go," Jethro told Herbie so that he would be sitting next to Judy too. Charlene and Jethro followed in that order. That was how we watched Clifton Webb do his best to make us all look less than forward to where we were headed during the next calendar month.

When the lights came up, Judy was the first to speak up. "Are we staying for *Ma and Pa Kettle*?" That was the other half of the double bill. "I'm hungry. Let's go to Sugie's."

"It's Monday," Herbie reminded us. "They're closed. Everything's closed, no?"

"I was craving their chicken curry. Do you like curry, Rafael?" She hadn't stopped pawing him throughout the feature. I had tried not to pay any attention, tried to keep my focus on the screen, but every gesture of her hands, her fingers, had set my stomach to churn. I hated myself for the predicament I was in.

"I don't think so. Is that Chinese?"

Jethro snickered but Charlene shushed him and said, "No, Rafael. It's Indian food. Quite spicy."

"Haven't had the pleasure."

We were all standing up now and I couldn't keep myself from checking every position Judy took towards Rafael. He had to have noticed me. How could he not have seen me doing *that*. "We could drive out to Malibu Inn," I suggested, wanting to draw a truce with my intense attractions.

"I know," Jethro said forthrightly. "Big Rock Café out in Malibu. It stays open late. We can walk the beach. Rafael will like that."

I wish I could have been better company that night.

At the Café, Judy practically sat on Rafael's lap. Our corner booth was tight but not *that* tight. The banter stayed relatively light. Questions about Ottawa brought up Lucille. I was like a hawk when Rafael mentioned her name; I monitored Judy to see if she had a conscience or any degree of propriety that seemed warranted, once a girlfriend waiting back home for Rafael was in the mix. There was none exhibited. She had glided over that technicality and moved on to talk of sororities, which ones she and Charlene would be pledging for.

"It's weird how Stanford starts so late. Is it always like that?" Judy asked me as we were paying the bill.

"It's later than usual this year. I'm going up early to stay with a cousin in San Francisco for a week. Get my bearings in the Bay area."

"How fun!" She leaned into Rafael so forcefully, I thought for sure they would fall down. He laughed and took her by the waist as though letting her know she was safe with him. I hated them both at that second in time.

Out on the beach, the cool ocean breezes made me happy that we had changed into our dungarees. Rafael had no suitable jacket with him so I lent him my cardigan, which he graciously offered to Judy when she began to shiver. She took his arm instead and huddled closer to him, like an appendage attached to his hip.

We walked a ways, going north, then came back down to where the Café lights made it safer to stroll. The surf was at low tide so that we had stretches of sandy beach before us.

"What are you all doing tomorrow?" Judy asked.

That was my cue. "Rafael and I are going to buy me a car."

"A car?" She was fascinated. "And then …?"

"I was going to drive around. Show Rafael a few highlights. Take him to Hollywood."

"You've never been, right?" she asked Rafael, already knowing that answer *and* some. He shook his head. "My dad's got tickets for a premiere. On Wednesday night."

"A premiere?" Charlene shrilled with excitement.

The girls grabbed each other's hands. "Nothing big. Not like Van Johnson or Bing Crosby are in the film. But they might be at the party afterwards. It's Paramount. You never know …"

"What's the movie?" Jethro asked.

"*Jolson Sings Again*. Larry Parks and Barbara Hale are the leads. Daddy says it's going to be a hit."

Everyone had questions, but I could tell that the prospect of a Hollywood premiere was beyond Rafael's ken. I was keen, as was Herbie, but I had Rafael to contend with. "How many tickets?" I asked.

Judy was quick to pull back. The way she looked at me—we were under the streetlamp so the white of her eyes were clear to see. "It was four tickets." She hesitated, almost as though it was on purpose. I had never thought of her as mean, but then, we hardly knew each other well enough for me to have formed that opinion. "But I'm positive if I ask Daddy, he'll come up with two more. We'll make a night of it. The after-party. We'll get in. Daddy will make sure we're on a list."

Our excitement was palpable as the girls sat together in the back and made plans about their dresses and their hair. Rafael was next to me, crunched up. I whispered in his ear, "You'll be fine. We'll get you duds tomorrow."

He never said a word.

EIGHT

Jethro's car pulled away leaving Rafael and I to our own ruminations. The quiet of Sunset Park was always welcoming at this hour. Far away from the hustle and bustle where the tourists crammed by the ocean. We had dropped Judy off at her mansion—hidden behind tall stucco fencing. Rafael had walked her to the door and been introduced to her mother. Charlene was then escorted to her door by Rafael, who got to meet a second mother for the night.

"How was she?" Jethro asked him as soon as he reached the car. "Did she ask a lot of questions?"

"Too many," he said before cracking up at our moxie, pulling the wool over these parents' eyes. We had parked on another block so that Charlene's parents wouldn't be suspicious, having refused outright Herbie's argument that this would be a dead giveaway.

"Did you have to explain not having a car?"

"I did what you all told me to do. We wanted to take a walk so I parked up the street."

"She bought that?" Jethro said. We all knew he would never have been given the benefit of *that* doubt. "You have the face of an angel, Rafael. You can't fight it."

We all jeered and made fun of him; the four of us happy to be off the hook from parental complications.

"My third mother tonight," Rafael said as we walked up the front steps of our bungalow. "You're positive this is going to work?"

"No clue. Going to have to wing it."

Mother always left the lights on so that the front and back porches were lit until I came home. It was our tradition that I shut them off after I got in. I opened the door and saw her asleep on the sofa. She often did that when she didn't know how late I was going to be. After that morning's bonanza, I wondered if she thought I'd been out showing off my car. "Mother …" I said gently, not wanting to startle her.

Her eyes opened and she saw Rafael and sat up. "I'm sorry. I must have dozed off."

I could tell she could not make head nor tail of Rafael's presence at this time of night.

She checked her watch. "Oh, my." She stood and pressed out the creases from her dress. 'Did you buy the car?" She went to turn on more lights.

"I know it's late. And no. We looked but we didn't buy." Before she could ask, I said, "Mother. This is Rafael Jerome. He's visiting Los Angeles from Canada."

"Canada? My. That's far. Are you here with your parents?"

"No."

I could feel the complexity of our situation and had no words that might comply with any acceptable explanation. I switched tactics instantly. "Rafael, this is my mother, Rebeka Silverman."

"Pleased to meet you, Mrs. Silverman." Rafael shook her hand.

"Are you boys hungry?" she asked, unsure of what else to say. She could see he had a backpack in his hands.

"No, Mother. We're stuffed. We were up in Malibu. That new place. On the highway?"

"How was it?"

"Great views. We went after the movies."

"Did you boys have fun?" She was addressing Rafael mainly, wanting a feel for her houseguest.

"We had a swell time. Met some nice people."

"Girls, I presume." She grinned as she said it and Rafael blushed. That won him *so* many brownie points.

"Charlene met up with us. She brought Judy Mosley."

"Judy Mosley? My ..."

"Guess what she's got for us this Wednesday?" Mother hated guessing, so I relieved her of the duty promptly. "Tickets for a premiere."

"Well, you're certainly coming up in the world."

I knew how little any of that meant to Mother, not in the traditional sense the expression was used. She may have wanted me successful and married to a good girl from a respectable family, but the flash and cash that was Hollywood did not impress her. Ivy league, a professional career, those were the aspirations she had always hoped for me.

"You'll be going too, Rafael?" The question was more about getting her bearings. I was savvy enough to grasp that she needed answers as to who this young man was and why he had luggage with him.

"Mother, if you don't mind. Rafael's going to stay with us. A few days. It's a long story."

"I have time."

She wasn't going to let me off this easy. I had no choice but to use the lie Herbie and I had invented for her ears only. When it was told, she gave him a pitiful gaze. "That must have been very frightening. We had a couple of scares in Paris. Years ago, when I took Gary on our adventures."

"Il m'en a parlé, Mme Silverman."

And with that, we were off to the races. The white lie about how Rafael came to us dissipated, and Mother was left with a soulmate, for that was all that she could see when someone spoke a foreign language she knew. Having mastered German and French as a young girl and picked up Spanish along the way, she thrived at every chance she had to converse in those languages, regardless of who with. Rafael was no longer a stranger. For now, he was ambassador to a world she wanted to explore.

It was going on one thirty and I could tell everyone here was exhausted. "Mother. We have a big day tomorrow. Rafael's coming with me to buy the car."

"You will be careful. I'd go with you, but I'd be a nuisance. Je ne connais rien des voitures."

Upstairs, in my bedroom—we only had two in the bungalow—and the couch felt oddly inappropriate. Herbie always slept upstairs with me when he stayed over so Mother never even brought up the prospect of making up the couch. "That went quite well, don't you think?" I had taken off my shirt and pants and was standing in my boxers.

"Yeah. She speaks French beautifully. She'd be right at home with my family."

That pleased me more than he could have imagined. I beamed and Rafael looked at me quizzically.

"What? Why are you making that face?"

I had never been good at hiding my true feelings and, now, I seemed caught without my wanting it. "It's nothing. Just … How strange this all is." I could see Rafael retreat. One moment he had been there with me. Now he was distant. "You all right?"

"Where am I going to sleep?"

I saw my bed and suddenly realized we were strangers. This wasn't Herbie doing a sleepover after an evening cramming for an exam. There was zero history to create such an intimate space between us. Not like this. Not like I supposed I had hoped for all that day. "I … uh …" I looked away from the bed as soon as I saw Rafael balk at even the possibility of sharing the mattress. "I have extra blankets. I'll set you up on the floor." I threw him a pillow from the bed and he grabbed it in the nick of time. I retrieved the winter comforter from the cedar chest and went to the hallway to fetch him clean sheets from the linen closet. When I came back into the room, Rafael had taken off his dungarees and put on the rinsed-out boxers from earlier that day. "Are they dry?"

"Uh, yeah," he said unconvincingly.

"I have clean ones." When he didn't refuse, I went to my drawer and tossed him a pair. "Here. These are tight on me. They should fit you well."

"I need to use the bathroom."

"It's at the end of the hallway. Be quiet. Mother's likely still up. She's finicky about her privacy."

Why had I said that? Rafael laughed and went outside, making sure she wasn't in the hallway before he scrammed. He came back in a jiffy wearing the freshly laundered boxers.

"You can keep those. I have plenty."

He lay down on the makeshift bedding, and I turned out the lights. We stayed in our respective hollows—mine on a comfortable mattress, surrounded by all of my familiar paraphernalia that summed up my high school years; Rafael on the floor, covered by the billowy down comforter that did little to mask the hard floorboards underneath him. I thought of where he came from. What had happened in Calgary that he hadn't disclosed, only alluded to. A few minutes went by when I said, "Was it really bad?"

"What?"

It appeared as though Rafael had already begun to fall asleep. I'd woken him up, if that was possible. "Calgary."

The longest silence prevailed before he said, "I don't want to talk about that."

Small snoring noises soon came from the floor and I was left to my own imagination. I had lived an interesting life up till then. I had seen parts of Europe. I had been back east once or twice. New York City and Chicago. Never Boston. Boston was still a city I wanted to see but for now, Calgary, farmland, the banks of the Ottawa River. These were where my dreams took me.

NINE

The morning light had been shining into the bedroom window for what seemed ages. I could hear the songbirds, could smell the scent of the ocean seep from the screen placed at the bottom where my window was left ajar, eight inches from the sill. Rafael's snoring had subsided leaving only shallow breathing that I associated with dreaming. What visions were rolling through his brain? Pretty ones? Pesky ones?

I peeked over the edge of my bed and saw him deep in slumber. He looked peaceful, younger than he had the day before. His five-o'clock shadow barely registered on his juvenile face. When was the last time he shaved? He hadn't shown any signs of facial hair the day before. I rolled onto my back and was planning our day when the phone rang. When no one answered, I jumped up and ran past Rafael who stirred with a start.

"What …?" he said, still mostly asleep.

I flew down the stairs and reached the phone before they hung up. "Hello. Silverman residence."

"You guys get to bed late?" It was Judy.

"Yeah. Kind of." I could hear Rafael using the toilet upstairs.

"Is my favorite French Canadian available?"

I became territorial in a heartbeat. "He's still sleeping," I said as Rafael descended the stairs two at a time. He was in his dungarees, bare-chested and looked as handsome and forlorn as the day before. I mouthed, "It's Judy. She wants to speak to you." He approached eagerly. "Speak of the devil. You'll never guess what the cat dragged in. Here," I said, handing him the receiver.

"Hi. Judy?"

I watched, adamant that Judy Mosley was not going to ruin my day with Rafael. He caught me staring and turned away, obviously wanting privacy. I would not give him that.

"I couldn't tell ya," he said. "I just got up."

He listened and laughed—the kind of laughter that guys did when girls were at their most mundane. I never understood that. The obligatory rules between the opposite sexes that left me cold if not downright confused much of the time.

"I'll ask him."

Rafael turned to see that I had not budged an inch. My house, my rules I would have said if he had challenged me.

"She wants our agenda for today."

I knew bold action was needed to keep my affairs on target. I snatched the phone. "We've got a pretty tight schedule, Judy. I'm buying the car later this morning. Then I thought I'd drive to Hollywood. We need clothes for tomorrow night. That's still on, right?"

"Yes. Daddy got us the extra tickets. We're in the balcony now." She had a wheeling-dealing sort of tone as she said it, which suggested I had to keep up with my side of a furtive bargain.

"That's great, Judy. Really." She asked where we were going to shop. "I hadn't thought about it yet. Why?" She proposed a rendezvous for late afternoon. "I'd like that. I'm sure Rafael would too." I detested lying but what else could I do now that she was vying for Rafael's affection. "My mom. She mentioned something about a dinner tonight. I'd hate to mess that up." We bantered back and forth before she asked to speak directly to Rafael again. "Sure. Of course. Here he is."

Rafael turned away once more as though *that* had worked the first time. He wanted me to leave him so he could talk in private, but a pettiness I didn't know I had within me had taken over.

"I guess so. Yeah. Okay," he said. "Maybe tonight."

He hung up and turned to see that I had barely moved. He walked to the stairs and I realized then that I had messed things up. Why had I done that? I marched behind him when he closed the door saying he needed to change. I stood in the hallway of my own house and debated how to play this. Give him space, my gut told me, so I walked downstairs, wondering where Mother was. I saw the note on the table. "Gone to my appointment. Won't be back till quite late. There's pot roast in the refrigerator for dinner. I'm dining out with the Barrys. Have fun."

I quickly crumpled the sheet of paper, aware that my lie, once discovered, could ruin everything. Rafael came sauntering in. He had his rucksack with him. "Going somewhere?"

"I ... I just thought ..." His sentence trailed to a whisper.

I had not anticipated this. But *why* not! I had no claims here. He was free to go. We both knew that. "I can be so stupid. I don't know why I do that."

"Is that what you call it?"

I wasn't sure what he was implying. "You want to go?" I asked hesitantly.

He put his bundle down on the chair. "Where's your mom?"

"She had a meeting."

"For work?"

"Yes and no." My ambiguity was no help. "She does insurance."

"A woman? Wow."

"She's more of a promoter. My dad had a firm. When he left us, she worked out some angle with his company. She gets commissions. I still don't quite understand what she does." What I said hardly mattered. All Rafael cared about were my intentions, and I was clueless as to how to proceed. "You want to meet up with Judy, right?"

"I'd like to."

"What about Lucille?" The about-turn from Rafael was shocking. For a second, I thought he might actually hit me.

"What's wrong with you, Gary?" He went out to the living room and I followed. He was looking for something. "Do you have cigarettes? I could use one."

"Here," I said, opening the silver box my mother kept

for entertaining since neither of us smoked. He took one and a wooden match and lit up. When he inhaled, I could see he was a smoker. "How come you never smoked yesterday?"

"I'm broke, remember?"

He had the money I had given him. That he could have bought a pack but didn't made me respect him even more. He had values that we shared.

"None of you were smoking. I didn't want to impose."

"It's weird, I know, that none of us smoke. Everybody else at my school does. Jethro's influence. He's a health nut. But Judy must …"

Rafael smoked in silence like he was weighing out all of his options. "So, your mom. This dinner tonight. That's on?"

Why had he asked *that* question! Anything else, I could have handled. He could have accused me of being attracted to him. I would have hemmed and hawed and said yes. He could have asked me if I was queer and I would have confessed. I was so smitten. He had a face that was pure gold. An innocence about him. Maybe it was the Canadian culture, a simplicity that was so appealing I couldn't stop myself even if I had tried. The way we had met. The serendipity of it. Seeing Rafael naked for that one instant in the men's room at the beach, the day before, had fed into my fantasy and I couldn't let it go. "I think so. Yeah. There was no note."

"Can you call her? Does she have an office?"

I shook my head. "Here, up in her bedroom is where she keeps her files." He could see he was stuck with my rendition. "Why don't we play it by ear? We'll eat breakfast. Go out for the car. You're into cars, right?" He nodded, aware that I'd seen how excited he had been during yesterday's test drive.

"That'll take us a few hours. Easy. I'll drive you through Hollywood. While you're out here, you *have* to see what all the hoopla is about."

He was settling into the picture I was drawing of our day together but he was no dope. I knew I had to add Judy into the mix to keep him on my course. "When Mom comes home, I can ask if Judy can join us. Last minute …? But first, we have to get you duds for the premiere."

"I don't think I'm gonna go to that."

I was astounded. "Why? Judy's setting this all up. In part … I'm pretty sure for you."

Rafael reached for another cigarette and lit up. He was tense as hell and I couldn't figure out why. A minute ago, I thought him angry at my being jealous of her. Now, this? "You're going to have to help me out here. I'm lost."

"You and me both." He puffed on the cigarette like it was made of a stronger substance than tobacco. "I promised Lucille …"

Ah, Lucille. I loved her instantly. "Yeah …"

"Before I left for Calgary, I told her I'd come back to her a virgin."

I didn't know men made those promises. I had no words.

"She's very Catholic."

"You?"

"Yeah. Sort of." He put out the cigarette. "We made a promise that we would both be virgins on the first night of our honeymoon."

"I see …"

"No. No you don't." Rafael rose, looking like a caged animal. "I gotta …" He went to get his kit. "I have to leave."

"What? We just planned …"

"No, we didn't. *You* did."

"Rafael. What's going on?" I asked but he was already on the front porch. "Where are you going? You don't even know where you are?"

As I reached for him, he turned and swung at me. We tousled on the walkway and fell onto the lawn.

"You don't own me," he said, all garbled as he tried to pin me down, but I was stronger, bigger than him, and got the upper hand. He went passive all at once and I could see him begin to shake. A shaking that came from … fear? From some kind of hurt that I couldn't pinpoint? It was not of *my* doing. Nothing I had done towards Rafael could have induced this. "Uncle," he said, as if we had been wrestling for real.

I let go and we sat side by side on the lawn. I couldn't tell if he felt foolish or not, but I was exhausted. That was my only feeling. A poor night's sleep after a confusing day, laden with a reach of emotions I had never experienced before, had me beside myself and I wasn't confident in what I might say. "Is there something you need to tell me?"

"You," he said. "You want to tell me something?"

This was where it could get tricky as hell, I told myself. "Can we go inside?" I asked, conscious that neighbors might be watching, listening.

"Why? So you can seduce me?"

I jumped up, angry and frustrated. He had no right to accuse me like that. I had been a gentleman from the start. He had to have grasped that. "Is that what happened in the restroom on the beach?" I walked away from him and onto our front porch hoping he would follow. I could hear his footsteps and opened the door and walked in.

Rafael was in my face as soon as we hit the living room. "You're queer, right? I'm not wrong about that, am I?"

No one had ever confronted me that way before. The manner in his question was not how Herbie would have broached the topic if he had ever had the temerity to do so. Even Jethro, I thought, would have been more empathetic had it ever been brought up. Rafael, however, had hatred in his voice; I could see how this might backfire. I couldn't have that in my mother's house. "No," I denied unequivocally.

"You're lying. I can tell. The way you've been eyeballing me."

"Is that what you've been thinking all this time? Why I gave you money? Bought you food and clothes?" Even as I said it, I could hear the phoniness coming from me. How ridiculous I must have sounded. But I had self-preservation to think of and quality acting was in order. "I felt sorry for you. Is that so wrong?"

I could tell Rafael was reassessing everything. He'd snapped his cap and was now reevaluating. "I'm sorry. I guess …"

I needed to assert my ascendency. "I think you owe me an apology." Was I going too far?

"I apologize. I'm more messed up than I realized."

His saying that made me curious. "I don't know you. But I'm sure you'll confide in me when you're ready." I wanted to say I was a good listener but that would have been mawkish.

Our standoff ended in the blink of an eye. There was a calm to the room where before only tension had resided. "Cornflakes or eggs?"

"Any bacon?"

"We're Jewish." Before he could apologize, I added. "Of course, we have bacon."

I made us breakfast and we ate as though nothing had occurred. We left on foot for Hastings Chevrolet on Euclid, enjoying the walk, talking about what we wanted from our lives. At the dealership, Scott Smith had prepped the '46 coupe convertible in anticipation of a sale. After a quick spin, the paperwork was drawn, some cash and a check exchanged, and Rafael and I headed to Hollywood.

TEN

We drove under the porte-cochere at Bullock's on Wilshire. The valet, outfitted in livery, took my keys—a first for me—and we walked inside to the smell of what money could buy.

"Gary. I really don't need anything fancy."

"You saw the Pantages Theatre we're going to tomorrow. Imagine when all the limousines come riding up there. We might not be in tuxes, but we want to look our best." I had a hunch this extravagance would not pass muster with Mother. All my college funds being squandered in this fashion, but I couldn't help myself. The day had been going splendidly, with our earlier skirmish having left no blemish on our budding friendship.

In the men's department, an attendant approached. With his slicked-back hair and a dashing Valentino style, I could tell he was going to be flamboyant by how he walked. "Gentlemen, what can I do for you?"

I studied Rafael, worried that he might be rude but only got a blank stare from him. Clearly, I was running this show. "We need suits. Shirts. Ties and shoes."

"The whole kit and caboodle?"

His fey delivery made caboodle sound dirty. "Yes, I suppose so."

"Follow me."

The flair in his step, as he walked us to the suit section, had me envious; how uninhibited he was!

"Do you have any preference?" He looked me straight in the eye when he asked. I blushed unexpectedly, something I rarely ever did.

"We're open to suggestion," I said, not the least tongue-in-cheek.

When he turned to Rafael, I panicked, sure that he would punch the clerk in the nose if the man even came close to touching him. "You look very familiar. Are you in the movies?"

"No. I'm not," Rafael answered him, unaware that the line was small talk, Hollywood parlance as an opening line.

Our clerk, whose name was James, began by asking our sizes. His devotion to detail was exemplary. I could see why Bullock's had the reputation it did, why the Hollywood elite shopped there. He took out a measuring tape when I told him my jacket size. I couldn't fathom how this might all progress when Rafael winked at me. The shift in him was nothing short of astonishing. There was no recoiling when James took our inseams once we were in the privacy of the fitting room, standing in our underwear.

In front of the mirror for a final check before getting

back into our civilian dungarees, I thought we made the handsomest couple I had ever seen. Our suits, pinstripes—mine a navy blue to match my eyes, Rafael's a dark gray. Our shirts with matching shades, lighter gray for me, duskier for Rafael to contrast with our ties. Our shoes, wingtips, black to go with both our suits. For the finishing touch, fedoras that fit us quite well. At the cash register, James threw in socks and boxers like they were Christmas morning stocking stuffers. "On the house," he added as he dropped them inside one of the bags. I wondered if they did that for all their novice customers who splurged, to get them to return and spend some more?

We were back downstairs waiting for the valet to bring my car. I had never felt as high and wild. It reminded me of shopping sprees back in Paris as a youngster when Mother would indulge and regret it as soon as we had gone back to our rooms. I hoped that would not be the case here. Buyer's regret was not something I had considered.

Rafael could see how excited I was. "You're a fool, you know that."

His words weren't disapproving. It was all ... what? What was it that I was up to? Did everyone react the same at found cash? The large sum of money Mother had given me barely twenty-four hours before had been without conditions. But she, I, had understood that it would have to take me through my first full year at Stanford. A car, tuition. Room and board. The sundry needs that any freshman had to purchase being away from home on his own for his first time. "You only live once?" I said as a way to appease any concerns over my folly.

"What's your mother going to say?"

"She doesn't need to know, right?" I said, making him an accomplice.

"She has eyes. She's going to see. I came in with a backpack. None of this …" He lifted the boxes and the bags.

There was merit in what he was saying. "I'll think of something."

Driving down Wilshire, the sun was ever perfect—the August Hollywood heat in the traffic that would be replaced by breezes once we neared Santa Monica and the ocean. As I chauffeured us, I pointed out any location that might have been remotely famous. We went through Beverly Hills and into Westwood for a detour to show him UCLA. "That's where Charlene is headed at the end of the month."

"Is that where Judy's going?"

I had to think for a second of where she had accepted admission. "Did she mention that last night?"

"If she did, I didn't pay any attention."

The poor soul had no connection to any of what my friends and I were about to face—neither the roads we were entering upon, nor the complexities that came with choices.

If Judy was scheduled to attend UCLA, it would have explained her shopping outing with Charlene. "Umm … I don't think so. Maybe headed for USC where Jethro's going?" I was up on Sunset and came back down to Wilshire where the traffic congested. The mention of Judy's name needed to be addressed when the brainchild hit me. Cockeyed as it seemed, I thought it worth a gander. "You were right, Rafael. Mother will be too suspicious by far."

"Yeah. So, what do we do?"

The idea germinated as I steered along in silence. He could tell I was hatching a plan.

"She's not going to be there?" he asked, recognizing my neighborhood as we drove closer to home.

I knew better but pretended we were taking a chance. "We'll leave the bags and boxes in the car."

"Won't she want to come out and see it? You just spent serious bucks on this."

Rafael was nothing if not meticulous in his worries. "We'll put the packages in the trunk. You'll see. I can pull this off."

When we drove into the driveway I said, "Wait here. Stash everything in the trunk. I'll see if the coast is clear." I went inside, aware that it would all be quite empty. I stepped back out on the veranda and gave him a thumbs up.

"What's the plan?" he said approaching. "I need to know what I'm getting into."

"You're going to love this. It'll make you very happy."

"Is Judy going to be part of this?"

His question depressed me, but I chose to rise above it. "I'm not sure. I haven't thought it out that far." My mind raced at all the possibilities of this going so wrong. "You won't have to sleep in my bedroom again. How's that for a start?" I could see he was intrigued. "We're going to get dressed in our fineries. You're going to take all of your stuff. I'm going to leave a note for Mother that we've been invited out. She'll understand. She'll be dead tired anyway. Trust me. She'll be relieved at not having to cook for us. I'll say not to stay up for us. That I'm going to be coming home very late." I could tell that part did not go well with Rafael.

"Where are we going?"

"Do you trust me?" This was definitely a stretch. He wavered, nodded grudgingly. "We'll go out for dinner and drinks. Then I'll drive to the Miramar."

"What's that?"

"A very fancy hotel here in Santa Monica. It's where a lot of stars stay."

"Yeah …?"

He was reticent as heck, like he thought it a ruse on my part to seduce him. "Relax. I'm not staying with you." His eyes did just that. The nervousness in them lessened, the pupils got smaller. "This way, Mother won't see the expensive duds. I'm going to leave my new outfit at your hotel room. We'll pack a suitcase. I'll change there and come back in my regular clothes. Then tomorrow, I'll meet up with you. I'll tell Mom that you bunked at Herbie's. I'll give him a head's up. We can call him from the hotel."

"You sure you can afford all of this?"

"Not really. I don't even know what they charge. But I bought a car today. Nice clothes. I'll just have to get a job when I'm up at Stanford. I'll manage."

"Do we have time to shower? I'm stinking again."

The thought of Rafael naked in my shower stirred something in me and I had to make an excuse to turn away. "Yeah. Go get the bags in the car. Shower and we'll get all dressed up. We have to skedaddle though. In case Mother comes back sooner."

I walked inside towards the kitchen. I took out a bottle of Coke and drank to get my thoughts in order. I heard the front door open and shut and Rafael's footsteps on the stairs, the noise of him moving in my room, along the hallway.

He was at the bathroom door when he hollered, "What towel do I use?"

I ran to the stairs and saw him again in his boxers. *My* boxers, the ones I'd given him which fit him to a T. "Uh, just use the one on the rack. That'll be fine. I'll toss it in the hamper."

He went inside and I walked upstairs to my bedroom. I could have used a cold shower but there was no time. The longer we stayed, the more complicated it might get. I returned to the kitchen sink with a towel and a washcloth and cleaned my armpits so as not to stink up my new shirt and suit. I was back in my bedroom, fully dressed, when Rafael walked in. He had the towel wrapped around him; his hair wet but not dripping. "I'll give you privacy," I said, not wanting a repeat of that morning.

"You do look spiffy."

"We aim to please," I said, containing my delight at his compliment.

Outside, in the hallway, I held my breath. That's all I could think to do.

ELEVEN

I toyed with taking him to Sugie's Tropics, the place Judy had suggested after the movie. Would Rafael recall the name? Ask to invite Judy to join us? I took my chances and drove to North Rodeo Drive in Beverly Hills. Their parking lot was packed. "We may have to wait awhile. Is that okay?"

"Yeah. I'm not starving." Rafael followed me inside.

"A table for two?" I asked the maître d'.

"You have a reservation?"

"No," I said, "last-minute party cancellation." The man looked at us suspiciously, but we *were* dressed the part.

"No one else joining your party tonight?'

I saw Rafael glance around, wondered if he was regretting going along with my scheme. "No. Not this evening. We're flying stag, I'm afraid. Just want to eat and celebrate."

"What's the occasion?"

His question stumped me, I had to think fast on my

feet. "Uh ..." I leaned in pretending I didn't want others to hear. "My friend here is in town for tomorrow's premiere of *Jolson Sings Again*." He was all ears. You could always depend on that hook in this section of town. Mother was forever using the tactic whenever it suited her whims. "He's related to Betty Garrett. Larry Parks's wife?"

"He is?" The maître d' examined his seating chart for that evening.

"Betty's cousin. A young actor. All the way from Canada."

"From Canada?" He checked off a box in his register. "I have a table. It's pretty tight. Not the best location."

"We'll be fine. Won't we, Rafael?" He stayed silent, making him even more mysterious to the maître d' who was walking us to our table by now. As soon as we sat down but before our waiter came with the menus, I turned to Rafael and said, "I think we need champagne, don't you?"

"I've never had any."

"Never? No bubbly ever?" He shook his head. "Well, you're in for a treat. I ordered the Veuve Clicquot, ignoring the cost per bottle. That it was the pricier of the bottles on the Tropics menu must have been why they never asked for IDs. The champagne arrived, chilled to perfection in its ice bucket. The pop of the cork drew us a few smiles. I saw some women fawning our way. I supposed we must have presented as eligible bachelors. The sensation was not unpleasant.

When I saw the curried chicken listed under the entrées, I knew there was no way Rafael wouldn't pick up on that, make the connection with Judy's comments at the Criterion, so I was relieved when he kept quiet. We settled on the deluxe dinner, which came with a glass of Bordeaux. He chose the grilled fillet mignon and I went with the New York sirloin. By the time dessert was on our table, we were giddy. The room appeared to actually be spinning, I was *that* intoxicated. Not so much by the alcohol—though it was flowing nicely through my body, but by my company. Yes, I had lied about my inclinations towards him, but what else could I have done that would have kept him close to me? Rafael had a way of making me feel comfortable in my own skin, but damned if I could have explained why that was. With him, I was both myself and not myself at once.

When the bill was placed on the table, Rafael took it from the plate. He studied the outlay.

"Are you keeping an account?" I asked him.

"I am."

No sooner said than he passed the bill back to me. What *were* we doing!

We walked out onto Rodeo Drive. The night air was cooler than I had expected and I was very aware that I couldn't drive safely. "There's a park just a couple of blocks from here. Let's walk. I need fresh air before I get behind the wheel."

"Good idea."

Beverly Gardens Park at night was not the same as in daytime. I had to focus to find my bearings. At one point, I stumbled and nearly fell.

"Whoa," Rafael said, catching me before I went down for the count. "You okay?"

I was and I wasn't. I was emotional and didn't care for Rafael to see me like this. I wanted to be the strong one here. "I haven't told you about my brother, have I?" The notion of bringing that up left me rattled. Why had I raised so sensitive a subject *now*?

Rafael stopped walking. "I thought you were an only child," he said, predictably perplexed. "Didn't you say that?"

I hadn't, but I had also not divulged what was rarely mentioned by me or Mother. "No. You didn't ask …"

"I think I did. No?"

I shook my head.

"So, where is he? Is he much older?"

"Steve was a year younger than me." The uttering of his name aloud sobered me up. "He died when he was thirteen."

"Sorry to hear that."

Did I want to go into all of that familial mess? Now? Tonight? Steven dying and Rafael at the Miramar should have been worlds apart.

"What happened? If you don't mind me asking."

Rafael was standing so that the light from the lamppost made the pomade in his hair gleam. I wanted to reach out and put my fingers through the slicked-back waves, see how that would feel, but had to resist at all costs. "He went to Cuba with my dad. He and Dad were close."

"When did your parents split up?"

"A thorny saga that. It went on for years. He left when I was very young. Came back. Left again. Mother *left* him. A dance made in hell." Did every child whose parents' marriage disintegrated have this refrain?

"Is that why you and she were in Paris? Was Steven with you?"

I shook my head. The regret of all that lost time was untenable now. "You remind me of him," I said, though why would not have made sense to anybody acquainted with either. Steve, blond, blue-eyed, and not that tall for his age, had nothing in common with Rafael on the outside. Not even on the inside, from what I could see of Rafael thus far.

Yet, that affectionate assessment of mine prevailed, this conduit that I had created between them. "He was a tough kid. He liked to box and wrestle."

"At thirteen?" Rafael asked, his voice inflected so that I could see he was having trouble with that.

"I get it. Dad … made him into a fighter is what I think. Is that weird?"

"Kind of. Your dad wasn't a boxer, was he?"

I laughed and couldn't stop laughing. My father, my monied father from old money that went back generations, a fighter! "No. He landed himself a desk job for the war."

"Wasn't he too old for the draft anyway?"

"No. He was only …" I calculated to verify my math. "He was thirty-six in '40 when the draft began. No. I remember very well Mom wanting him to go and fight." I chuckled, conscious of how crass that must have sounded. "Mother can hold a grudge like no other."

"She seemed pretty nice to me."

"She is. She's swell, as far as mothers go. But she's not great wife material. I've come to understand that. Sort of …" I saw a bench and we walked and sat down. I could see a few men walking further into the park, away from the street lamplights; I wondered what they were up to at this late hour. "My brother went with my father to Cuba. Right after the war ended. There were enormous money opportunities on the island apparently. Father had some business deal, and he took Steve along to see some fights down there."

"At thirteen?" Rafael wasn't the first person to react this way.

"Nobody liked how Father was with Steven. Too Hemingway by far." The entire episode was coming back in a flash, as though a cherished possession from a deeply fought custody battle.

"He was disappointed in me, his first son. That was obvious from an early age." I could tell Rafael was attaching innuendo onto that statement, but I didn't care anymore. "They had only been there two days of a week-long trip. They were out on a boat, deep-sea fishing, and poor Steven slipped and fell into the ocean."

"Wasn't he wearing a Mae West?"

"He was. But he got entangled in the fishing gear. And sadly, a houndfish—they're bloody awful. Likely attracted by the silver chain he had around his neck. At least, that's what the inquiry suggested. He got maimed, lost too much blood and drowned. It happened very fast." I neglected to mention that the men were drunk, and that no negligence charges were ever filed.

"Jesus, Gary. I'm *so* sorry." He put his hand on my back. I could feel the warmth it brought to my skin, the impression it made against the wool of my suit jacket.

"You can imagine Mother. She hated Father before. But that sealed everything. That's how she obtained the job she has. When Dad … disappeared the next year."

"What do you mean?"

"He left for good. We think he's in Europe. We don't know for certain. Could be in Timbuktu for all I care."

"Jesus. And I thought you had it all." Rafael took his hand away and, for a split second, I was convinced he was going to hug me. It's what I wanted. What I would have done with anyone else confessing their woes the way I was.

He stood up. "I think we need to drive. Drive fast and far." The look on his face was magical. "Are you up for that?"

I had sobered some and the diversion he proffered made me ready for an adventure. We went to get the car. At the wheel, I peeked at my watch. "We should check into the Miramar first. Just to make sure we can get a room."

At the hotel, the valet came to greet us. Inside, at the reception desk, I tried the same approach I had used at Sugie's since the lateness in the hour put us at a disadvantage. "For two nights?" the clerk inquired.

"I believe so. Yes. Two nights. Possibly three. We really can't confirm until after tomorrow's premiere." The bait was so effective, I reminded myself that I needed to thank Mother down the road.

"Premiere?"

"Yes. That's Rafael Jerome," I indicated my companion. "I'm booking the room for him. He's in town for the *Jolson Sings Again* premiere tomorrow night. At the Pantages."

"Is he in the film?"

I smiled as docile as I knew how in order to ingratiate myself as smoothly as I could. "His uncle. Larry Parks. Well, actually, he's Betty Garrett's relation. Mr. Parks's wife's nephew. From Canada."

"We have many Canadians stay here." The clerk examined their availability. "We're quite booked up. I'm sure you can understand."

I didn't. I thought of August as not that popular a month for travel to Los Angeles, too hot and muggy. But what did I know of these things!

The man, an Italian if I guessed his accent correctly, asked, "We have a bungalow that's available. But no longer than three nights. No more."

"A bungalow?" I repeated. I could just imagine the cost. Didn't dare to ask for fear of having the wind taken from my sails. All I wanted was to persevere with this crazy design of mine. "Mr. Jerome would love that accommodation. It'll be more convenient if his party wants to move here from Romanoff's tomorrow night." The clerk smiled politely. I couldn't tell if he saw profit or problem and I didn't care. I looked at Rafael who had stayed a few yards away, waiting to see if any of this could be pulled off. Without even showing my driver's license, I signed the register. My age was never questioned as I produced sufficient funds for the first two nights, cognizant that my cash flow was shrinking.

The bellboy accompanied us to the car for the one suitcase in the trunk and shepherded us to our bungalow. Inside, the luxury was beyond my own expectations.

"Jesus," Rafael exclaimed.

"You're sure you're not very Catholic? You say that word a lot."

"Jesus," he repeated, with a punch to my gut this time, a fake jab that made me buckle back onto the bed.

"I'm still in shock at the sticker price."

"How much?"

"I'm not saying. This one really took me for a loop."

"Can't be more than the suits?" I hesitated so that Rafael fell back onto the bed next to me. Collapsed like he had fainted from the blow. "Yikes. What are we *doing* here?!" He jumped off the bed and for a moment I wasn't sure where this would go.

"I don't care anymore," I told him. "I just want to live. See what you've done to me, Rafael Jerome. Nephew of Betty Garrett."

We screamed with laughter. "Should we call Judy?" he asked.

A pall came over me but I quickly recovered. "No. It's

too late now. What would you say if the mother answered? Worse, her father! He might cancel the whole shindig. We wouldn't want that." Clearly, I wasn't beyond using guilt.

Rafael reconsidered. "No. Of course not. Not now." The inference being all the cash I had spent on this madcap caper of mine. "What time is it?"

It was going on eleven thirty. "I could try Herbie. In case Mother calls for me there," I said, as unlikely as that was. We didn't need more drama. "His family stays up pretty late." I dialed and he picked up. "That was fast. Your parents not home?"

"No. They went to a movie and out for drinks. Did Jethro reach you?"

"No. Why?"

"He wanted to see if you'd bought the car. He thought you'd call him today with the news."

I felt terrible. "Totally forgot," I said, remembering now that he had wanted me to do that. "It's been quite a day."

"Uh huh?" he said, with a question mark that could only mean one thing—what had gone down with Rafael and me.

"I got the car."

"The '46?"

"Yeah. Then me and Rafael picked up some suits for tomorrow. You're all ready?"

"Expensive duds?" he asked, dodging my question.

I wavered. "Not as expensive as the hotel room I rented for our party tomorrow night." The silence at the other end was so long, I thought Herbie had fainted. "Herbie?"

"You what?"

"It's wild. Guess where I'm calling from?"

"San Quentin? That's where you're going if you don't end this romp of yours."

I hadn't committed any crimes but his comment made me stop dead in my tracks. "What?"

"Does your mother know about any of this?"

"Herbie."

"No. Gary!" he said, upping the ante like we were playing poker.

Herbie could be such a nitpicker. Any of the pleasure I'd had from that day's outings—the car purchase, shopping at Bullock's, the champagne, the weight lifted off my shoulders unburdening myself to Rafael about Steven—all of it went away, like an inflated balloon fizzling at the end of a fantastic party. "I'm at the Miramar. We rented a bungalow. Judy's going to flip out. *And* Jethro."

"Remember senior prom? Charlene is not going to want to go there unchaperoned. I can tell you that much."

He had a point. I had not considered all the angles here. "Okay ... Listen, Herbie. Mother thinks Rafael will be staying at your house tonight."

"Oh, is that why you got yourself a hotel room for the night? Just the two of you?"

I worried that Rafael could somehow hear what Herbie was saying. He was paying attention but not that closely. He had already taken off his jacket and tie, and was unlacing his shoes. He looked sleepy to me. I put up a finger to let him know I'd be done in a jiffy. "I'm headed home now. Rafael will get a good night's sleep."

"Why? Didn't he get a good night's sleep *last* night?"

I was astounded. It was as if Herbie could read my

innermost thoughts, suspected the most egregious behavior on my part. "The floor in my bedroom's not that comfortable," I said.

"Oh. Sorry. Of course."

Herbie reacted like he had crossed a line, though he really hadn't. He had guessed my ulterior motives from the beginning. He knew me better than I knew my own self. "Mother won't call tonight. But just in case, Rafael's at your place. You met him first. Just like we talked about it."

"You went with that story?" he said, proud that his ruse had been useful.

"Yup. I'll call you from the house before noon. See what we want to do about cars. I think we'll use both cars. Make it easier. That way there'll be fewer complications."

"Is that what *you* think?"

Herbie was teasing me now. I liked this latest freedom in our friendship. When I hung up, Rafael was in the bathroom taking a leak. He came out, his dress shirt unbuttoned. The T-shirt underneath, his own from Canada, was faded. The contrast to the expensive articles was stark. I took off my jacket and undid my tie. I slipped out of my shoes and went to the suitcase. "I'm going to change into my dungarees." When I came out of the bathroom, I hung the suit in the closet. "Can you call room service in the morning and ask them if they can launder our shirts? They'll need to be fresh for tomorrow night."

The bungalow accommodation was roomy—a living room with a kitchenette, a bathroom, and a bedroom with a large dressing alcove. The décor was out of a movie set, I thought. Was it any wonder that you read about stars who stayed here months and years on end, a home away from home! I went to get my knit shirt from the suitcase when Rafael turned towards me. He had that vulnerable air about him, the one he'd had on more than one occasion since we had met. "You can stay here tonight," he said. "If you want. I'll take the couch."

His offer stirred up more feelings than I could have ever anticipated. Nerves in the pit of my stomach did somersaults, so frightened was I of what might take place. I stupidly put on my knit top, tugged on it so that it covered my abdomen fully, so that he couldn't see my muscles trembling. "I … Mother …"

"Forget it. That was me being stupid."

Was this the right time to ask about Calgary? Before I could resolve that for myself, without my wanting to, I began my story of Paris. "The third time I went to Paris with Mother. The time when we got an apartment, not a hotel …" I could still see the high ceilings, the windows with the shutters that we used to close before going to bed. "I was nine. No, eight. It was in 1939 right before the war. Steve stayed behind with Dad's parents. No clue as to what went into that decision." I gulped for air and wet the inside of my mouth with my tongue, I was so nervous about what I was going to reveal. "There was a boy. A few years older than me. Not by much. Maybe eleven. Twelve tops. We played together in the hallways. Down and up the stairs. We weren't allowed to use the elevator, for some reason. Nor run around out on the streets. You needed to be with adults for that." Rafael's eyes were poised on me so I continued. "One day. We decided to go up on the roof. That too wasn't allowed but we were bored. We were kids. I was just following him."

I wondered if Rafael could guess where this was going.

"The sun had retreated. It was cloudy with rain likely on the way. There were clothes lines up there. I don't know who put them there or whose clothes they were. They could have been his. Cleo," I said. I hadn't uttered that proper name in years. "Cleo told me to go into the corner. He pulled a sheet from the lines. I saw that there was straw where he had indicated. As though it was used to lie down on. I'm not sure why I listened to him. Sitting on straw was not that appealing. But," and I hesitated for what seemed an eternity before I added, "But Cleo. He appealed to me." I wanted to check in with Rafael to see if he was revolted but I didn't dare. "I went and sat down on the straw after he laid the cloth over the mound. The sensation was warm and moist. Probably musty too. The sheet wasn't completely dry. Cleo sat down next to me and before I could say or do anything, he had his hands inside my shorts pocket. He wiggled and slid it so that he found my privates. I recall thinking, 'Uh-oh.' The thought of running away was there, but something stronger kept me immobile. He never said a word. He just proceeded to undo his own shorts. The buttons … There was no zipper on his. It all took no longer than minutes. Ten maybe. He said nothing, just moved and fondled me and I sort of did the same with him. Whatever it was that happened between us. I guess it was sex …"

I thought the ceiling would collapse, thought Rafael would murder me on the spot. Hit me, at the very least, but all that followed was the longest of silences. I could hear his breathing. Not belabored. Not heavy. Just regular breathing that calmed my own. When I looked up, Rafael was crying. His cheeks were wet and I couldn't tell what was causing that.

Was he feeling so sorry for me, disgusted beyond the pale? Had I sickened him with my lies and my manipulation? *Say* something, I thought. We just stared at each other until I finally added, "My life has always pulled me towards guys. Boys my own age. I can't explain it any differently. It's what I am. What I've always known myself to be." I leaned back into the sofa chair and let out a small moan. I wasn't about to lose it entirely but I was overwhelmed by my disclosure.

"In Calgary," Rafael said, and placed his elbows on his knees, his head in his palms. "There was a bad man. A politician."

His revelation captivated me instantly. "Yeah …?" I quickly forgot everything I had just said.

"There was a fight one night."

"You get into a lot of those, don't you?" He raised an eyebrow, exasperated, and I apologized silently; mouthed "sorry" twice.

"No. I don't ever fight. Never fought until Calgary." He went to the door and for a second, I thought he was going to open it. Instead, he checked the locks. "There was a bar I went to with my cousins. Real rough-and-tumble cowboy stuff. Nothing like what we had in Ottawa. There was a girl there. A real looker."

I was entranced by all that he was sharing. "Go on."

"I still don't know exactly who did what to who. All I know is that this guy started in on me. I was sauced. Did I say that?"

"No."

"Well, I was. I got kicked out. We both were."

"And your cousins?"

"This is where it gets very muddled." He had a pitiable air about him. "They didn't come out. I waited and I got angrier and angrier. So, I began to walk home."

"Was it far?"

"Very. We'd come into town by truck."

"Did you know how to get back home?"

"No. Not at all. I barely knew Calgary." He came and sat across from me on the two-seater sofa. "Have you ever felt like you were the last person on earth?"

The weight of his question shook me to my core because I felt that way all the time, yet I had never heard it expressed with such despair. My problems paled in comparison. "Not in the way you're suggesting … I don't think."

"I was walking along a main street. There was traffic but I didn't have a clue where the hell I was. Or what I was doing. What I wanted to do. I just thought of walking." He wiped his forehead, which had begun to perspire. "That had often worked for me to let off steam."

"And …? The politician …"

"I'm getting there." He lay back and rubbed his scalp so that all of his hair was disheveled, with a wildness to it. "Have you ever been inside a limousine?"

"No. I haven't."

"Well, a limousine drove up. The window came down and a pleasant fellow peered out the window."

"No!"

"Kind of like a scene. From a movie."

"Like a movie star?"

"Well, that's the only thing you think of when you think of limousines, right?"

I nodded, since that was the only plausible scenario.

"You'd be wrong." He exhaled and took in a deep breath. I could tell he was holding back tears. Didn't want them to come out. "Politicians ride in them too."

He stood and paced. I so rarely did that. Did it even work if you were anxious? Watching Rafael suggested otherwise. "Are you okay?"

"Do I look okay?"

"No. You don't. You're scaring me, Rafael." As soon as I had said it, I regretted it.

"Maybe I should stop. No need to actually."

"No, Rafael. Tell me. I'm here for you. I want to hear."

"Is there liquor in this joint?"

"We could call room service …" It was late and I suspected that was more complicated than it seemed. "We could try. I don't really know the liquor laws for hotels."

"No. I need to be sober for this." He sat back down again in front of me.

I wanted to reach out, hold him in my arms, aware of how unrealistic that was. "You can go slow. I have all the time. I can stay the night. That's no problem."

"When the guy offered me a cigarette …"

"From the car window?" I asked, thinking that peculiar.

"Yeah. From the window. I thought, 'Why not!' I walked over. Took the cigarette and he lit up a match. That's when I saw his face. A pretty big face. He was a bruiser. He said, 'Need a ride?' 'Hell yeah,' I said. The door opened and I got in."

His eyebrows rose again. His brow furrowed and I waited with bated breath.

"He said, 'Where to?' I told him the general location and he told his chauffeur to drive on out. The ride into town had been a good twenty minutes. As we drove, he talked and I listened. He had a bar in the back. This shelf with bottles and glasses. He poured us scotches. I've always liked the taste of scotch. It's what my dad drinks on special occasions."

I made a note to buy scotch for tomorrow night.

"The booze hit me hard. I'm not a big swigger. And I was already buzzed from all the cheap beer from the cowboy saloon. At one point, I *had* to take a leak or piss my pants. We were in the middle of nowhere. You can't imagine how deserted it is out there. At night. In the dark. I said, 'Sorry, but I need to take a piss.' 'No problem,' he says. He tapped on the window. I still don't know how the chauffeur knew what to do. The limo stopped by the side of the road. When I got out, he came out too. 'I'm about to bust, myself,' he said. Or words to that effect. We were standing by the ditch pissing away when I thought I heard an animal in the field. I must have panicked and he picked up on it. He moved before I knew what was up. He had me. In a grip. He was a big fella. Right away, he had his mouth on my mouth. His tongue was inside me and his prick was against mine. Piss everywhere. He was almost erect and my cock got all the signals twisted. It got hard too. Before I realized what was happening, my pants were around my ankles. I thought, 'Shit! I'm going to get a blow job.' I still think he spiked that scotch whiskey because I got weak all of a sudden. Next thing, my face is flat on the ground. It's wet and the smell of dirt and gravel and the exhaust from the idling car is going up my nose. There was this searing pain."

I gasped. I couldn't believe what I was hearing.

Rafael was beyond tears as he finished with just a few more sentences. "He did that. To me. A man! It was no blow job, Gary."

We stayed motionless as I tried to unravel the horror. My feelings for Rafael had only grown. All the feistiness that I had thought problematic in him had materialized into a compassion that belonged to brothers, not a two-day-old friendship. "Is that when you left?"

"No," he said, trying to replace defeat with defiance. "I lasted two more days."

"Your cousins ... Did they know?"

"The politician was smart. He left me there. He didn't let me back into the limo so that there would be any evidence."

"How do you know he was a politician?"

"The fucker. He was so stupid. As if I wouldn't be able to recognize him in the papers!" Rafael thumped his right fist against the couch. "The very next day. At suppertime, my uncle Julien was reading the newspaper. Right there. Bold letters. "Senator Clinton Burnshaw."

"That was his name?"

"Yes it was. I'll never forget that face." He teared up. "That pain."

I had no recourse. I inched towards Rafael and put my arm around his neck like he was my best friend in the world. His pain felt like mine. His torment, my own. Unlike his agitation that morning, Rafael was calm as could be. He allowed me to be the Gary I wanted to be. Loving. Approachable. Understanding to a fault. I was being aroused and did all within my power to calm my own reactions. When I let go, I asked. "What did you tell your cousins?"

"Nothing."

"Nothing? How come?"

"What did you want me to say? I was buggered by Senator Burnshaw out in the ditch somewhere?"

"So, none of your cousins …"

"Yeah, the smarter one. He may even be like you? Come to think of it, I'm convinced he's a lot like you."

His equation was unsettling. To be compared, already, with someone else after admitting aloud my penchant for guys, minutes prior. *That* was quick. "What did that cousin say? What's his name?"

"Lionel."

The analyzing of the puzzle appeared to give Rafael a boost of energy. He was up and inspecting the hotel bungalow like there might be hidden treasure. Was he going to suggest another wild outing, that proposal of his to go driving fast that we had pledged to do a few hours before but hadn't?

"Lionel and his older brother, Luc. They picked me up along the road. Didn't ask a lot of questions when I said I'd prefer riding in the cargo bed."

"'You're gonna freeze your balls out there,' Luc had said. 'This ain't Ottawa. This here's Alberta. The nights are cold.' Luc revved up the engine promising a rough ride either way. I could see that Lionel was watching me. The way I'd walked funny up to the side of the truck. The way I must have come off as timid when, before, I'd been just one of the guys. He *knew*. I think he might have seen the blood on my underwear later on. I tried to hide it good. Washed them myself using lye soap to get the stain out. Said to my aunt it was shit. I'd had bad diarrhea from too much booze and messed myself."

"Well. You'll have Lionel to testify if ever you decide to go back there."

"I'm ... never ... *ever* going back to that shithole province. Made that promise to myself when I snuck out of there two days later, way before dawn."

"What do you think they thought? They must be worried senseless. No?"

"They're cowboys. I got my ass whipped. I looked like a fathead ... Worse, a chicken in front of a popular gal. In front of all the guys my cousins knew or worked with. They just assumed I set off for back home with my tail between my legs. Which I was. Sort of. Until the first ride that picked me up was headed straight to Butte, Montana. That's how I landed in the United States of not Canada!"

I loved his corny humor. "And then you hitched where?"

"Montana into Idaho." He used his finger to trace an imaginary map. "Then Nevada and finally Santa Monica, California, to meet you. My guardian angel."

The sweetness to his compliment made me blush with pride I hadn't earned. I *so* did want to be this man's guardian angel. I could feel it my life's calling. If only ... "I promised you that we'd drive fast and far. You still want to?"

"Hell, yeah." He put on his shirt and I suggested we put our suit jackets back on.

"With the top down, it'll get chilly." We got to the bungalow door. "Where to?" I asked him.

"Hell, if I know. But I'm sober. You're sober. What could go wrong?"

TWELVE

Swimming in the Miramar pool at dawn was its own soothing reward. Apart from a couple of staff walking the grounds, cleaning up, and gearing for the chores of a new day, Rafael and I were in our own private oasis. We had raced up the coast and walked along a darkened beach north of Malibu. I had wanted to skinny-dip, thought of making the suggestion, then refrained. Why ruin a perfect evening?

The smell of the Pacific Ocean at low tide had always left me feeling lonely as though the temporary loss of volume, combined with the powerful waves scattered so far from the shoreline, might be permanent—a consequence of planetary misalignment that mankind could not brook. I associated the loss of Steven with the ocean but did not blame its repository. I had Father to blame for that.

Rafael and I had talked about what he would say upon his return to Ottawa. How he would handle himself. Explain that he had stayed in barns along the way, worked a few days for room and board, then stopped in Toronto and befriended some people in the downtown core. That seemed viable enough—replace Santa Monica for Toronto; maybe even explain away his tan lines. When he asked me what my plans were for Stanford, I told him I had no clue. I was going to university because it was the thing to do. Not the thing that *I* wanted to do necessarily. If he had asked me to go with him to Ottawa, would I have done so? That night, under the starlit sky, with a full moon and the lowest tides that stretched to infinity … I might well have. And what of my life then?

We got out of the pool when we saw a gardener staring at us strangely. In the bungalow, I went to shower first and came out to find Rafael fast asleep. I scribbled a note, "Will call you in the early afternoon. Don't forget the shirts!"

As I drove home, I realized I would have a lot of explaining to do. It was nearing seven when I walked into the house.

"You must have had a doozy of a night." Mother was sipping her morning coffee with the *LA Times*, a ritual of hers.

"You didn't stay up, did you?"

She shook her head. "You must be tired."

"I am. But I have a lot to do."

"The premiere still on?"

"Yes." I was waiting for more questions but none came. Was this what happened after you turned eighteen? Owned your own car? I was unaccustomed to this laissez-faire attitude. "I should probably get some shut eye." I took a few steps toward the living room.

"Set your alarm. I'm leaving early again. I have a lot of appointments today."

"I will." I was at the bottom of the stairs when she called out.

"Will you be out again all night tonight?"

The tone was not at all judgmental. I *liked* this a lot. "Well, there are a couple of parties after the premiere. Everything depends on Judy's father. And his plans for us." The lie was so boldfaced.

"Well, if you meet Greta Garbo, give her my regards."

I was in the middle of a gorgeous dream about Rafael. We had eloped and were in a Venetian gondola, listening to Vivaldi coming from a window along the Grand Canal when the phone ringing downstairs woke me up. "Hello, Silverman residence," I answered, aware that I had to pee.

"You're a knucklehead. You know that."

Jethro was pissed off and I didn't blame him. "Sorry. Is it past noon?"

"Are you still in bed? It's one-thirty."

I heard some clattering in the background. "Where are you?"

"The payphone at the beach. Getting in a workout. What's the set-up for tonight?"

I sat down on the settee and tried to organize my thoughts. "Well … Let's see. Did you speak with Herbie?"

"I did."

His curt reply made me wonder if they had discussed my association with Rafael. "So, you heard about the Miramar?"

"So, it's true. You booked us a bungalow?"

"I did. I splurged."

He whistled. "I like this new Gary. Where have you been hiding him all this time?"

"All it took was a large infusion of greenbacks."

"I'll say."

We made our plans and I called up Rafael who picked up on the very first ring. "Judy?"

I was stunned at hearing him say her name. "Sorry to disappoint."

"Oh, Gary. I was wondering when you'd call."

How to proceed? I couldn't ignore the elephant in the room. "Did you call Judy? Is that why you thought it would be her?" I didn't need to be told that I sounded like a nagging girlfriend.

"Umm, yeah. I had her number, remember? She gave it to me on Monday."

I had forgotten. It added up. "You slept okay?"

"Like a baby. You?"

"I just got up. Jethro called me."

There was a pause, as though the previous night had barely happened between us. Why did men *do that* to themselves! The awkwardness of disaffection passed when he asked, "How was your mom? Any snags?"

"None. Remarkably so. She didn't even seem interested. I suppose she's getting ready to let go." Saying that left me sadder than I could have imagined. To think of Mother letting go that way. Did all mothers prepare like this for the day when their children left home? In increments, a day at a time, so as to make the break easier on all parties concerned? "So, here's the skinny for tonight."

At four, I arrived at the Miramar with sandwiches and Cokes. I had taken a bottle of wine from the house and bought a bottle of scotch and one of gin along with some tonic water. "It's going to have to do. I don't know how to mix martinis," I said. "Do you?"

"Not really. Rye and ginger. Rum and Coke. Beer. That's about it. And scotch on the rocks. But that's no cocktail."

"No. It isn't." We ate our snacks and sat at the kitchen table, each of us in our own little world, thinking about the night ahead. "You'll be okay picking up both ladies?"

Rafael smiled like he had won a contest. "You don't think their mothers will talk?"

"Beats me. I hope not." We laughed at that. "As long as it's not *before* tonight. You'll be fine." We giggled even more now, thinking how ridiculous our charade was. "Just don't mix the last names. "Charlene Bennett. Judy Mosley."

"Good evening, Mrs. Bennett. A lovely house you have," he said, practicing. "Mrs. Mosley. This is so nice of your husband giving us these tickets." He glanced at me for approval. "How's that?"

"You'll have them swooning. No doubt about it."

The RKO Pantages Theatre on Hollywood Boulevard was a logjam of limousines and fans that night. We had parked around the corner, a few blocks away. Me and Rafael with Judy in my car. Herbie with Charlene and Jethro in his.

"You have the tickets?" Jethro asked Judy when we were out standing on the sidewalk.

"No, dum-dum. I left them at the house." She was sporting a stunning dress with taffeta and silk that tapered below the knees. "And anyway, there's a name list at the box office. There are studio people there who check us in."

"Your dad not going to be there?"

"No. Thankfully. He hates all of this stuff. So does my mom." She took Rafael's arm. "Not unless his name is in the credits. Then … yes. Of course."

Rafael was in awe of his date. I could tell by how he tried not to stare only to look again, almost salivating. This *was* going to be a trying night all around for me.

Jethro took the lead with Charlene who had on a black velvet dress with pearled sequins above the waist that shimmered under lights. It was still early, with plenty of time before the start of the feature, but we had to be in our seats by an allotted hour or else our places could be given away. Judy had emphasized how the theatre had to be standing room only for publicity's sake. Rafael, in his stylish suit and freshly laundered shirt, walked with Judy, with Herbie and I bringing up the rear.

"You get any sleep?" Herbie asked me, under his breath, worried that Judy might hear.

"Some. Not a lot."

By the time we hit Hollywood Boulevard, the razzmatazz spectacle had begun. "Wow, will you look at that." We all saw Ginger Rogers stepping out of a limousine.

Rafael turned to me and smiled excitedly. His eyes said it all. We managed to get through the melee and reached the ropes. Jethro handed the six tickets to an attendant and gave them Judy's father's name when asked. We were ushered into the lobby. "Have you been here before?" Rafael asked me.

"Once. When I was a kid. You, Judy?"

"Yeah. Plenty of times."

Her reply came off as rehearsed, grandstanding for Rafael's behalf, I thought. I did not like this woman for too many reasons. "I'm impressed," I said, though I wasn't in the least. The women went to the ladies' room and were gone for ages.

"I'm thirsty," Herbie declared. "Will they serve booze here?"

"I think after the movie. Not before," I said. Jethro took out a flask. "Put that away." He did so very quickly with a "what gives?" look. "I don't want us getting kicked out of here."

"Sorry, Mother."

"That's Captain to you, ensign," I said, aiming for the upper hand.

Seated in the mezzanine in the same order as on Monday night, the six of us gawked at the array of celebrities below. "Look, your cousins." I got Rafael laughing when he saw who it was.

"What?" Judy said, overhearing me. "That's Larry Parks. The lead."

"No," I corrected her. "Rafael's related to the wife, on his mother's side. Betty Garrett."

"No!"

I could see how riled she was when I told her and the others how I'd used that fabricated connection to get us seats at Sugie's and my bungalow at the Miramar.

"You need to be careful, Gary Silverman," Judy warned. "You may have crossed a line."

I thought about it for a second. "Well, not a big one. It's done all the time in this town, no?" Herbie's "I told you so" glance brought up images of San Quentin momentarily. "All right. Agreed. No more of that." I took a beat. "Unless we need to get something special at some point."

"Like …?"

"Fancy champagne?"

"Maybe for that …" Judy said. She smiled broadly and I felt some reprieve.

Charlene whispered, "Kirk Douglas," and all eyes darted in that area of the orchestra section. "There's Roddy McDowall. Who's he talking to? The guy looks very famous."

Jethro stood to get a better angle. "Wow. That's Jolson himself."

I looked down and could see that he had aged. "Is Jolson big up in Canada?"

Rafael had to think about it. "The name, yeah. My parents' generation, right?"

The movie went by fast, the audience taken by all the songs. The standing ovation was long and the speeches many. I had no idea how it compared to other premieres, this being my first, but Jolson addressing the audience moved everybody. The second standing ovation just for him blew the roof off the joint. *This* was a Hollywood legend, and we were present for that.

Outside, after being denied access to a private party in the mezzanine lobby, we were shepherded out and gathered by our cars. "I am so thirsty," Herbie said for the umpteenth time. Jethro passed his flask and we all took sips of vodka.

"I hope there's more booze at the bungalow," Judy said, looking my way.

"There is. Not much food though. If we want to eat, we'll have to pick up more supplies."

Jethro opened the trunk and took out a bottle of champagne. "I snagged this one from the house. We can stop off at Canter's and pick up deli."

"I'll head on out with Judy and Rafael," I said. "We'll set up the place, put the champagne on ice, and wait for you three. How's that?"

By eleven thirty, the radio was playing a brand-new Andrews Sisters song, "I Can Dream, Can't I?" They might as well have tortured me! Rafael and Judy were dancing quietly in the middle of the room while I tried to pretend to be busy with nothing. When the others arrived with food, we popped the champagne that was much too warm but it didn't matter. With only two girls with four guys, the reality soon sunk in. We took turns, depending on the music, trying to make the best of a knotty situation.

After the champagne, Rafael and I switched to scotch, with everyone else more inclined to gin and tonics. "Do your moms know each other?" I asked Judy during a lull. It was already one in the morning. Our faces were flush and I could tell that Charlene had her guard up when she came over, a signal that she was annoyed with Jethro who had drunk too much without enough food in his stomach.

"Our moms?" she repeated, indicating her and Charlene.

"Yeah."

"Why do you ask that?"

I glanced at Rafael who had this boyish smile when he was drunk. "Well, Rafael picked the both of you up tonight. Won't it seem weird, if your moms discover that?"

The girls suddenly grasped the implication and giggled uncontrollably. "No. They don't travel in the same circles. Right?" Charlene agreed. "But my mom," Judy explained, "she knew I was going out with Charlene. She *does* have their number."

"Oops," Jethro said crashing in, "busted." He took Charlene by the waist and tried to kiss her more passionately than might have been appropriate with all of us present in the room.

"Don't, Jethro," she said.

We saw her check the clock on the kitchenette wall. I felt uncomfortable for her, but I was more upset with Jethro's Lothario. I did not want the night to be over this early. I quickly intervened, not wanting a replication of prom night. "Can I freshen your drinks?" I asked, always the perfect host. Judy gave me her glass as did Jethro and Herbie. "Charlene?"

"No, I'm fine. I should eat something. I'm too drunk as it is." She sidled to the table where the cold cuts and cheeses were and made herself a plate. "Anyone?" she asked, lifting a container of dill pickles.

Rafael joined her. I poured alcohol, scotch on the rocks for me and blends of gin and tonic for the others. The music of Bing Crosby singing "Far Away Places" came on the radio and Herbie asked Judy to dance. The lyrics made it irresistible; I *had* to glimpse over at Rafael. He must be thinking of home, I thought. He was in conversation, a tête-à-tête with Charlene. What *were* they discussing?

When the song ended, an upbeat number came on and we all joined in together, swapping from partner to partner, a jitterbug version of a square dance. When the tune came to a close, Jethro was all sweaty, as was I, and he took off his tie. He slugged his gin back and took hold of Charlene who was not in the mood.

"Don't," she said.

"Why not? We're a couple again. What's so wrong with a bit of smooching." He gazed at her like he was about to pounce.

"Jethro Beauregard," Charlene said, but she had the giggles now, so her credibility was on the line. "Don't. You. Dare," she threatened and began to run; into the other room they went, and we all waited to hear what would come next. When there was only silence, I saw Judy inch toward Rafael on the settee. Her fingers lay gently on his lap and I could tell that Herbie and I would be third wheels soon enough. I signaled for him to join me at the cold cuts to make ourselves as scarce as we could.

"We can't make a habit out of this," Herbie said. "My manhood can't take this."

I kept my snickering to a hush. "It's not like we had many options. Only six tickets, remember?"

"You should have found a date for yourself, Gary. That would have been the wiser thing."

"Yeah. But since when am I wise, right?"

Herbie's manner was edifying. He had miscalculated the evening and was living to regret it.

"I'll tell you what," I said, "if it gets steamier … which I doubt it will …" I hadn't begun to finish my sentence when the bedroom door slammed open and a frightened Charlene stood in the doorway.

"I want to go. *Now*," she announced.

We were all taken aback. No one wanted to leave. I would have sworn that on a stack of bibles.

"I can drive you home," Herbie offered, just as I was trying to reconcile Charlene's wishes with mine. "I'm not too drunk. Honest."

With no Jethro coming from behind, and me still lost in my own fantasy about the evening, I said, "Why don't you take my car?" I fetched my keys and gave them to him. "You can just leave the car at your place …" By saying that, I was implying what I knew deep down he wanted, which was to leave too. "Jethro can drive me to the car. Unless you want to come back. Of course …"

"I'm beat. I'm helping Dad early in the morning. I should be off." He nodded to Rafael and Judy and never bothered with Jethro. I was surprised at how little support Judy gave to her friend. Didn't women always stick together? She never got up. Stayed by Rafael's side—who was too confused, clueless about what generally transpired in our group to voice an opinion. He was as quiet as a church mouse.

Charlene and Herbie had been gone for no more than seconds when Jethro appeared from the bedroom as if on cue. His hair was disheveled and red lipstick marks were on his lips and cheek.

"Have you been misbehaving, Mr. Beauregard?" Judy said, so mischievously that I expected Rafael to react. I could only think of Lucille back in Ottawa, disillusioned if she had known the female company he was now keeping.

Jethro refilled his drink. I noted that he hardly put any tonic with the gin when he slurred, "I thought we were past this …"

The unfinished hinted at sex. What other conclusion could we make? Time and place, I thought. *Time and place.* He went and sat opposite the couple, with me still standing by the food. I walked to the radio console and turned the dial to see what else we might find. A jitterbug tune had Jethro pull Judy up who let herself go. She and Jethro cut a rug like I had never seen before. She was all Rita Hayworth in *Gilda*. "Put the blame on Judy" came to mind right away. The joy in their steps made me want to dance too. I picked up Rafael—his jacket and tie already off—who looked like he might have been falling asleep and I spun him around.

"No, Gary. Don't."

"Why not! It's a party." Before I could entice him some more, Judy switched and took Rafael into her arms and gave me Jethro who willingly swept me into his. My imagination swirled as he partnered me with more finesse than I would have thought him capable. When the coupling didn't break up as a gag guys played on each other, when the rhythm of the beat had firmly taken hold in both of us, he did not shy away from leading me, and we jitterbugged like we had been going steady for months.

When the music came to a stop, a slow song, Perry Como singing "Bali Ha'i," was next, and all four of us made a kind of grouping. We were soused by now. Embroiled not simply by the alcohol, but by all the made-up notions of what sex would be. No one knew what it was. Or if one of us did, the others were not privy to that. I never thought of Calgary. Never recalled Rafael's trauma until …

When we began to embrace, it was Judy who led us on. She kissed Rafael passionately, the way Jethro had tried with

Charlene. Rafael gave the impression that he was into the experience and I was turned on without realizing how much. We transitioned to the bedroom without a word spoken. Clothes items came off and before anyone had grasped the degree to what was happening, we were all in our underwear on the bed. I was so enthralled with the titillation, I didn't notice that Jethro had removed my underwear until it was done. I could feel his appendage on me when he moved, and he and Judy took off Rafael's boxers before Jethro removed her bra and panties.

He slid down and tried something when she pushed him away. "No,' she said. "Rafael. You …" And she took him. They were having sexual intercourse and I could see it before my very own eyes when Jethro, who had been on a tear all night, took hold of me and forced my head down on his cock. The abruptness was as shocking as the act. I wanted to do this with Rafael. I *knew* that. But did I want to do this with Jethro? I was as confused as I was drunk, and gave in to my baser instincts until I realized that this was not what I wanted and pulled back. I saw Jethro's puzzlement. The deriding was all over his face. What, you don't want this? is what it said. I felt saddened by how crushing that was. Had he known *all* along? That that was what I was? What I had wanted—maybe not from him, not now. Perhaps before? When I hadn't yet met Rafael.

When Jethro saw he had nothing more forthcoming with me, he did the most outrageous thing and tried to mount Rafael. Before I could react, Rafael screamed, "*Hostie*! What the fuck?!" He flew off the bed and everyone sobered instantly. He ran into the other room.

"What did you do?" I said. I was at the side of the bed, fumbling, searching frantically for my underwear when we all heard the door to the bungalow open and slam shut. "What …?" I mumbled to myself. I needed my clothes. All I could envision was a naked Rafael running out onto the Miramar hotel grounds, cops being summoned. I could tell that the others thought much the same.

We got dressed with what items we could find—impeded as much by drink as by mortified bewilderment—and went into the other room. I saw that the closet door was open and my suitcase was gone. My clothes were on the floor.

"Did he leave for good?" Jethro asked.

By now, Judy had recovered most of her senses. She was sipping water from a glass she had poured. "He'll be back. Right?" She looked at me for an answer, but I was too numb to reply. "Doesn't he have his stuff at your house?"

How could I explain what was impossible to explain? That I felt I knew him better than I had ever known another man before, without even knowing where he lived. What his phone number was. Who his parents were. I had no answers for Judy. None.

THIRTEEN

Jeremy sat frozen in his chair at the table. The hour he had spent listening to Gary recount his story had gone by inexplicably fast. He had traveled through time; that was the only way Jeremy could claim to understand what had just occurred. He could see—he *saw* Santa Monica in an entirely immovable light now. The texture of that section of Los Angeles would never be the same. He started to hyperventilate when Gary approached and Jeremy pushed him away. "Don't!"

Gary saw the overwrought reaction and stepped back.

"Did you rape my father?"

"What …? No!" Gary was utterly distraught that his narrative could be this misconstrued. Had Jeremy thought Calgary a stand-in for a transgression of *his*?

"But you had sex with him!"

"No, Jeremy. Not really."

The younger man rose from his chair and went to the window. He opened it. The sounds of Paris at night, the traffic below, were not as noisy as he might have thought in a city this size. The heavy rain had slowed so that barely a drizzle fell against the glow of lights outside. "Did you …" he began to ask when he grasped that would have been too impossible. Unless Gary was some secret agent, a spy with sophisticated connections, their meeting had to have been random. He quashed that as idiocy on his part. Instead, he went with the more mundane. "When you saw me …"

Gary nodded, having anticipated the question.

"You knew?"

The other man nodded again, moved his head to indicate his own inability to comprehend the odds of their encounter. "The minute I saw you from the side, my heart beat. You were too young to be your father but that didn't register right away. You were Rafael." He teared up and wanted to run away, to come back to find history unchanged, locked in a time warp so that Jeremy could be Rafael. *Had* to be Rafael. 'Til his mind couldn't play those tricks on him any longer. "When you exclaimed aloud, the spell broke. You didn't sound like him."

"No. I sound more like my mom. That's what people tell me. Not great for the ego."

Gary came to Jeremy's side. "I wanted to tell you."

"Tell me what! That you saw my father naked once upon a time?"

"Well, technically … Not fully. In passing. Bits, I suppose."

"The bits that mattered, right?"

Jeremy saying it that way made it all tawdry and Gary felt compelled to clarify. "It was not at all like that."

"If I'd been ready to bed you, would you have?"

The sixty-four-thousand-dollar question, Gary's very own life-lived conundrum befell him! "Thankfully, I'm not your body type," he said, evading Jeremy's question.

"I don't have a body type."

"Just a Justin type, is that it?"

Gary, provoking him with that, seemed overstepping. "Yes! God-fucking damnit."

"That just leads to madness, Jeremy. Trust me, I know that only too well."

Jeremy wondered if he was referring to the long-lost eighteen-year-old ghost of his father. Had Gary been carrying around *that* delusion? "Well, it's only five years for me. You?" he said, wanting to be mean, should his instincts be correct. Punishing Gary for having pined for a straight man, for a bond that could never have materialized, was justifiable to Jeremy.

The baiting was undeniable. "That's cruel," said Gary. He thought of pouncing. Forcing himself on Jeremy, making him succumb. Make *his* needs Jeremy's needs by sheer strength. This primitive urge that had been plucked from obscurity—a tender yearning unfulfilled from years prior, and resurrected with the telling tonight. But he saw his mother disapproving all the way back from 1949 and his self-control prevailed. A need to placate took over instead. "You'll like this." Gary went to get himself another drink from the minibar. "You want one?" Jeremy declined. "It's because of your dad that I took up photography."

The announcement was peculiar. "Was Dad already into photography back in '49?"

Gary turned as he poured his liqueur over ice. "Did Rafael get into photography too?" His mind raced with all the interconnectedness of their lives.

"I'll say. We were the most photographed kids on the block. Dad did home movies. Slides. Photo shoots. That's what he enjoyed to do the most. He was very visual, now that I think about it. Did you teach him stuff?"

Gary was stirred into a reverie—Rafael and him opening their own studio. How life might have given him entirely other purposes than the ones he had come to choose. "No. I didn't even own a camera back then. That's why I said what I just said. I had no photos of Rafael at all. When he left, that was it. There was only a void. I swore I'd never …"

The two men mulled over that in total silence. Jeremy with questions he didn't know how to phrase. Gary with a pining that had never subsided. Finally, Jeremy spoke. "You never tried to look him up?"

"Have you ever gotten out of your clothes, left them in a pile somewhere? And you come back to them a bit later. You're surprised to find that they still hold some of your heat? The heat's there like a bubble, captive. You can even recall and think to yourself, 'That's me. That's *my* body heat,' you think." His eyes wandered around the room before returning to Jeremy. "Your dad came into my life. Stayed for three days. And he left this unsettled package of human heat." The man did everything in his power not to cry, though his insides were all mushy. "Mother was a ball of contradictions. Full of love. Love of life. Open-minded …"

"Did she have something against my dad? Is that it?"

"Not about your dad specifically." Gary went to sit down

on the sofa. What he wanted was to lay down his head but he had to resist, otherwise fatigue would overcome him. "Not about him. But it's what he represented." Gary knew how lost he had been for the next few years. His freshman year at Stanford had not been successful. He had wanted to bail more times than not. With his money squandered even before arriving, dwindling to scarcely a few hundred by late October, he had struggled with two part-time jobs while taking a full class load. He elucidated for Jeremy.

"I'm impressed, Gary. Stanford couldn't have been a cakewalk."

"Mother was worried of losing me. That was why whenever I'd try to reminisce with her, she'd discourage me from finding your dad." Gary had this harsh manner to him that only rancor could explain. "The word *homosexual* was never, ever used. It was all understood and never mentioned. She *might* have relented …" Gary took in a breath of melancholy and continued. "When I had come home on that morning after. With Jethro driving me to my car."

"Did you three stay over at the Miramar that night?" Jeremy's question made Gary frown. He nodded. "Did you three …" Gary bobbed his head once. "You dog, you." Jeremy went to the minibar and helped himself. He sipped the liqueur. "Well, dish, man. I want to know."

"You'll think this odd …"

"Try me."

"We went out in Jethro's car and drove a mile or two when we realized this was not going to do anything. Rafael could have been anywhere by then. It's not as if your dad didn't have any experience getting around. He was probably on side streets hiding. Hell, he'd hitchhiked all the way from Calgary to Santa Monica. This is before there were decent highways. At eighteen! And he was broke. Then, at least. When he left, he had the cash I'd lent him in his pockets."

"Did Jethro and the girl …"

"Judy?"

"Yeah. Did they know Dad's story by then?"

"They learned that night." Gary sat up straighter, tipped at the edge of his seat. "When we got back into the bungalow, Judy said, 'I really liked him.' And I said something like, 'Me too. A lot.' Jethro found it funny. I can't exactly recall how it went down from there but he kidded, 'Me too. But not in that way.'"

"Wasn't he the one who tried to fuck Dad up the ass?"

"I'm getting to that. Up until that night, the only thing I knew about Jethro was that he was *totally* into fitness. Did he hang around with a lot of hot guys, comparing bodies and muscles? He did. And I was always the recipient of his comments when I'd ogle any of them for too long. But it was never mean. Lighthearted stuff. So that night, when he'd been so open to group sex, it had tripped me out. I was a virgin. I'd never kissed, been kissed …"

"What about that boy in Paris on the rooftop?"

"Really, Jeremy? Kids' play. That was it. That was my formation until that night. When Jethro got me to go down on him." Gary, recollecting the act, made him fall back against the sofa. "My mind exploded."

"And …"

Gary could see that Jeremy wanted dirt and details. "I'm getting there. We decided that the story would be that Charlene became sick at a party and went home with Herbie driving her. And that Rafael offered the Miramar bungalow to Judy for the night while he went to stay with a friend. That was the official story for the parents. That your dad left for Canada the next day without saying goodbye because Judy had rejected him because he wasn't going off to college."

"Were there any complications?"

"Oh, Jeremy. So many …" Gary rose and stretched. He wanted fresh air and suggested a late-night walk. They dressed and were outside when Gary continued the telling of his story. "Judy had a past that none of us knew then. No surprise there, right?"

"None. You made her sound like a pro."

"She almost was. Not my place to share. Back in the bungalow, everything fell into place as Judy and Jethro initiated the intimacy. It turned out that Jethro had been diddling a few of the bodybuilders and Judy was no virgin. So, they took me by the hand and led me on my journey."

The upscale neighborhood of Gary's hotel had little foot traffic at this late hour. The men strolled the perimeter like the town was all theirs. "Was it pleasant?"

"For my first time?" Gary considered the momentous aspect of losing his virginity. "Yes, it was remarkably nice."

"Did you diddle with both of them?"

"I did. Which is why I was not in the least bit interested in women from then on. Not their bodies, not what they could bring me. Though, to be fair to Judy, she was magnificent. She did everything in her power to turn me on and with Jethro doing his thing all over us, it truly was a come-to-Jesus-moment for me. I knew, then and there, that men were my only calling."

"You didn't suspect before that night?"

"Of course. But there were no names for it back then. Even in Hollywood. You can't fathom how difficult it all was in those days. You kids!" he said, making Jeremy laugh aloud.

"Are you still friends with them?"

"Was. Am."

"Well, that's clear."

"They got married."

"Jethro and Judy? I *did* not see that one coming."

"You, me, and everybody else." Gary turned so that he was walking backwards as they continued down the sidewalk. The moon was visible and peeking from the clouds, playing hide-and-seek with the shadows. "She got pregnant that night."

"No! Who's kid?"

"Not mine, that's for sure. Jethro's."

"Are they still together?"

"No. They lasted quite a while though. But Jethro was never one for being faithful."

"Is he straight? Gay?"

"He'd never admit it. What with grandkids … But I have a hunch he swings both ways." They had reached the Seine. "You going back to your hovel, I presume?" Gary had been dreading this.

"I should. With this backstory of yours …" Jeremy stopped them in their tracks so that Gary worried briefly. "Are you still going to shepherd me about town?"

"Why wouldn't I?"

"Well … Isn't this painful for you? I must remind you of my dad. Is that fair to you?"

Gary made a "can I hug you?" gesture and Jeremy complied reticently. "Let me finish the story. Maybe that will help you understand better."

"Uh-oh. More story …?"

"In the morning, when Jethro drove us back home, I went by the reception desk and paid for a third night at the Miramar."

"Wh-what?"

"I had to. Just in case. I wasn't sure if your dad would be back."

"Had he left anything behind? Why would he come back?"

Gary's disappointment was on his face. Rafael had left *him* behind. The air of hopelessness that all unrequited lovers had that dug deep into their psyches. "He had left his army surplus boots. They were in the bedroom under the bed when he ran out. But that's not why I thought he might return."

Jeremy pitied Gary. Knowing his father, the life that his father eventually led, there was no way that Rafael Jerome would have done that. To have returned to the Miramar would have denied Lucille Leclerc her rightful place back in the social strata of the Vanier section of Ottawa. His father's sense of obligation was stronger than any sexual dalliance or misadventure, bar none. "He didn't, did he?"

"He did not. I sat all night. Every little noise outside made me sit up. I had never prayed very much at all. Never have much since. But that night. That night, I prayed. I made pacts with God. I promised a life of virtue if only Rafael could walk back into my life. Just for one night so I could explain everything to him. Tell him I loved him. Tell him we were made for each other. That I didn't expect him to reciprocate with sex. I didn't need that. (Even though, after the night before, that part of my prayer was likelier weakened!) But I prayed, invoked whatever the Hebrew God let us sinners raise. I just wanted to make amends. Let bygones be bygones if he needed to leave me behind. I could almost agree to that. As long as we kept in touch. A letter now and again. I wanted *so* much to see him smile at me. Tell me it was all going to be okay. That him in Ottawa and me, wherever I might land, that it would be all right between us."

A strong wind came up the Seine. Both men felt the cold against their backs. Jeremy couldn't tell if Gary had shivered or was holding back sobs.

"When dawn arrived, I understood that I had lost him. I imagined him in the Midwest by then. In some truck or car. Having conversations with new strangers I had to fight not to be jealous of—those lucky saps who had him in their company even if for a short while. How fucked-up is *that*! When the sun was pawing its way through the bungalow window and my eyes had drained of all the water they would hold for days to come, I took one last shower. I remembered the first morning, when I'd come out of the bathroom and your dad had totally crashed out. He looked so beautiful on the bed. Like he might have been able to hold me in his arms had I had the courage to approach him then. After our middle-of-the-night stroll on the beach, after the secrets we had revealed to each other, that possibility seemed feasible." Gary glimpsed at Jeremy to see how much of a fool he was making of himself. All he found was encouragement. "I didn't dare lie down on that bed. Had I done so, I would have had a total breakdown. I was a mess." He took a few beats to compose himself. "I walked out of there and made a promise to myself. I wouldn't hurt myself. How crazy is *that*," he told Jeremy. "I was batshit over-the-moon for your dad. Maybe … If we'd fought in the war, the time together with your dad in '49 would have purchased us a different story."

"But my father wasn't gay."

"No, but I couldn't fathom that, not then. I thought love attracted love."

They were at the bridge and Jeremy needed to pee—head off to his hotel or else relieve himself by a tree—but he didn't want to stifle the mood. He put a hand on Gary's forearm. "If it'll make you feel any better, that suit you bought him …"

Gary's eyes narrowed some, a squint that said, "yes?"

"I may be wrong. But I have it back in my closet in Los Angeles. At least, I think it's the same one. Dad never said much about it. Never threw it out though. Never let Mom give it away. It was kept in one of those suit bags. An heirloom almost."

Gary was speechless.

"You'll have to come over when we're back stateside. We'll know then if it's the real deal."

FOURTEEN

"Can we just leave the story be for one day?" Gary asked of Jeremy at their rendezvous at the Metro on their way to Versailles.

"Is that fair?"

Gary thought he understood how it might have been for Jeremy. Would he have wanted to hear more if someone had approached him with news of his father, years after the man had left the United States for destinations unknown? He believed, though, that his father was not in the same category as Rafael, not in relation to sons. "Let's take the train and just stay on neutral subjects for now. Give me time to place things in perspective. I didn't sleep that much last night."

"And you think I did?" Jeremy replied.

That was the last of the topic until they were on the palace grounds. They had opted out of a tour, deciding to walk on their own to get the sense of history. Standing in the Cour

Royale and then onto the Cour de Marbre, the men were reminded of the excesses that had led to revolution, the interiors that left no doubt as to the root cause that popularized the guillotine.

Gary and Jeremy were in the Hall of Mirrors, engrossed by the glut of overindulgence, their reflections all around them. "I have to ask," Gary said.

"About?"

Would he regret opening the can of worms? "The suit."

"Oh. We're ready *now*, are we?"

"No. But if we stay in public, it'll be safer."

"Safer? Were you planning on hurting me?"

The joke, meant as a pleasantry, reminded Gary that they might very well be coming at this from divergent angles. "No. I was thinking more of tempers. Being riled by unexpected discoveries."

"I see." Jeremy stepped away and turned so that he could have been starting a match of some kind. Fencing? Wrestling? "You go first."

"If your dad kept the suit."

"That's if the suit is *the* suit." Touché, Jeremy thought. How many more of these before he might count himself victor?

"Well, it's not the suit he wore for his wedding, right?"

"No. I'm pretty certain it's not."

"And it wasn't a suit that he wanted to be buried in?"

"Too late for that." Jeremy had to think for a moment. "My brother, Matthew, was in charge of the will. I hope he didn't fuck that one up." He considered the possibility. "No. But we fought over who would get to keep the suit."

"Why is that?"

"I have no idea. Matt would never have worn it. That's for sure."

"You?"

"Worn it?"

Gary nodded.

"Maybe. It doesn't fit me but the material and the cut. It's quite beautiful."

"Rafael was stunning in it. You can't imagine how he stood out. I still see him in the Bullock's dressing rooms. Him coming out and showing it to me. Quite the stud."

"My father was many things but never a stud."

"You didn't know him when he was eighteen. On the loose."

"Is that how you see him back then? On the loose?"

Gary and Jeremy were sparring. Their banter, the back and forth. Even their bodies, how they approached and circled. The game was set with no one keeping score. "Why would your dad keep the suit? That's what I'd love to know." Gary lunged smoothly so that he came very close to Jeremy and whispered, "I'll bet you he never told your mom."

"About the suit?"

"The suit. Santa Monica. What happened in Calgary …"

The mention of Calgary gave Jeremy the opportunity to pivot. "How can you be so certain that the Calgary story Dad told you wasn't just made up? That he picked up on your gay vibe and made it all up so you'd keep your hands off of him."

The rebuttal, for Gary, was too easy. "For one thing. You had to be there." He walked away to see how bright the sun was shining from the window onto the wall of mirrors next to them. All the tourists seemed to be lit by klieg lights, the brightness was that intense. "The way your dad spoke. The words he used. His body language conveyed …" Gary remembered the speed at which Rafael had skedaddled from the four-person orgy. The instant Jethro had propped himself against his buttocks had spooked Rafael. Prudishness would have reacted earlier, very differently. "I don't think so, Jeremy. Your dad *was* traumatized. That's how I found him. He was a lost soul. I'm not saying I saved him, but …"

Trying to square that imagery with the father he had lived with for his entire life was all too rigorous. Jeremy inhaled like he was about to run a marathon. *How* to find the strength to face this head-on? "Well, I doubt he ever told Mom anything."

"Why do you say that?"

"She wouldn't have understood."

"The rape? His time in Santa Monica?" By that, Gary meant meeting him. Being changed by him.

"All of it, I suspect." Jeremy could not envision his mother accepting any of what his father had done.

"Do you think your mother thought he was a virgin on their wedding night?"

"That's what they always bragged about. Not bragged. Wrong word. They just talked about it like they had achieved a goal that was rarer than you would have thought back in their day."

"Well, that was a lie on your dad's part."

"Was it?"

"Technically. Yeah."

"Well, maybe, technically my mom wasn't a virgin either."

"You think?"

Jeremy guffawed; the notion was so preposterous to him. "No. She was *so* a virgin on her wedding night."

They had left the Hall of Mirrors, seen all of the palace that they had planned to see and went walking on the grounds. The view from anywhere in the gardens, between the layout of the plantings to the sculpted fountains, was breathtaking. They had settled on a bench and were resting before deciding on their next move. "I think your dad was bisexual."

"No, he wasn't. You're mistaken. It's … What do they call that in psychology?"

"Projection?"

"Yup."

"Maybe. But why keep that suit? How did he manage that with your mom? Didn't Lucille need answers for that?"

Jeremy tossed around some possible explanations that might make some sense to him before he argued them out loud. "They were always very frugal," he concluded.

"Yeah. I'm listening."

"If … And I haven't a clue here, how he pulled it off. If he showed up back in Ottawa with a tall tale. Some concoction about … I can't fathom what he could have said so that his parents wouldn't look at that suit and not ask him questions. But … He must have had a plausible story."

"And …?"

"Well, that story must have worked on my mom. Right?"

The men mulled over that likelihood. "Was your mom gullible?"

"No. Not that I ever thought. No more than most women from her generation. Her background."

"And they weren't religious?"

"At the beginning. Sure. But what's that got to do with it?"

"Well, if your mom had been very religious …" Gary treaded lightly here, for fear of offending. "Religiosity often has a lot of gullibility that goes with it."

"Yeah. Could be. Early on, maybe she just accepted what Dad told her. He brought that suit into the house. Into that marriage somehow. It wasn't hidden away. Not totally, at least."

"When did you learn about the suit?"

Jeremy paused to consider. "Can't recall. Somewhere along the way. At some point I was aware that there was this old-fashioned suit at the back of their closet that he never wore." Jeremy remembered something and blurted it out like it was a piece to the puzzle. "I wanted to wear it once."

"You did?"

"Yeah. It was for a high school function. A costume party? He flat-out said no."

The two understood the clue even with the great chasm between what Gary presumed and what Jeremy thought. "It meant too much to your dad. He was afraid you'd ruin it. That's what I think."

"No. I think he might have been afraid that I'd start asking too many questions." Jeremy was finally accepting the reality that all of Gary's chronicle was commensurate with the burden his father had carried to his grave. He wanted to be back in his condo in North Hollywood to try on the suit. Pictured himself traveling his father's journey all alone from Santa Monica back to Ottawa with so many secrets that would have undone most men his age. That affliction he had carried. The experience of rape in a darkened field back in

1949 for a straight boy just on the cusp of manhood. The disgrace, if anyone had ever discovered his ordeal. His father had preserved the suit because it had to have represented recovery of some kind. He told Gary that.

"You think so?" Gary asked, open to the idea. Married to that hope like an action that could validate what he had carried with him near on fifty years.

"I'm tending to see this your way, Gary. I don't have any answers. But I'm going to start investigating.

"For what?"

"Your guess is as good as mine."

The sun over Versailles was warm and blissful as they sat on the bench. The birds by the water chomped hungrily on the food the visitors fed them. "Can you ask your brother?"

"No. Not him. He'll just freak out and …" Jeremy shook his head. The idea of Matthew hearing what Gary had told him gave him a frisson like spoiled food as it went down before you realized it was rancid. "No. But I can start with Paulette. My sister. She won't appreciate it at all either."

"She's okay with your being gay?"

"Yeah. They both are. In their own way." Jeremy stood, signaling he was ready to depart. "I'll have to broach it very carefully."

"Over the phone or in a letter?"

"Not sure. I'll have to think on that."

Gary rose and stretched his legs since one had begun to fall asleep, a function of getting older. He shifted from one leg to the other to work up the circulation. Tapped and massaged the thigh, hating that his muscles did that now and again. "Is there no one in your dad's generation that could have information?"

They began to walk without ever discussing the fact that

they were leaving the palace grounds and heading into town to catch the train. "An aunt or two. Maybe an uncle." He thought of which ones who might have a connection with that past his father had hidden so well.

"On your mother's side? It was her family that Rafael stayed with, no?"

"You probably know that better than I do!"

How could he? "No," Gary replied. "No. I remember what happened to him. What your dad told me. But not the specifics. Not the family stuff."

"I'll have to really think all of this out. I have my work cut out for me."

They were at the train station when Gary asked, "When do you think you'll be back up in Canada?"

"Next summer. Unless I go home for Christmas."

"Do you? Go home for Christmases?"

"Not a lot since Mom died. Not every year. On occasion. Depends on work. If I have a lot to do during the Christmas break. Every year is so different." Jeremy thought of the coming academic year, his new responsibilities as department head. A Christmas up in Canada seemed out of the question though, now, with this family intrigue … This mystery that definitely needed solving. "If my sister. Or an aunt—any relative has information. That'll guide me."

Did Gary dare to presume he would be kept abreast? They had taken their seats. The air conditioning in their passenger car was a welcome relief from the heat. Both men had questions that wouldn't be revolved any time soon, but Gary wanted to make sure of one thing. "You'll come to visit me in Santa Barbara. Promise?"

Jeremy turned slightly in his seat. "Gary. You've made a friend for life."

PART II

OTTAWA, WINTER 1997

FIFTEEN

Ottawa was never a great destination at Christmas. The snow and ice, the likelihood of snow storms, and the constant flux in weather forecasts were enough to drive any traveler up the wall.

"Who's picking you up at the airport?" Gary asked. He had called at the last minute to wish Jeremy a safe trip.

"It depends."

"On …?"

"On people's schedules for one thing." Jeremy had been putting his suitcase in order when the phone had rung. The carry-on bag made packing for six days an art form he did not possess. He was bringing too much and had to pare down. He threw everything out of the overstuffed leather case back onto the bed and began putting articles in piles of yeses, likelys, and maybes. "On who can drive to the airport when I get there with the least amount of hassles." He would be on the lookout for either a nephew or his sister, he said.

"When will you spring your news on them?"

"At Christmas Eve dinner, I thought. While pouring the gravy."

Gary knew his younger friend enough by now to appreciate his humor. "You'll be using a slideshow presentation?"

"Yes. That way, they can all see the visuals. Dad naked in a bed with two other men and a woman. The Calgary rape in flagrante delicto."

Gary chuckled at the grand gesture with the Latin phrase.

"That should do the trick, Gary, don't you think?"

The commuter flight he had taken from Toronto to Ottawa was encountering a lot of wind turbulence on its descent. Jeremy found himself white-knuckling the armchair rest trying to breathe as deeply as he could, his stomach worse for the wear and tear. At the arrival gate, Jeremy spotted Paulette. "I love the color," he said, running his fingers through her hair.

"Yeah ... Not too obvious?" she said.

Her tight hug reminded him that distance *did* make the heart grow fonder. Theirs was a good relationship, not too close, but close enough to matter. With the occasional letter and cards for birthdays and some of the holidays, they spoke over the phone on average once a month. When Rafael had died, and for the year afterward, their calls had been more frequent—that need to compensate for the tragedy of losing their last parent so prematurely. Not living nearby made the loss slightly easier, Jeremy had determined in the end. He had been grateful, if you could say that and mean it in a positive way about the loss of a father. Had he been nearer geographically, would he have been bent more out of shape from the sudden loss?

"Is that storm still coming?" Jeremy inquired once they were in the quiet of the car.

"80 percent chance, the radio said."

Why did Canadians have to use percentages when talking about weather? In Los Angeles, the skies never deviated much. There was never any need to verify what the projections were. Sunny and hot nine months out of the year. Rain and Santa Ana winds in parts of the winter. Winter! Jeremy laughed inside, thinking about winters in Los Angeles. There *was* no winter. It was green and warm with flowers of some kind yearlong. Or so it seemed to him, after growing up in the Canadian snow deserts, a wilderness that could frighten—the long haul that could only be described as cruel and unforgiving compared to the temperate conditions in which Jeremy had been luxuriating since his move to sunny California in his late twenties.

"If we're lucky …"

"You always say that, Jeremy. You have the worst luck with weather every time you travel up here."

She *was* right. How many times had his travel plans been delayed! Cancelled at the last minute for hours or a day or two due to weather systems that made flying ill-advised. She never understood exactly why Jeremy bothered with Christmas travel. Not that she wasn't happy to see him, only … this! The roads were icy after the dip in temperature the night before, which had left black ice under the snow that made driving precariously dangerous on streets that saw little traffic.

"Well, maybe this year will be different." Jeremy rubbed

the passenger side window with his glove to see how bad it was outside. The sky was a bland gray-black with clouds that had no hint as to what they held in store for them.

Jeremy's niece and nephew came to greet him as soon as they were inside. "Is that tan for real?" Gisele asked. She smudged his face, insinuating he might have been wearing makeup but when she checked, her fingertips were clean.

At sixteen, she was coming into her own feminine wiles and Jeremy could not believe the growth spurt since he had last seen her. "It sort of comes with the territory in LA. You just haven't noticed before." He gave her a hug and stood back to inspect his nephew. "How old are you now?"

"Fourteen," Larry answered, his voice just in the throes of changing registers. The cracking was endearing.

"Come here, young man." Jeremy pulled him by the neck and gave him noogies on the head. "You're not too old for these, are you?"

"Ouch," Larry yelled.

"Boys." Paulette tapped her brother so that Jeremy stopped the roughhousing. She took his coat and scarf and hung them in the foyer closet. "Larry, take your uncle's suitcase to the guest bedroom." Her second-born did as he was told.

The siblings went to the kitchen with Gisele in tow. "Is Fred joining us for Christmas Eve?" Jeremy could see his sister communicate with her eyes and he retracted by changing subjects. "Matt's coming with the boys, right?"

"And their girlfriends," Gisele said.

"Girlfriends?" Jeremy felt mischievous for no other

reason than he was back on home turf. "So, it's settled. Eric is straight then?"

Gisele looked at her mother who stared disapprovingly at her brother. "Jeremy!"

"What?! We always suspected …"

"No. Not me. *You* did."

Jeremy could see that the orientation theme might be off-limits because of his niece. "My bad," he said, apologizing so as to include the teenager.

"I always thought he might be, too." Gisele went to the fridge and took out a can of Sprite. "Want something, Uncle Jeremy?"

"Uh … Yeah. I'll have one of those. I'm thirsty."

"No wine?" Paulette went to get some cheese and crackers and put out a plate. She poured cashews in a crystal dish and placed it all on the table set against the rectangular banquette.

"I'm fine." They settled on munching their late-night snack with Larry joining them. "So, who's all coming tomorrow night then?" he asked.

"Matt. Eric with a girl." Paulette pointed at Jeremy to behave. "Marc with a girl."

"Do these girls have names?"

"I haven't met them."

"Mom, yes you did. We met Rachel at Thanksgiving."

"Oh yes. I stand corrected. Sorry, honey. You're right. You. Me and the kids. Nine total."

"Matt's not dating anyone?"

"If he is, he's not bringing her." She seemed happy with

that, as though that complication would only add to her stress.

"And you?"

"Mom's not dating anyone," Larry said emphatically.

Jeremy got the message loud and clear; he sympathized with Paulette, who must have been lonely. He knew his sister had gone on dates. Obviously, she hadn't let the kids in on that. Or maybe she had, hence Larry sounding dictatorial? Her Fred had not been a bad man, just not an easy sort to get along with. His menial jobs, which had always paled in comparison to her great-paying government job that utilized all the benefits of her bachelor's in economics, had been the bane of their fights—the disparity in incomes that faltered so many marriages. Jeremy felt especially sorry for Larry, understanding how important that lack of a father role could be in the day-to-day.

"Are *you* dating, yet?" he teased Larry, aware that this was the worst thing he could do for the boy at that age. "I'm kidding. You're too young for that. Plenty of time." He glanced at Gisele, who gave him a wicked smile. He liked *that*. "You?" he asked. "Any cute boys you want to talk about?"

His niece conferred with her mother, all nonverbal. "A few..."

"Too many," Paulette said. "She takes after you, I'm afraid."

"Me?" Jeremy exclaimed. He had no memories of being wild in high school. That period in his life had been the dullest on earth.

"Well, maybe not in high school. But you certainly made up for that in college."

"Okay. Guilty as charged."

"You had a lot of boyfriends in college?" Gisele asked, primed for more.

Paulette cleared her throat, cuing her brother to watch what he might share. *As if* he was about to provide a play-by-play of any sexual encounter from his youth! "I was … checking out the merchandise to see what suited me." He looked back at Paulette to see if she approved. She did by nodding.

"And what suited you?" Gisele asked, mocking his turn of phrase.

"Boys. I liked boys." He turned to Larry. "Hope this isn't grossing you out?"

"Nah. I'm used to it."

"He has a buddy who just came out to him, to the whole school, right before Christmas break," Gisele announced, like it was a banner on the five-o'clock news.

"No!" Jeremy was fascinated. "That's pretty brave. Catholic school. In Ottawa?"

"He had no choice. Some girl outed him."

"Ooh, that's terrible." Jeremy knew how cruel high school could be. Back in his Los Angeles district, the laws were changing fast. Protection for the LGBT kids was just taking off. "I'm sure you were very supportive, Larry."

"He's my best friend. What did you want me to do?"

His answer, followed by a question—was it rhetorical or demonstrative? In Jeremy's day, the best friend would have surely disappeared, *and* fast. "Well, he'll need all the support. You don't have to be alone for that. You can always reach out." He had meant with other staff at Larry's high school but the offer suggested he was there for him as well. "What's his name?"

"My friend? Humphrey."

"Humphrey turned out to be gay?! I would never have guessed."

"You and me both."

Larry grinned and his uncle understood completely. Humphrey was a tall, muscular, sporty kid from the neighborhood who had been best friends with his nephew for as long as Jeremy could recall. "I would have lost that bet, Larry. Hands down. How are his parents?"

"They knew. At least, he said that." He shrugged. "It wasn't obvious to anyone."

"Well, teenage girls …" he began to say when he stopped himself.

"Yeah, what about teenage girls?" Gisele inquired.

"Oh, nothing. I don't know what I was thinking."

"Yes, you do. You were going to make a point."

"She's right, Jeremy." Paulette was proud of her daughter standing up to her brother. "Do tell. About teenage girls."

"Well. It's my experience. Not so much from when I was a teenager," though it truly was, "but from now. Since I've been teaching high school." He paused to choose every word as accurately as he could. "Sometimes, when girls fall for a boy and they find out that he's gay, it can get ugly."

"Has that happened to you?" Paulette asked.

Jeremy considered for a second. "Not that I can remember. If it did, I was clueless. No girls ever fell for me that way."

"That you know of," his sister added.

"You're not going to tell me you know something I don't?"

"No, nothing like that. But with your looks and your manners …"

"My looks and my manners?"

"You were cute in high school. Very polite with the girls."

"Yeah, but I didn't really date."

"You didn't go to prom?" his niece asked.

"I did, Gisele. But it was with a lesbian." Before Paulette could object, he added, "No, I wasn't aware of it at the time. Hell, Bella didn't know that about herself either. But we went together because it felt safe. It was what you did if you were gay back then. So that you'd have a memento. A photo. Some memory down the road."

"It doesn't sound very romantic," Gisele said.

"No, it wasn't. But it was fun. I could—we both could say we went to our senior prom."

The nostalgia topic seemed perfect for Jeremy to broach the issue of their father. "Paulette, do you still have all those photos that Dad had when he died?"

The swivel in topics surprised Paulette. "Yeah. They're in boxes in the basement. Why?"

The Jeromes were not photo-album-family types. She hadn't even gone through them like she had meant to when Rafael had died back in 1992. Five years had come and gone, and the prospect of ever doing that chore was highly unlikely now.

"A funny thing happened in Paris."

"Paris?"

"Yeah. I wasn't going to talk about it …" Jeremy suddenly regretted raising that now.

"What happened, Uncle Jeremy?"

He could see his niece was very curious. "I probably should be talking with your mom first."

Paulette's vigilance spelled misgivings in abundance.

"It's nothing … salacious," he said, though it all absolutely was. "But, kids. Sorry to do this to you. I wasn't thinking. You'll know all about it eventually. It's just for now, better that your mom and I discuss this in private."

With that sober stipulation, Jeremy rose from his seat.

"Maybe you can show me where those boxes are?"

"Now?" his sister asked.

Larry sprang to his feet. "I'll show you, Uncle Jer."

Paulette got up to get herself some more wine. "Be careful. There might be glass in there."

She watched her son and her brother walk to the basement door, shut it closed, leaving the women to consider their options.

SIXTEEN

Matt was summoned to Paulette's the very next morning. Never a pushover, still, he had been left in the lurch when Paulette refused to tell him why it was paramount that he come over.

"But I'm going to *be* there by four. Can't it wait?" Paulette's vagueness had irritated Matt. "You're not going to give me a clue, are you?"

This was important was all she would say. "The kids shouldn't be around to hear it," she added.

The eldest had become portly during his forties. The extra twenty pounds were carried at the waist, a potbelly that was more noticeable when he wore jeans that were too tight, which is what he had on that day. He walked in from the front door that was seldom locked and saw Jeremy on the sofa. They nodded and Jeremy thought of waiting to be greeted, to see if Matthew had been given any hint as to the nature of their dilemma. Matthew walked towards him.

"Don't you ever put on weight?" he asked, and struck his paunch with a palm, proud of his heft. The brothers hugged.

"Never." Jeremy could see how chubbier he had gotten. "Not allowed in my sort of crowd." He did a silly pirouette to accentuate the gayness of his clan.

"Yeah, so I've heard." The insinuation was blithe, no more meaning to it than a "pass the salt" at the table—all fraternal. "You're not helping Paulette with the cooking?"

"I'm doing desserts. I'm going to start …"

Paulette walked up to Matthew and pecked him on the cheek, which was rarely done since they saw each other often. Born less than a year apart, with only a few neighborhoods between their houses in the west end of Ottawa, the elder siblings were close. The kiss on the cheek told Matthew something was certainly up. "So, what's this big to-do?"

Paulette put up a finger to indicate the kids upstairs in their bedrooms. She escorted them down to the basement, aware that the news might destabilize the first-born in their family. They sat down on the sofa and chairs by the gas fireplace and she turned on the mechanism to get more heat going, get the bite out of the dampness in the room.

"You wanna begin?" she said.

Jeremy had had an entirely different vision of the telling of his story. He had planned for less presentational, more conversational. A "so, a funny thing happened" remark just like last evening, done in passing, that would grow into more specifics once the parties had accustomed themselves to the content he had to share.

"Well, for starters. I need you to keep an open mind."

"You're a woman? You want a sex change, is that it?" Matthew said in all sincerity.

Jeremy looked askance at his brother. "Is that why you think Paulette asked you over here? For me coming out as trans?" Matthew's arms went up with a "yeah, why not?" gesture. "No, Matt. This isn't that." The youngest wondered if the man was relieved that this was not *that* hurdle.

Though the Jerome siblings didn't smoke anymore, the duress made them all wish for a cigarette.

"Go on, then," he said to Jeremy. "Why did I have to drive over here so quickly? You can't be pregnant." The reticent smile was his attempt at lightening the mood. "Shit, you got someone pregnant? No, dude. That can't be. Can it?"

"Matthew, will you just let him speak?"

The three sat back in their respective seats and took in the silence in their own way. Paulette, having previously heard the incredulous tale, had again been disinclined to believe any of it. She had wanted her older brother there for guidance, to stand up to the hogwash Jeremy was about to spew for a second time in her home.

"Someone say something. I have a lot of preparations to do. The boys are coming over for drinks and open presents around two today." He glanced at his watch. "It's a tight day, that's all I'm saying."

Paulette told Jeremy to repeat what he had disclosed to her in the privacy of the guest room late into the night.

"First. I'm only going to say it once." He made sure that his brother knew this was directed at him. "I don't want any screaming or fighting."

"You're not starting with your rules already." Matt stood up. "I'm not one of your high school students. I'll do what the hell I want."

Jeremy thought of leaving. Walking back upstairs, apologizing to his niece and nephew and catching the next flight back to LA. Ever since Paris last summer, he had held off saying a word over the phone or in a letter, exactly for *this* not to happen. Miscommunication and supposition that could lead to hostility towards him who, after all, was only the messenger. "I met this guy in Paris." Matthew's obnoxious expression made Jeremy cut him off at the pass. "No, Matt. Nothing like that."

"Good. I don't need to hear that stuff."

"What stuff? The gay stuff? What we all do in the privacy of our bedrooms?"

"I don't do that."

"I'd love to know what *that* is." Jeremy was being spiteful now.

"Guys, come on," Paulette said, playing referee. "Jeremy. Just spill it out."

"This guy, Gary. Knew Dad. Way back in the day."

"Here? In Ottawa?"

"No. That's the crazy thing about all of this. Not Ottawa. Not Canada. California."

"What do you mean, California? Dad never went to California."

"Matt, that's what I told Jer. I knew I was right about this."

Jeremy had grasped from the outset that the Santa Monica part would be a stretch for anyone to believe. But

Calgary, on the other hand, *that* was conceivable. Calgary, time spent in Alberta, was part of their father's legacy. As little as they knew—what little there was in the family's lore—Jeremy understood that this part was not as contestable. "Apparently he was. According to Gary."

"Does he have photos?"

"No. No photos."

"Then how can you be sure he's not lying. Is this about money?"

"No, Matt. This isn't about money. If anything, Dad owed him in a big way."

"So, it is about money. How much does this … What's the guy's name again?"

"Gary."

"How much does this Gary say Dad owed him."

Jeremy rose from the side chair and went by the gas flames. The chill in the basement rec room had been replaced by a toasty heat. It felt good to not have freezing toes. "Gary is loaded. Trust me. The last thing that man needs. Or wants. Is more money. Our money."

"We don't have any money," Matthew stated for the record.

"Tell him the rest, Jeremy."

He knew intrinsically that this was not going to be pleasant for Matthew. The incident had repulsed him, too, on hearing it initially. It never got any easier, not the description or the imagining of it being done to his poor, defenseless father at eighteen. "When Dad was in Calgary."

"He wasn't in Calgary."

"Where was he then?"

Matt had that "I-don't-know-but-you-know-I'm-correct" look on his face. "Near Calgary."

"Fine. Near Calgary. It fits with what I'm about to tell you." Explaining the rape of their father at the hands of a big-shot politician was as absurd to Paulette and Matt as it had been when Gary narrated the episode to Jeremy. The Jerome trio stayed quiet as everyone processed the account.

"There is no way that happened." Matthew stood up and pulled at his belly, lifting up the blubber with his belt. Tongue-tied was never a penchant of his, but he was now, caught off-guard. "Why would you entertain this kind of wacko bullshit?"

"I was as shocked as you were. But it all fell into place. Once I heard the whole story. Got to know Gary."

"Did you fuck this guy? Is that why you think he's telling the truth?"

Jeremy and Matthew rarely saw life from the same lens but this was untoward. "You know, Matt. You can cross a line too often."

Paulette who had played peacekeeper for years said, "Stop it. This is Christmas Eve, for God's sakes." She went to Jeremy and told him calmly, "Tell him about the suit."

"What suit?" Matthew inquired.

"The one you wanted to give to the Salvation Army. The one you didn't want me to keep," Jeremy said. He could see his brother trying to place the article of clothing. "When Dad died. We were cleaning up the house. You found it …"

"No, I'm the one who found it," Paulette said. "Dad had it in the back of his closet because when Mom died, I'd seen it and asked him what it was. I thought he wore the suit for his wedding."

"That old thing?"

"That old thing, Matthew, was bought for Dad at Bullock's in Lost Angeles. A fancy store. Fitted for him. On the spot. They did that back in the day. He wore the suit for that flashy premiere." Because Jeremy had the outfit in his closet in a suit bag back in North Hollywood, had it confirmed by Gary that it was indeed the same suit, he could state it as a fact. "Gary paid for it. Dad was supposed to pay him back but that never happened. He took off. Gary never heard from Dad again."

"Any wonder, if …" Matthew left the sentence as it was. Finishing it would have made him describe sex with a group of people, which was inappropriate given that they were talking about their dad. "This is too much." He went to the stairs. "I have too much to do to handle this."

"When do you want to *handle* this?" Jeremy asked, the emphasis on handling since that had not been any expectation of his. All he had wanted was assistance in figuring out the genesis of this family mystery, not have him conduct the investigation.

"What's there to handle?" Matt began to climb up the stairs.

"There's a lot to handle."

"Whoa. What do you think you're going to do with this little nugget of yours?" Matthew had returned to the bottom step, pointing a threatening finger at his brother.

"I want to see if anyone can help us with this."

"Help us?!" By now, Matthew had heard enough. "You're going to keep your mouth shut, Jeremy. Dad's memory. Don't you have any respect for that? For the sake of Mom's memory at least. What do you think this will do?" He walked up the stairs and said as he was leaving, "Don't you bring this up at dinner. I'm warning you. You hear?" He didn't wait for an answer.

By four that afternoon, Jeremy had settled down in the living room with his cosmo, compliments of Jennifer's talents. "You've been together how long?" he asked, making small-talk. Everyone had arrived within the last quarter hour.

Jennifer checked in with Eric who took the floor. "Depends on which date you count."

"Okay, I'll bite." What else could Jeremy say without being rude? Didn't all couples agree on what constituted their first date? Hadn't he and Justin seen eye to eye on that, at the very least?

"We met at a mixer on campus."

"A Christian sorority," Jennifer explained.

"Is that where you learned how to mix this mean cosmo?"

Her smile widened to a grin. "Never." She appreciated Jeremy's wit.

"Didn't think so," Jeremy replied with a wink.

"I don't think they were even serving liquor at that function, were they, Eric?"

"That explains our not hooking up then."

Jeremy was surprised at his forwardness, an emulation of Matthew not his mom.

Jennifer slapped Eric's wrist playfully. "We didn't hook up then because *I'd* just broken up and I wasn't into finding anyone."

"No. That took two more weeks."

Jeremy had never seen Eric this spirited. How *much*

liquor had the boys consumed prior to their arrival? Or was that what new love could bring? Jeremy suddenly wanted some for his own. "And how long ago was that?" he asked.

"That was late last June," Jennifer said. "The official date."

"But I had totally tried to pick you up at that mixer."

"You had." Jennifer rubbed Eric's forearm, catching Jeremy's glance as she did.

Suspicions of his nephew ever being gay went to the wayside. The boys, Marc and Eric, had turned into handsome young men, the uncle thought, on the cusp of their adult lives. He credited their mother's influence in their success to date. Not that Matthew was a bad father, but Elizabeth and her PhD had encouraged and guided the boys to successfully complete their undergraduate degrees, find work in the public sector that made Ottawa what it was today. Jeremy had finished his cocktail when Jennifer asked him if he was ready for a refill.

"Wouldn't say no to that." His drink refreshed, he asked, "What do you do, Jennifer?"

"I'm a lawyer. Well, will be by next year, once I'm finished articling."

"Impressive."

"Eric told me you teach history?"

"I do. AP US history is my favorite. I also teach US Government and Politics. At the AP level. But not every year. It changes." He sipped from his drink, savoring the Cointreau aftertaste. "What does Rachel do?"

Rachel looked over. "Did I hear my name?"

"Yup. I was asking Jennifer what you did."

"I'm just finishing my BA in psychology at Carleton. I'm going for my PhD afterwards."

"Impressive." Jeremy was aware that he'd repeated himself. What *else* did you say to high-achievers? "Where are you planning on doing that?"

There was hesitation as Marc leaned into their circle of conversation. "All depends …"

"On …?"

"On if we want to move or not."

"Oh," Jeremy said. "That's always tough."

Rachel rose from the couch and came to where Jeremy was seated at that end of the living room. Larry upped from where he was and joined them, squatting beside his uncle. Jeremy was tempted to play with the boy's hair but refrained, not wanting to make anyone uncomfortable.

"I'm applying now for grad school. I sent out a half-dozen applications. I'd love McGill, but I'll take wherever I can get. The financial aid package will be the deal breaker."

"Always is." Jeremy knew how tough it was to fund an education in Canada. "A shame you're not in the States. A lot more access to financial aid down there."

"I've been told. I have an aunt in Rochester. She wanted me to apply to Cornell. But the out-of-state tuition would have killed me."

"I'm sure you'll get exactly what you want." Jeremy turned to her partner. "Marc, you'll relocate too?"

There was more hesitation. "We're gonna wait and see. Montreal to Ottawa is doable. We can survive that, can't we?" he asked his girlfriend. Rachel nodded but the wooliness was unmistakable.

As a lull set in, Paulette came in from the kitchen. "Jer, I need your assistance."

"Sure thing, Sis." He walked into the kitchen to the turkey on top of the stove. "That looks yummy."

"Let's hope it's not too dry. Matt so hates dried turkey." She basted as Jeremy began to cut slices of white and dark meat with the electric knife. They joined forces to make the gravy a perfection. "You want to bring that to the table, Jer? I'll call everyone in."

The meal was served with holiday carols playing on the audio system. "When was the last time you were here for Christmas, Uncle Jeremy?" Gisele asked. "I forget."

"You were starting junior high. The year your granddad passed away. I traveled to Ottawa on three occasions that year." The mention of Rafael made Paulette and Matthew tense up. Jeremy saw it immediately. The last thing he wanted was a quarrel. He took his glass of wine and raised it. "A toast." Everyone around the table followed his lead. "To Rafael Jerome. A super guy. May you rest in peace, Dad."

The clinking had stopped when Larry asked, "Did you find what you were looking for, Uncle Jerry?"

"What?"

"The pictures. You said you were hoping there might be some from Calgary."

Matthew's knife banged against his plate and all eyes went to that end of the table. "Uh, sorry," he said. "It slipped."

Marc, who was seated next to his father, continued to stare at the cutlery, as though an expletive rather than an accident had occurred. He suspected his father of having begun to drink too early in the day. "You okay?" he whispered quietly.

Matthew gave him a brusque glance, clearly meant to dissuade him from further bother, so Marc ventured, "Uncle Jeremy. What was that about Calgary? Who went to Calgary?"

"Don't we have family out there?" Eric joined in.

Jeremy knew how quick to anger the boys' father could be. His expression pleaded with his sister to intervene. "Nobody went to Calgary," Paulette said. "Anybody want more tourtière? I baked plenty this year."

"I'll have some," Jeremy said. He got up. "Anybody? Seconds?" He could see the knives coming at him from Matthew. Did he dare test those waters? Fuck it, he thought! "Matt, you want some?"

His older brother, seated at the end of the table, looked apoplectic. With Paulette at the other end, they were like the matriarch and patriarch in charge of the proceedings. "No. Jeremy. I don't want any more tourtière. I'm stuffed."

"You've hardly eaten, Dad," Marc said. "Are you feeling all right?"

Matthew's deep, in-and-out breath was heard by everyone at the table. The newer members, the girlfriends, unfamiliar with any of the family drama from years past, knew no better.

"I love Calgary," Jennifer said. "I have two uncles who farm out there. Well, ranch. They have herds of cattle. I went there when I was a kid. Got to go to the Calgary Stampede."

"You did?" Jeremy asked. "Do tell."

Matthew's knife clanked again, this time on purpose, calculated to intimidate, but Jeremy would have none of it. He had a Bullock's suit back in his closet in North Hollywood, in near-mint condition that screamed out for attention, and he had every intention of airing it out for all to see.

SEVENTEEN

Boxing Day—the day after Christmas in Canada—was typically set aside for shopping. Unlike the previous morning where the drapes to the guest room had been drawn tightly, ceremoniously, very late on Christmas Eve to curtail any daylight from disturbing him, Jeremy was bright-eyed and bushy-tailed today. No hangover for him *this* morning.

Matthew's combativeness on Christmas Eve had caused Paulette's nerves to take a turn for the worse. Her stomach had barely settled down these thirty-six hours. She had taken sleep medication and was feeling her old self again when she entered the kitchen to the smell of fresh coffee and bacon and eggs.

"What a difference a day makes," she said, inadvertently sarcastic. She could see Jeremy's excitement. "Tell me again why I'm doing this with you?"

"Because we need to. We have to do this."

"Matt's going to have a conniption when he gets wind of this."

"What else is new!"

Paulette poured herself some hot water, opting for peppermint tea to work on her stomach. "He didn't want the kids alarmed. That's all. That's why he freaked out the way he did." She sat down after popping slices of bread in the toaster.

"Is that all you're having for breakfast?" he asked.

"You don't have kids, Jer. You can't understand."

Why did parents use that trope? He had hundreds of kids on his rosters. Handled every teenage emotional need that presented itself. With each subsequent year, he was as much social worker as history teacher as his skill-set required updating to accommodate every socioeconomic obstacle the kids brought with them to campus. His homeless students, of which there seemed to be more every semester, were the hardest, most wrenching cases. He thought of those kids, bit his tongue, and simply replied, "I think Larry is a very mature kid. If your fourteen-year-old son can handle the truth, then the others can too."

His sister knew he was right. "It's just … It's our dad, Jeremy." She was beginning to suspect that this was a gay-versus-straight thing. That for heterosexuals, the rape allegation—if that was what they were dealing with, male-on-male aggression—was too cringe-making to cope with.

"Eric sure picked a feisty mate."

"Yeah. She's going to make a humdinger of a lawyer."

"A good thing it was her saying what she said. It really shut Matthew up." Jeremy giggled and Paulette joined in. "Do you think Matthew will hold it against her?"

Paulette got her toast and buttered them. "It's up to Eric, don't you think?" She drizzled a teaspoon of honey, spread it with her knife, and took a bite.

"If Eric mans up and stands up for her, yeah." Neither believed that would happen though. "How's the stomach?" he asked her.

"Don't ask."

As Paulette drove them to the Ottawa downtown core, just east of the ByWard Market, the weather had turned overcast again, with a gentle snow falling down. The senior residential manor, by its very location on the waterfront, denoted it as top-of-the-line. "She wasn't surprised when you called?"

"No. Why? She hasn't seen you in ages. She was happy for the company."

They parked and signed in at reception. "She must pay a pretty penny for this," Jeremy said. The elevator and the hallways were spotless, the furniture in the public areas collectibles that were inviting.

"She has Uncle Marcel's military pension. And the money from the sale of all that land."

"Oh, yeah that property. How much do you think they got for that?"

"Over a million. There was a subdivision coming in just a mile or two down from them. Maybe two million? Dad would have known."

With that apt reminder of who owned the past, they reached Thérèse's door. Their aunt answered quickly. Her gray hair was perfectly coiffed. She wore a flowery-patterned shirt with charcoal slacks and lovely satin pumps that matched the lilac and pink from her top. The three settled in at her kitchen table to tea and homemade cookies.

"You're still baking?"

Their aunt laughed. "Oh, go on with you! Not in here, not at my age, Jeremy. My baking days are all behind me." She lifted the plate up. "These are from Carole. They're addictive. Peanut butter and toffee. A bit too sweet for me."

Jeremy bit into one and swallowed it whole. "These are tasty, Aunt Thérèse. Not too sweet for me."

"I'll make sure to tell Carole." She sipped from her tea. "You look so young, Jeremy. How old are you now?"

"Forty-three next May."

"Doesn't he look good, Paulette?"

The siblings exchanged rivalrous glances. With no gray to his hair and with a tan on his face that suited his features, Jeremy looked ten years rather than only twelve months younger than his sister—the *one* bone of contention between them that never ceased.

"That's what happens when you don't have kids!" she replied.

The mothers laughed like it was their own private domain to flaunt at the childless. "So, no girlfriend, Jeremy?"

Jeremy's second cookie almost dropped from his mouth as he peered at his sister. Hadn't she been told he was gay? He was certain that she had at some point or other. Their mission suddenly became a bit more delicate. "Uh, Aunt Thérèse, you must have forgotten. But I'm gay, remember?"

The sexagenarian put fingers to her mouth to cover her faux pas. "I'm sorry, Jeremy. A senior moment there."

"No big deal," he said. "It's nothing, ma tante," reverting to the French diminutive.

"So, no boyfriend then?" Thérèse asked, pleased that she could transition effortlessly.

"No. Not anymore."

Paulette stared at him, hoping Justin's name would not be brought up. She had never forgiven the man for deserting her brother the way he had. Cowardly she had said at the funeral.

"Well, you'll find someone. You're young. You're handsome. I'm sure there's a nice fella in your future."

The affirmation touched him. Jeremy knew how religious his aunt had been once. Her husband, his Uncle Marcel, had been a member of the Knights of Columbus. She probably *still* attended Mass. "I'm still window-shopping," he said making light of it, though he could feel Gary's tut-tutting all the way from Santa Barbara at this white lie of his. He took his third cookie and wet his lips with the Earl Grey tea before he disclosed what they were after. "I was looking at old photos at Paulette's a few nights ago."

"That's always fun. I gave all the photos to the kids when I moved in here. Didn't want there to be any squabbling when I died."

Paulette frowned, the futility of a goose chase in her eyes. "So, you don't have any photos of Dad here?" she asked.

"Here?" Thérèse considered the possibility. "Maybe one or two in frames from when we were younger. Why?"

"Jeremy wants to …" Paulette stopped herself. She couldn't lie. She was too fond of the woman.

Jeremy jumped in. "I've started to put down our family history. On paper, to pass on to the kids. I wanted to make sure we have all the facts about Mom and Dad's lives. When you were all kids."

"Better now. Before it's too late." With two of her seven

siblings already deceased, the last of their stories lay with whatever the remaining could recall. "I taped some stuff for my kids. After Marcel passed away. They asked me to. Just to have some souvenirs. Carole typed it all up. She's a godsend, that one."

Paulette reflected on their cagey reasons, digging for dirt in their roots that day. Were they the opposite of a blessing, abutting more ruin than good? "Do you have any recollections of the summer Dad spent in Calgary? It was after his last year in high school."

Jeremy saw Thérèse's bearing change. "You remember that?" he asked.

Thérèse stood and went to get a pack of chewing gum on the counter. "Anyone?" She offered pieces to her guests but both declined. When she sat back down, she seemed to be thinking about what to say as she chewed. "That's a funny thing you ask."

"It is?" Jeremy was at the edge of his seat and wanted to blurt out a dozen questions but refrained; he stayed as calm as could be so as not to let the cat out of the bag too soon.

He and Paulette had not agreed at all on the tactics for this meeting. "*Only* if she knows something. If she hints at something. Only *if!*" she had reiterated, insisting that their aunt was too elderly, possibly too religious to be apprised of the gruesome details.

"I will not lead the witness," was all Jeremy had conceded, as if he had been a lawyer about to go to trial.

"Why do you say that, Aunt Thérèse?" Paulette asked.

"Your dad was the life of the party when he was a teenager. He'd been a gawky, skinny kid and then he started going out with Lucille in high school. We all knew each other from the neighborhood. He just blossomed with your mom."

Neither Jeremy nor his sister had heard this before. The picture they had of their father was of an older version. A decent man, a family man, but gentle and reserved. Boisterous with liquor in him but otherwise rather genteel. Insecurity is what both of them had decided along the way. That their father had lacked a certain kind of self-confidence to make it further in the world. Now, with Thérèse saying what she was saying, they wondered what role their mother had played in the evolution of their dad.

"Are you saying Mom changed him?"

Thérèse considered that premise. "No. Not exactly. I think he just came into himself when he fell in love. Isn't that what often happens with guys? The woman in their life compliments them. Makes them better. Or is that too old-fashioned?"

"No," Paulette answered. "I think that's still the case for a lot of guys."

Jeremy disagreed but kept his mouth shut. He had more important fish to fry. "So, about Calgary? What did you mean …?" He tried to be as nonchalant as he could with his question.

"I was pregnant with Willie. All hormones, like I had this sixth sense about me. When your dad came back, I felt it right away. He was different. Quiet. What's that word …?" She searched for the expression. "Introspective. Is that right?"

"He was more like … thinking more?" Jeremy suggested.

"Yes. Something like that. Measured. He was pacing himself. A bit unsure of things. We all noticed it."

"Did anything happen in Calgary?" Paulette asked, unable to mask her anger that none of this had ever been spoken about in their presence until today. And only with them asking about it now!

Thérèse shrugged. "We never got the real deal."

"What do you mean?" Jeremy was adamant that if answers existed, they would be forthcoming here. If his aunt or any of her sisters or brother had any knowledge of events, he wanted that information before going back to California.

"Well, I don't want to be speaking ill of the dead."

"Who?" Jeremy and Paulette said in unison.

Thérèse had regret in her eyes. It was apparent by how she studied them, the vantage point of an elder. "Listen, I always admired your mother. Lucille was the perfect wife for Rafael."

"We know that," Jeremy said.

"So, you won't get upset if I say she put the kibosh on all that."

"How?" Paulette asked. She had never known her mother to be that demanding. On the contrary, Paulette had thought her mom too passive for her own good; feminism was not a state of mind for women of her class in her generation.

"Well, out west, Rafael had stayed with her side of the family …"

"They weren't married right?"

"No. Not even engaged. Not officially."

"Is that weird? Him going to stay with relatives of his girlfriend like that? So far away."

"That was your grandmother's doing."

"Grand-mère Alice?"

"Yes. She gave Rafael the idea. Told him he should travel. He'd just failed high school. That had been a big disappointment in the family. Money was tight. The family needed cash. Rafael had to find work. Going to Calgary served those two purposes."

"And you have no clue what might have happened?"

"I asked Lucille one day. Couldn't have been more than a month or two after Rafael was back home. She'd come over to the apartment to help with the baby things. I remember 'cause I'd wanted her to come over just so I could get answers. Dad had wanted me to try."

"Grandfather Jerome?"

Thérèse nodded solemnly adding to the gravity. "I asked how her family was doing. Any news from the family back in Calgary. Not a word. A wall of silence at first."

"What?" Paulette said. This was not her mother's ways. Her mom had always been a friendly, easygoing woman.

"She said, 'We don't talk much about them.' Like there had been a rift. I assumed, maybe, that there had been a letter. We didn't make calls in those days. Not like today. I really can't say …"

"Didn't you ask?" Jeremy inquired. "Didn't you want to find out more? I mean, what did Grandpa say?"

"If Rafael wasn't saying a word, it wasn't your mother's place, right? Not back then. Not where we lived. As for Dad, he didn't appear too upset. He let it go somewhere along the way. Or maybe he got his answer. If he did, he never shared it with any of us." Thérèse looked at her niece and nephew and realized they were keeping something from her. "You know stuff, don't you?"

Paulette vigorously shook her head, denying to her aunt, threatening Jeremy to no avail. "It so happens, Aunt Thérèse, that I met someone who was acquainted with Dad back in '49?"

"In Calgary?" She stopped chewing her gum.

Paulette popped a few antacids as Jeremy told of Gary and Santa Monica. He mentioned only a terrible bar fight over some girl in Calgary and some repercussions that sent him on his wild adventure to the United States. No sexual assault to upset their aunt, to color any of her memories she had of her younger brother.

"I'm so happy, Jeremy."

Paulette had not seen that reaction coming. "You are?" she said, grasping to better understand.

"I always thought Rafael had given in. Not that he didn't love your mom. He utterly loved Lucille." The widow thought for a moment. "If you say that this occurred. It does sound a bit mysterious … But if Rafael sowed his wild oats, did what our mother kind of wanted him to do, then that means …" She was at once emotional and content. "He chose. He didn't just give in. I don't feel so bad. Your dad. Rafael. He was *such* a good boy."

PART III

CALGARY, SUMMER 1998

EIGHTEEN

The school year had come to a close on Thursday and by Saturday Jeremy was on a WestJet nonstop flight from LAX to Calgary. The family tragedy—as Paulette was wont to refer to it now—though front and center on the minds of Jeremy and his sister, had seen little progress towards any resolution. As he got off the plane and collected his luggage, Jeremy wasn't sure of anything. Lionel, first cousin once removed on his mother's side, was waiting with Jeremy's name in block letters on a cardboard he held in front of him. Jeremy waved.

"Little cousin," the man said and hugged him.

The tall, elderly man in his cowboy hat and boots had not seemed the hugging type but what did Jeremy know of cowboys! When he had reached out to Lionel by telephone, his distant relative had sounded pleased as punch that Jeremy was tracing his family roots. "You want to come out here?" Lionel had asked when Jeremy said that he was thinking he might. "To Chestermere?"

"Is that where you live? Where is that from Calgary?"

"Not far. You can stay with me. I have a big house. All to myself."

"Oh, I wouldn't want to impose. I'll get some hotel."

"Jeremy. I won't take no for an answer," he said, with a firmness that came from sincerity.

"Uh … That's very generous but I might want to stay a few weeks. Are you sure that's okay?"

"A week. A month. Ya like dogs?"

The question had come out of left field. "Yeah. I love dogs."

"Good. 'Cause I own three. Big ones. They bark but they don't bite."

The Buick Regal sedan drove quietly out of Calgary, the Alberta landscape all foreign to Jeremy. Apart from the Rockies that he could see in the side-view mirror as they went eastward, the land was somewhat flat. The luxury interiors with leather everywhere reminded Jeremy—oddly enough—of the limousine in his father's account. He erased that idea straight away. "Was Calgary very different when Dad came out to visit?" he asked, aware that he could not afford to ostracize the only lead he had. His approach to discovery would have to be very slow.

"Night and day. This town is like a yo-yo. Boom and busts with oil."

"Were you … Was the family into oil?" Jeremy had never heard that.

"No. Never. The Dussaults were always farming and cattle. All cattle in the end."

They drove through Chestermere and went by a lake. "You don't expect that here."

"The lake?"

"Yeah. It comes as a surprise."

"It's why the town's here." The turn signal resonated in the tranquil interior. Tic-tic. Tic-tic, as they made a left into a very long driveway, up to an old-fashioned farmhouse. "Home sweet home."

The barking dogs were unnerving even though Lionel had promised they were sweet as hell. The German Shepherd looked ferocious enough that Jeremy hesitated.

"Rex. Behave." The Shepherd sat on command, waiting for another order or a treat, but the long-haired breed that resembled a movie prop, a cross between a shaggy dog and who-knew-what other variety, jumped onto Jeremy. "Suzie!" Lionel shouted. She stood on her hind legs and licked the man's face.

The stone masonry on the fireplace was where Jeremy's gaze went once inside; the trophy antlers on the walls such a sharp contrast to what he was accustomed.

"Follow me. I'll show you to your room. Decent views of the lake facing south, you'll see." On the second floor, he pointed to the bathroom down the hall. "Only one up here. That's how they built 'em back in the day."

"When was this house built?" They were in his room.

"1930s. Late in the decade. '37 maybe?"

"Is this where Dad stayed?" Jeremy was putting his clothes in the chest of drawers, hanging up the shirts he had brought.

"No. Bought this beauty for myself in my forties. After Dad died and Luc took over the farm."

"You worked on the farm?"

"I did. We all did. A family business. But after Dad passed away …" He took a break from speaking, like there was too much to tell all at once.

"I don't mean to pry. We don't know each other. It's okay."

Lionel, who had sat in the high-back chair as Jeremy made himself at home, rose. "It's all right. You'll be hearing all the stories anyway. We got plenty of time." He went to the door. "I hope you like steak?"

The way he phrased it; Jeremy understood that he needed to declare, "I'm not a vegetarian, if that's what you're worried about."

"I was sure hoping not. What with the California address …"

Did Jeremy need to disclose his orientation too, get it out in the open and out of the way? "No, I'm a lot of California things, but not that one."

"Good, 'cause I bought great steaks for the grill. What do you drink?"

"Whatever you're having."

"Beer it is." He stepped out into the hallway. "I'll be in the kitchen. If the dogs come up," he was saying as Suzie swept by him and jumped onto the bed. "Git," he said but she stayed put, prone against the bedspread.

"It's fine," Jeremy assured. "She's adorable."

"A pain in the butt, but she sure keeps you warm at night. If that's your cup o' tea." He smiled and went downstairs.

At dinnertime, sitting out on the back porch, a breeze brushed against the eaves and the host felt obliged to comment. "It gets chilly. Calgary has warm days but the nights can really dip."

"I packed two sweaters." Jeremy went and fetched one. On his return, Lionel had served up their plates. "Bon appétit." He lifted his beer. They toasted to good health and ate.

The night was clear, the stars vibrantly visible from where they were. "You never came back east on visits?" Jeremy asked. The dogs had settled around the table, eager for leftover scraps.

"My grandfather left the Gatineau area on bad terms with his dad. They never patched things up."

"A shame," Jeremy said. "Happens in every family, doesn't it?" He wondered if back then was any different, what with the insurmountable distances and no money to speak of.

"My grandad was a scrapper. I have some memories of him. I was a teenager when he passed away. But my dad took after him. Made money. Lost it. Made some more. It was just the way it was out here. You could try anything. Mining, oil, farming, cattle. You name it. It took off. Sometimes it worked real good. Most times it didn't. Not the way you'd planned. There's a real independent streak out here."

Jeremy had no inkling of that. Before Gary had dropped his father's bomb on him back in Paris, all Calgary, Alberta, had stood for was the annual Stampede celebrations. Perhaps something about a tall tower and cheap oil but that would have been it. His virtual ignorance about the place that had likely been the source of creating him, directly or indirectly, was appalling.

"I went back east once, when we were young. Before your dad came out here. I think I was in high school. Maybe grade school? We took the train. It was very exciting." Lionel swigged his beer and nibbled on the apple pie on his plate. "Mind you, everybody fought with everybody. That part of the trip was awful."

"Do you remember my mom, Lucille, when you visited family?"

"No. Not as I recall. She was my dad's cousin."

"Oh. I thought … Does that still make us cousins once removed?"

"Beats me, Jeremy. I never put much effort into that. Cousins is cousins, right?" He lifted his beer to toast again.

"Here, here. To cousins," Jeremy said and chugged. The sound of some animal howling in the distance made the dogs perk up. "Was that a wolf?"

"Coyote, I think."

The quiet resumed as the men settled in their chairs. Suzie came up to Jeremy and he snuck her a rind of fat. The dog gulped it in one swallow.

"She won't leave your side now. You'll see."

"I could do worse." Jeremy petted the furry dog who plopped right on his feet. "You never married?"

Lionel grinned as though he had been found out. "You?" he retorted. Jeremy shook his head. "Confirmed bachelors, I guess."

"Well, I was in a relationship for five years."

"Yeah?"

No pronouns made it rather juvenile so Jeremy took the plunge. "His name was Justin."

"I see." The Albertan looked up combing the sky, and

pointed to a shooting star. "See that?" Jeremy had, and smiled. "Make a wish."

The directive seemed mismatched coming from a big man in cowboy attire. Jeremy wondered if this was Lionel's colloquial way of outing himself. "You ever had …"

"A Justin?"

Jeremy nodded.

"Not openly. It wasn't done."

Jeremy felt sorry for that generation of closeted homosexuals. Lives lost to secrecy and oppression, to fear and the loathing that followed. "A shame," he said.

"We adapted." Lionel fetched them fresh beers. He opened the bottles and passed one to his guest. "It wasn't all bad. Especially after buying here. With no one watching my every move. It got better."

Did *no one* in his family know he was gay? "No one special?"

"Lots of special ones. Just none of them stuck."

"I see," Jeremy said, though he really didn't. He had not the faintest idea how a man born in Alberta back in the twenties, raised on a farm to be a cowboy, could transition with the times and make a life for himself. Confirmed bachelor took on a too-compromising tone suddenly. If he could, he would have rejected the moniker now. "How did you manage?"

"It wasn't easy. There were places you could go to. But you had to be careful. You could be arrested if you even looked the wrong way. Especially if it was a cop."

"Undercover?" When Lionel nodded he asked, "Were you ever …?" There was another nod, this one with a twinkle in his eyes.

"We had a gay bathhouse, Goliath's. Back in the late sixties, early seventies. By then I was feeling pretty brave. I'd done all the cruising a person could do in Memorial Park. Had fun swimming naked at the old Y during guys-only swims." Jeremy was all ears. "Oh, you betcha. It was frisky." He chuckled, swigged back more beer. "This one night, at the baths. I'd brought this guy with me from the steam room. I think we'd fooled around. Enough to know it was gonna work between us." He raised his eyebrows. "I'm a big guy. I don't scare easily. Well, we got into the room. More like a locker. Not big at all. And this guy was built. He had muscles." Lionel pumped up his arms to indicate the size. "You didn't want to mess with him, that was clear. We'd taken our towels off. I was stunned by the pecker on him. I must not have realized it back in the steam room …?"

"Or maybe you had!" Jeremy said, cracking both of them up.

"Anyway, we hadn't done much. When he said, I was under arrest."

"No!"

"Oh yeah! I wasn't fifty yet. I was still working the farm. My nephews and nieces at my house all the time. It would have been the end of me."

"What … what did you do?"

"I gave him a blow job. I figured I could use that against him if he tried to take me in."

"He let you?"

"I think he was one of those sickos."

"Was he a real cop?"

"Beats me. I *thought* he was. He damn well looked the part. All that was missing was the badge."

"You never got his name?"

"As soon as he came, I put on my clothes and pretended I was going out for a drink. I still have no clue how I pulled it off. I ran out of there. Swore I'd never go back."

"Did you?"

"Not for a very long stretch."

The ensuing silence filled any generation gap that existed between the men. Jeremy felt quite safe to ask his question now. "Were you aware that Dad was assaulted back in '49 when he stayed with your family?"

Lionel stood and Jeremy wondered if he hadn't squandered everything. His heart was beating faster than he would have liked. The blood was rushing to his head as he went over what he might do to smooth things over when Lionel returned, huffing and puffing a bit. His hair was messy. "Oof. Haven't looked at these in ages. Had them in a trunk." He plopped a pair of scrapbooks on the table and moved the lamp to shed light on the materials.

"What is this?" Jeremy asked. He opened to find an article on Senator Clinton Burnshaw at an inaugural for some gala.

"You wanna know about *him*, don't ya?"

NINETEEN

Their conversation faltered initially, in fits and starts. The clippings, glued clumsily onto album pages, could have been a family scrapbook collected for posterity except that they were not about the Dussault family. These records concerned one powerful clan, the Burnshaws—landed gentry with more color to them than European nobles, if the headlines had any credibility.

"I didn't realize. Not right away, Jeremy. When your dad wasn't at the breakfast table that morning, I went to his room. His bed hadn't been slept in. When I told my dad, he was raging mad. He swore to high heaven. Blamed Luc."

"No one thought of calling back east?"

"Calling? No. Don't think we even had a phone back then." Lionel considered the likelihood. "We must have. But no one called. Long distance was for a death in the family. And anyway. We didn't know what to make of his departure."

"*You did know*, though. Didn't you?" Jeremy had already

surrendered the entire tale; he described events according to Rafael that had happened nearly fifty years prior.

"And Gary said that Rafael thought that *I* knew?" Lionel had asked, confounded by that improbable fact.

"Gary seems to remember it like he'd written it down."

"Did he?"

Lionel's hunch had merit. "If he did, he didn't say that to me. I just think his feelings for Dad were *that* strong …"

"You're sure your dad and he never …?"

"No. And Gary would have said it. He's a no-holds-barred sort of fellow."

Lionel continued. "When we didn't hear a thing—a good month went by—my mom wrote a letter."

"To whom?"

"I couldn't say. Not Rafael. It was on our side. I'd bet money on that 'cause she wrote letters often."

"My mom's family, the Leclercs?"

"It could be, yeah."

"What did the letter say? Did you read it?"

"I kinda recollect that I did. Or Mom asked if I wanted her to include anything on my behalf. I might have said, 'Say hello to Rafael if he was around.' I didn't want her to let on about a thing. I just didn't know how the situation was being taken care of back in Ottawa."

"It wasn't. Nothing was ever, ever said."

Lionel had shown Jeremy the news articles—society columns and front-page headlines to give him an idea of what they were against. "You see this," he pointed to a gossip piece dated three years after Rafael's assault. "That. That piece there from '52." He read aloud a sentence about mischief at a club. "That's what got me thinking about it all over again. In those days, to me that would have been code. The word mischief. These are men we're talking about. Not boys. It didn't set right with me."

"But you have articles from 1949? The same year Dad ..." Jeremy thought that peculiar.

"Yeah. That is odd ..." he said, skipping over the discrepancy, "I assumed *something* bad had happened. Just not exactly what. Maybe the guy he'd fought with roughed him up some more. Drove out here the next day when we were out working the fields. Rafael had stayed home. That much I recall. I did suspect that the cowpoke had scared him worse than we realized. We didn't ..." He was trying to arrange his thoughts to fit his memories. "That night, at the bar. It was Luc's fault. He set your dad up." The years between then and now faded away. Considering the confirmation of his worst fears, pangs of guilt washed over Lionel, removing the element of distance. What mattered now was restitution. "Poor Rafael," he muttered. "Your dad never saw it coming."

"Luc ... did it on purpose then?"

"Hell, ya. My brother could be a real son-of-a-bitch. He'd lost the girl to that cowpoke. And here, Luc was to inherit a lot of land, but the girl only had eyes for the cowpoke. What could you do?" Lionel poured himself another coffee. They were inside, at the kitchen table. "That night. At the honky-tonk. Luc saw your dad flirting with the girl. She *was* a catch. He knew the cowpoke was a jealous SOB. Still, he encouraged Rafael. Goaded him to make a move. He might as well have beat him up himself. What a licking."

"Why didn't you help him?"

"Why!" Lionel repeated. He sipped his coffee struggling for an answer. "Afraid, I guess. Back then. It was different times.

Men were men. Didn't take too kindly to their women …" His coffee was too bitter and he added sugar. "I thought Rafael would just sit out there and wait for us. He was so drunk. I sure thought Luc would come around sooner than he did. But then he got to playing blackjack and …"

Jeremy could see how fate had played into all of this. "Dad's pride must have been hurt. I can just see him. How he must have reacted being thrown out of the bar. You guys not coming to his rescue. In that city …"

"Town really. Calgary back in '49. Not much there."

"He didn't even know where he was … To take off like that. He must have been a mess." Gary's story took on so much more meaning now that he was here, breathing the Calgary air. "That fucker must have been cruising the streets hunting for vulnerable kids in his classy limousine."

Lionel pulled open the album nearest to him, to another clipping detailing a money scandal. "The man was a scoundrel. Plain and simple."

Jeremy found the senator's obituary and read a few sentences. "But he was praised in here. He went to his grave without ever paying any price."

"No. The Burnshaws don't pay the price. They *name* their prices. They run Calgary. Ran Calgary." He flipped through to more contemporary material. "Look. The son, Bernard. The grandson, Jason. They're all millionaires. Probably billionaires now. What with the oil business."

"Do you think I could approach one of them?"

"The Burnshaws?"

"Yeah. I just want to speak to the son. Maybe the grandson?"

"And ask them what? Did you know the Senator raped

my daddy?" Lionel stared at his guest like he was off his rocker. "No. It ain't done like that. Not here. Not in Calgary. Not unless you want your ass whooped. Or land in jail."

The defeatist attitude did not bode well for Jeremy's plans.

"You didn't come out here thinking that, did you?" Jeremy's muteness stunned Lionel even more. "Well, how would you manage to do that? You don't have any contacts. You don't have money, do you?"

"How much money would I need?"

"I don't know 'cause I don't know what you're proposing to do."

"If I could attend a fundraiser. Maybe go to a golf club they belong to."

"You're real serious about this, aren't you?" Lionel was suddenly very awake and attentive. "How would you go about this?"

"I could go to the library. Or check with the newspaper. A social columnist? Do a bit of digging around. There must be a way to do this."

"The Palliser Hotel."

"What's that?" Jeremy asked.

"It's where a lot of powerbrokers meet. At least, they used to. We could research that, see if that's still the case."

A shroud was lifting. Jeremy sensed some leverage, as though his father was reaching out to him from the grave with a pat on the back: "Go get 'em, son."

"You're welcome to stay here as long as you'd like."

"I think I will."

TWENTY

Calgary was in a heat wave that first week in August. "I love this." Jeremy had the car window down, lapping up the dryness of the air.

"This has the feel of Palm Springs. In the winter," Gary chimed in. The men were dressed in high-end business attire.

"How's your stomach, Zach?" Lionel asked.

"Better," the twenty-two-year-old replied, patting his abs, pleased with himself that his twenty-four-hour bug had vanished. Zachary Beauregard, just out of Stanford, had traveled with Gary up to Calgary. "Last night's upchucking did the trick."

"Must have been something you ate driving up."

"We never stopped for cheap food anywhere," said Gary.

"Maybe you should have," Jeremy said, argumentative when, really, all he was fretting about was that their organizing might all be for naught.

"In a Rolls-Royce? I don't think so, Jeremy."

The '69 Silver Shadow had a cachet that suggested Hollywood not Calgary. "Isn't this a bit conspicuous?" Jeremy asked. They were driving up to the private club, about to put to the test his and Lionel's meticulous preparations during the last month.

"This is Calgary. You *want* to be conspicuous," Lionel professed, from the back seat. "We're the Dallas of Canada. Can't catch fish without a bait. She is a beaut, Gary." The African burl walnut wood on the dash and console shined in the daylight. Turning to Zachary, Lionel said, "As is you, young man."

The off-the-cuff compliment to Zachary, seated next to Lionel in the back seat, made Jeremy cringe—he worried that it was too forward, too misjudged, enough perhaps to set the young man off his game.

"I come from a long line of classic beauties," he said, suave as could be.

"That's something Jethro would have said," Gary remarked. "You're more like your grandfather with every year. He was so proud of you."

Jeremy so regretted not meeting Jethro. "I can't make it to Santa Barbara this weekend, Gary," Jeremy had demurred in late September, stretched to the limit with all that the school district had piled on him to meet the latest California Standards implemented for the 97–98 academic year. "Maybe we can go out for drinks after the holidays? When things have settled down for me here. Let's see what January brings." As a new department head, his duties made for endless, politically driven days that ate into his evenings and weekends.

Jethro's untimely death last October had come as a shock. Back in the dog-days of Paris, the thought of meeting

Jethro and Judy at Gary's for an evening of drinks and reminiscences in Santa Barbara had seemed reasonable. "I was sorry not to have met him," Jeremy said. He turned to look behind. "Zach, he sounded like a fascinating guy."

"He was. Larger-than-life character, one hell of a hero to me," Zach bragged and wondered if that was being disrespectful to his father, Benjamin, who had had an acrimonious relationship with his father right to the end. "It's because of him that I lettered in tennis, squash, swimming, and soccer at Groton."

"No polo?" Lionel asked, being sarcastic.

"Not at Groton. I did that at Stanford. Along with golf."

Lionel had been apprised of that already—all part of their opposition research that had brought Zach into their scheme—and, *still*, he was impressed. Handsomeness in men of a certain age had always made him a soft touch. With Zachary Beauregard at his side—this near, close enough that the boy's deodorant wafted his way—Lionel was fighting for willpower. "If Jason Burnshaw doesn't fall for your wiles, he'll be as crazy as they come. Which for the Burnshaws is saying some."

The sable-brown Rolls came to a stop. "Do they have valet parking?" Gary asked.

"Don't ask me," Lionel said. "Are we ready for this, fellas?" He got out first.

Inside the establishment, Gary's membership to the University Club in Santa Barbara was honored, reciprocal admission being one of its privileges. The men settled down to a relaxing lunch in the dining room. Their only goal that day was to make contact. They would talk shop about their Hollywood projects, loud enough to be heard but not to be obnoxious, and draw attention to themselves for all the acceptable reasons. Money, status, a curiosity item to get people gossiping.

They had been there a half hour, drinking aperitifs and just beginning main courses when their mark arrived. Lionel tapped Zachary and nodded for him to look in the direction his eyes indicated. "How's your beef?"

"Perfect medium rare." Zach cut into the center to display the hint of red where it should have been. He chewed and sipped from the Merlot their waiter had poured. At one point, he caught Jason Burnshaw gazing his way and feigned disinterest. He had never tried any of his seduction tricks with men before. He could see this homosexual strategy was going to be a hoot!

"Are you sure about this, Bubbe?" he had asked earlier that summer in July.

Judy Mosley had been a *macher* in Hollywood, in her own way, for years. Her father's daughter, she had jumped into producing as soon as Benjamin, her eldest, was old enough to be with a trusted nanny. While Jethro worked as a stockbroker to keep them in plenty of money, she had tackled Hollywood and made a name for herself. "Honey," Judy said, "I wouldn't be asking you this huge favor if this wasn't important."

Zachary had not had time to grieve Jethro's passing. All his grades counted that fall quarter and, with the need to excel at his varsity sports, he had barely taken any days away from school to sit shiva for his grandfather. It was not until a full month after the funeral that he began to rethink graduate school.

"Son, you need a master's degree at minimum,"

Bennie—as everyone called him, said. "Poli sci was fine. But it won't get you shit out in the real world."

Zach was home from Stanford for winter break. His idea of landing a low-level job, even an internship in D.C., hadn't so much fizzled out as it had receded in importance by December. With money not an issue—a liberal inheritance from Jethro that had left him independent—he was unsure of what to do next. "But Dad, I don't know what I want to do yet."

Bennie had not insisted. How he had hated his own father doing *that* to him! His mother's Hollywood had never appealed to Bennie, and finance—the stockbroking industry his father had made their fortune in—was the last thing on his to-do checklist. With medicine a stretch, he did the only thing a good Jewish son could do—become a lawyer. "You have time, Zach. Just don't waste it. It's a precious commodity."

That was the topography of Zachary's life when his grandmother had called him to come over in early July. "You ever thought of working for me?"

"What?" Zachary found her proposition humorous. "What do you mean? You landed a hot project all of a sudden?" Movie properties had become scarce in her career so her offer was unexpected.

"Something like that. Can you come over? I want to discuss it in person."

At the Holmby Hills estate where Judy lived, Zach was stumped to see Gary seated with her out on the lanai when he arrived.

"My, you've grown."

"Not since the funeral, I haven't."

"Really? Maybe it was the suit. I didn't stay long. I had so much stuff back in Santa Barbara that needed tending to."

Gary's nerves were on edge, had been ever since Jeremy had called from Calgary to tell him he was extending his stay with Lionel, then shared the hoax he was hoping to execute.

"In cargo shorts. With that top. You look taller, Zach. What can I say?" Gary wished he hadn't uttered such inanities.

Judy came to his rescue. "This is the scoop, darling. I have an acting job for you."

"Me? Acting? No way, Grandma."

Judy accepted *bubbe* or grandmother graciously but she detested the shortened version that made her sound too old. She winced. "It's not for film, honey."

"Stage? That's even worse. I did a play back at Groton. I stunk. Not in my wheelhouse. Sorry."

"But I bet the girls loved you anyway," Gary said, aware that disingenuousness was not his forte.

Zach took it as a compliment. "Maybe …"

"This is to help out Jethro," Judy said. "And me."

The mention of his grandfather had puzzled him at first. *How* could that be?

In the Calgary dining room, the quality acoustics kept the room's conversations and the classical music from being too loud. "If you'll excuse me," Zach said. He went off to the men's room.

"Any luck?" Gary asked, sotto voce. His back was to the party they were interested in poaching. Jeremy shook his head and smiled as though pleasantries had been exchanged rather than tactical maneuvers, when Lionel cleared his throat.

"*Yes*, I'll be having dessert soon," Lionel said, pretending they had coded all of their verbal exchanges—which they had not!

"No!" Gary exclaimed at the confirmation.

In the men's room, Zach was at the urinal finishing up when he heard the door open. Had his teasing from a distance ensnared him his catch? He was incredulous as he zipped up and saw Jason at the urinal right next to him. He went to the sink to wash his hands.

"Did you try the lamb chops?" Jason said, over the music coming from a discreet speaker. "Never tasted anything so sweet."

Zach was relieved not to have made the first volley. "I did not."

Jason joined him at the sinks. "You're new in town?"

"Checking out the city." Zach couldn't be drying his hands for much longer. The thick cloth napkins had done the trick already.

"From …?"

"L.A. Santa Barbara."

Jason gave him a winning grin. "Well, which is it?"

The man's pearly whites belonged on screen, Zach thought. "Both."

"Both …?" Jason wondered at the game the stranger was playing. "Okay. Both it is then." He tossed the used towel into the appropriate bin. "Your first time at the club?"

Zachary nodded.

"Who did you come with?" Jason asked and quickly tried to rescind. "Not that I know every member here."

"But you probably do, don't you?"

It was Jason's turn to nod and try to be humble.

"I came with my uncle. Well, not really my uncle."

"Oh, I see," Jason said, unabashed with innuendo.

Touché, Zachary thought, but jumped in swiftly. "No," he said, holding back on using *dude*, not sure how the term played up there in Calgary. "*Nothing* like that. He's an old friend of my grandmother's. We're up here on her behalf. Doing business."

"What kind of business? Oil?"

"No …" Zach had begun to edge towards the door, wanting to be chased. "Film. My grandmother's a producer."

"Would I know any of her pictures?"

Zachary had memorized the most noteworthy with A-list stars. DeNiro, Nicholson, Dunaway, Taylor and Burton, along with a few younger legends from the eighties since his grandmother *had* slowed down in the last decade.

"Should I be intimidated here?"

"Don't be. She's just scouting for fresh prospects. If you know what I mean?"

"Why Calgary?"

"Location. Location. Location."

"And the exchange rate. I'm sure she's thinking that too."

"That too." Zach opened the door and Jason walked out with him.

"How long are you in town for?"

"Open ended."

"Where are you staying?"

"Out of town. With friends of my uncle. But I think we'll be moving to the Palliser tomorrow, maybe the next day. Better for business deals."

"You should."

They had reached the dining room. "Why?"

"You play squash?"

"I do."

Jason took out a card. "Call me. Set up a time with my secretary."

"A secretary? I'm impressed. What do you do that you've got your own secretary?" Zach glanced at the card that had no details—just a name and a phone number. "How old are you?"

"Old enough to have a secretary. You?"

"Me! A secretary?"

"Oh … You're going to make me fight for everything, are you, Mr. …?"

"Beauregard. Zachary. I'm twenty-two," he relinquished, enjoying their give and take. "Just graduated."

"From?"

"Stanford."

"In …?"

"Mostly polo playing," he exaggerated. "A bit of poli sci."

"Politics. My granddad was a politician. A senator."

"You didn't say what you did."

"This and that." Jason patted Zach on the back. "And the secretary is my dad's, but she takes calls and does appointments for me."

The men shook hands and went their separate ways.

That night, Gary and Zach booked separate suites at the Palliser Hotel in downtown Calgary for the following day.

TWENTY-ONE

"You'll call him tomorrow?" Jeremy asked as the two men were getting into the Rolls to drive to their downtown destination.

"I should. Yes," Zach said. He pushed the switch to lower the window. "His dad's offices aren't that far from the hotel. It may all work in our favor."

Jeremy propped against the glass. "Be careful."

"That's why I have Gary by my side."

That evening, Gary and Zach were dining in the hotel hot spot when a commotion arose from a corner of the room. "Somebody had too much to drink," Gary commented as one of the well-dressed patrons was being escorted out by management.

"I can walk by myself," Gary heard her say. The woman pulled her arm away and caught his eye. She winked at Gary who fought not to chuckle. He lifted up his glass to her as if to wish her good luck when she stopped. "You look *so* familiar," she said.

Gary was accustomed to high-end clientele with demanding personalities and turned on the charm. "Santa Barbara perhaps?"

Their exchange put the administrator on the spot, placing the onus on management to reconsider its intercession.

"Perhaps ..." she said and extended her hand. "Natalie Springs."

"Gary Silverman." They shook—the finger equivalent of a curtsy—and Gary had no choice but to continue their conversation. "I own La Maison in Santa Barbara. Perhaps you've dropped by on some occasion?"

"I *adore* La Maison." Gary had no reason not to believe her, but he didn't. It was all a ruse to not be led out, he suspected. Their food arrived. "A good choice," she said. "The trout is always done to perfection here." She bent closer. "That couscous will melt in your mouth. They add a secret ingredient to their butter." She eyeballed the manager who was now disinclined to continue with the mandate he had thought unfortunate but necessary moments ago. Gary's options were limited too, but he was always fascinated with the rich and wacky, so he barely checked in with Zach before saying, "You're perfectly welcome to join us. Zach?" he asked.

"Oh. Yeah. Sure, of course."

An extra chair was brought, along with another place setting. Her food was retrieved from her former table.

At the other end of the room, the woman Natalie had

clashed with was doing a lousy job of ignoring them. "You mustn't mind my friend over there. We get into these silly arguments."

Gary could tell just by the way she wavered, the lilt in her speech, that she was not only drunk but stoned. Pills, if he had had his druthers. "Friends for long?"

"For ages," Natalie said, drawing out the expression melodramatically.

"It seemed you were ..." Zach realized how inappropriate it would be to say what he wanted to say.

Natalie chortled, put her hand on his arm. "Dear, you can't insult me. You're too young and handsome. Whatever you wanted to say ..." Her martini arrived and she sipped from it. She dangled the olive around in her glass before finishing, "Say it."

"You were having a doozy of a fight."

"We were. Emily Clark can be very vexing."

The name immediately sprang the guys into action. "That name ..."

"You know her?" Natalie asked Gary.

"No. But it rings a bell."

She leaned into the table to bring them into her confidence. "You must have heard of the Burnshaws? The Alberta Burnshaws?" Having said it like it was a trap that no one should fall prey to, she sat back waiting for their reactions.

"Well, this is a strange coincidence ..." Gary began when Zach looked at him like a deer in headlights. For an instant, Gary wondered if he was about to make a misstep when he felt Zach's gentle kick under the table, which shut him up.

"Zach?" said a voice coming from behind Gary.

"Jason. Hi. Uh ..."

"She's over there, Zach." Natalie pointed to Emily's regular table. "She *really* needs your help tonight. Sorry, dear."

Zach noticed how embarrassed Jason was as he said, "Uh, just give me a sec'." The Burnshaw heir went to his mother's table and sat down. Zach could hear their conversation that should have been private; he could see people at the tables whispering, doing everything but minding their own business.

"So, Gary," Natalie asked, "are you in town for long?"

"Not too long. Depends on prospects."

"Oh, I do love prospects," Natalie said and tried her hand on his. Gary's removing it promptly told her all she needed to know. She smiled wickedly at him and finished her martini.

"Do you think your friend will be okay?" Zach asked.

"Hard to tell. She should really be in rehab. Simply refuses to go."

"In denial, is she?" he said.

The throaty laugh almost scared Zach. "No, darling. Emily Clark is many things. In denial is not one of them." She peeked to see how Jason was managing. "Poor boy. I don't envy him his burden."

"Why won't she go into rehab?" Gary asked, just to take the focus away from Zachary.

"She's been. They don't work. Not the therapy. Not the one-day-at-a-time crap. Certainly not the higher power bullshit." Natalie tucked away the remainder of her martini. "She loves what she loves. What can I say?" The conspiratorial lilt, the ever-wanting-never-getting that addiction brought, gave her away again. "If I didn't think management would object, I'd walk over there again myself."

Zachary rose and made his way. "Jason, it's nice to see

you again. Just moved into my suite today. I was going to call for squash. Tomorrow. How's the schedule?"

The relief on Jason's face was apparent. "Zach. This is my mom. Emily Clark this is Zach …" He stumbled on his last name.

"Beauregard."

"How could I forget! With a lovely name like that."

"Not in high school it wasn't." The guys laughed.

"Try Burnshaw. Back in Toronto."

"You went to high school in Toronto? Where?"

"Upper Canada College."

"I went to Groton."

The twentysomethings recognized their pedigrees in spades. Before their bonding could continue, Emily stood up. "Mom, where are you going?" Jason could tell she was still itching to fight. Management had not phoned him as a last resort for nothing. "Mom. No! I'll leave you." The threat worked. His mother sat back down. "Why don't we bolt from here, Mother? I'll have the Bentley sent."

"I haven't finished supper yet."

"Are you really going to eat any of that?" Jason could see she had picked at but hardly bothered with the cut of beef she had ordered. In his experience, under-the-influence was not conducive to much sensible eating. She pushed the plate away as if to prove his point.

"Fine. Let's go."

"Tomorrow afternoon. Works for you, Zach?"

"What time?"

"I'll pick you up at one? In the lobby here."

Jason escorted his mother like a defenseman protecting

the net. Natalie and Jason coordinated their eye contact so that no more scrapping would take place in the restaurant.

"Good riddance," she said as Zach rejoined them. "So how do you know Jason?"

"Just met. Last night. Calgary must be a smaller town than I realized."

"It is when you've got money." She caught their waiter's attention. "I'm having another one. Anybody else?"

"We're good. We still have wine," Gary said, indicating their bottle.

"So, what brings you to town, fellas?"

"The movie business," Gary said. "You interested?"

TWENTY-TWO

"Gary, it's pushing one. You need to go in case he shows up at the door."

Gary was buzzing around Zach's suite, coaching him on how to execute their next steps. "I can be here. As far as he's concerned, we have nothing to hide, right?"

"Yeah. I suppose."

"Let's go over what you should do. One more time."

"I need to let him win at squash," Zach said, like it had been ingrained in him by an instructor. "Why again?"

"If he wins, he'll feel good about himself. It will give him the confidence that he can win with everything else you might propose."

"What if I'm much, much better than him? I may not be able to fake-lose that way."

"Really?!"

"You obviously don't play a lot of squash."

"I do. I did. You'll pretend to trip up. Make it seem like you're more into him than the game."

"Won't he lose respect for me if he sees I'm not competitive?"

Gary stared back at him as though dealing with a combative five-year-old.

"We don't even know that he's gay."

"We sort of do," Gary said. He could see that Zach was losing his eye on the prize. "Lionel says he plays the field. That it's rumored in the gay community."

"Like the gay community doesn't think every rich, hot, straight guy isn't gay."

"Okay ... In that regard, you're correct."

"I know I am. I haven't been around Hollywood and Bubbe's cronies to not know that." He looked at himself in the mirror, arranged his crotch which was bunching up.

"Why did you do that?" Gary asked, curious now.

"What?"

"You just checked yourself out in the mirror."

"And you don't?"

"Maybe. If I'm going out on a date, I do."

"Well, this is a date, right? Sort of. That's what I'm doing here. Setting myself up as eye candy to catch a Burnshaw." The stating of their sting operation made Zach uncomfortable as hell. Jason seemed decent to him—not the type of fellow his grandmother had described about a long-dead ancestor of Jason's. He was regretting having agreed to the unsavory charade.

"You're having second thoughts, I can tell." Gary knew what card he had to play. "All I can tell you is this, Zach.

Think of Jethro. Your grandfather. If he was here, he'd tell you these sons-of-bitches have to pay." The phone rang. "I'll let you go." He got to the door of the suite. "You can do this."

The squash rounds were take-no-prisoners aggressive, with Zach utilizing all of his skills to play well while still landing at the bottom of the leaderboard. "Dinner's on me, I guess," Zach said as they left the court.

"A bet's a bet." On their way to the dressing rooms, Jason asked, "Any preference where we eat?"

"It's your hometown. You decide."

They were getting out of their sweaty clothes. "I was sure you were going to win," Jason said. He had wrapped his towel around his torso.

"I could blame it on …" Zach began and switched tactics. "You won. Fair and square, dude." In the showers, Zach was cognizant of being checked out, fleeting glances that communicated desire more than once. He did not respond; he did what all straight men with manners did in situations like that and ignored them. Though, now, the stakes had grown.

They drove to the same private club where they had met. "So no chance of Leslie coming back into your life?" Jason asked.

The Californian had been waiting for the topic of girlfriends to resume. "We *just* broke up. The before-last week of our final quarter at Stanford. Too soon to say …"

The subject appeared concluded, like the boys' histories were concentric circles rather than players on opposing teams when Jason asked, "Do you want her to come back to you?"

The combination of exertion and a hot shower had

relaxed Zach. He was in his comfort zone and could forget momentarily that there was entrapment in the cards, and just appreciate the gourmet food that tasted even better at this outing. He made a noncommittal shrug with his shoulders.

"Yowch." Jason chewed a few forkfuls of food. "What happened?"

"I wasn't going off to law school. That's what happened. No graduate school …"

"She said that? She called it off because you had a change of heart about your future?"

"Well, to be fair. I'd been saying law school for most of the time we were together. I'm the one who altered the rules."

"You're allowed, right? Your life. Your rules."

"You're not in a relationship."

Jason chuckled. He lifted up his scotch. "I'll drink to that." He scarfed back the booze like it was edible. "You saw my mom. Imagine her and my dad. Any wonder I'm not into relationships." He ate the last of his lamb and chomped on some bread. "I don't do relationships. Not well, anyways. Maybe if the right person came along …"

"How is your dad? Your parents don't get along?"

"Bernie? Bernard Burnshaw hardly ever sees her. If he can manage it."

"They're divorced?"

"No. Just don't see each other."

"They live together?"

"Oh, God no. That would be catastrophic. Biblically so. No. They've been separated for … ages. I can't even remember them together."

"Oh … Sorry to hear that."

"*You* saw my mother. Difficult doesn't even begin to

describe." He interrupted his sentence to order another scotch. Zach got another bourbon. "Between you and me, she has dirt on the old man."

"No ...!"

"Who knows? You'd think he'd divorce her. Or her him. He's got one lady after another in his penthouse. It's not even a secret."

"Maybe your mom likes being Mrs. Burnshaw?"

"She *never* used the name. She kept her maiden name. She's always been Emily Clark."

Zachary wanted to ask so many questions, but he couldn't quite discern how to play the game he had been assigned. That night was supposed to be all about the film business, not chaperoning and playing therapist to Jason Burnshaw. "She must have come from ..."

"No. Not a penny. She was a dancer. Met Dad at some convention."

"Wow. She must be independent."

"That she is."

Jason leaned in closely and, for a second, Zach thought he might have been in for his first male-on-male kiss. "So, tell me all about LA. *Orrr*, Santa Barbara." The Gaelic inflection on *or* made Zach question how intoxicated his squash partner was.

"What would you like to know?"

"Well, how much are you looking for people to invest? That's what you're up here for, right?"

The trap could not have been set any better. Kudos to Jeremy, Zach thought. He had not expected it to be this easy. "Money. Prospects. My grandmother wants us to assess if Calgary is doable."

"Doable?" Jason repeated, with a teasing that surprised Zachary.

The male energy was too dominant, recognizably heterosexual. So why this coquettish wordplay from a jock? "Film-wise. Can it accommodate a film company with some soundstages. That kind of doable," Zach underlined, convinced Jason was straight. "Dude, you're drunk."

"Am not. Am I?"

"Why don't we switch to coffee?"

"That'd spoil the mood." Jason seemed to pout. "I always thought you movie people were big on drink, drugs, and sex."

"All of the above. But time and place … right?"

"How about my place. Now?"

"Jason. You really are drunk."

"Maybe I am." He pulled away from the table, his entire countenance changed.

Zach saw it form before his very eyes.

"Are your mom and dad still an item?" Jason inquired.

"They are." Zach felt bad for having a more functional family than Jason's. "Bennie and Martha Beauregard," he said, wanting to give them more flair than they had. "They're pretty stable. At least, on the outside."

"Bernie and Bennie. That's weird."

Zach laughed, not having paid much attention to that commonality. "They sound like they could be a comedy duo."

"Not *my* dad. Trust me. Not much comedy there."

The phrasing augmented more dysfunctionality in the Burnshaws. "You're not close?" Zachary asked.

"We are. Just not in the fatherly sense, if you catch my drift. Buddies, if you will."

Zachary wasn't sure what to make of that. "You said your

grandfather was a politician the other night. Were you closer with him?"

"No. Died way before I was born. My dad's seventy-one. He had me with wife number two. He was old. I was an accident."

"Says who?"

"What do *you* think?"

"Did anyone ever say that?"

"His first wife!"

"Okay, well that's not very reliable."

"No. You're probably right. She was barren. Couldn't give Bernie the goods." He paused and sipped then said very candidly, "But it hurt just the same."

"Dude. You've got quite the family. Don't get me wrong. Mine was a doozy. My great-grandfather was old-Hollywood. I've heard lots of stories …"

"Yeah? Tell me some."

"I have a better idea. Let's leave here," Zach said, picking up the bill.

"Where to?"

"Let's have an adventure." Zachary had been told not to go over to Jason's unaccompanied until the lay of the land had been thoroughly assessed. "The night's still young."

"My place or yours?"

"Are you too drunk to drive?" Zach asked.

Jason blew air his way. The smell of alcohol *was* strong but Zach ignored the signs, discounted the advice from the gay conclave who had sent him on this vengeful scam. It all seemed irrelevant under the convivial circumstances.

"Your place it is."

TWENTY-THREE

They were driving down a ramp under a railroad bridge, taking a sharp turn that caused Zachary to brace. "What happened to 'a house'?" he asked. They were edging towards downtown Calgary.

"Mom's house is too far," Jason said, slowing down. "This is nicer."

"What is this?"

"Dad's penthouse." They were at an underground garage entrance and Jason keyed in his code. "I'm too wasted to drive all the way out to the house. It's all the way back where we played squash today."

"Won't your dad mind? Will he …"

"Chill. I live here too. I go between Mom's house and Dad's here. He won't even be there. He's always out carousing. A regular tomcat."

The private elevator took them to the only apartment in the building. "What is this?"

"I told you. The penthouse. You like?"

"I thought penthouses were higher than this."

"You would be mistaken. This *is* the top floor. Actually, there are two floors." Jason pointed to the semicircular stairs. "That goes up to a cool billiards room and deck. Wanna check it out?"

Zach followed up the staircase. "What's below us?"

"It's a securities firm. It used to be a bank. Built back in the thirties. My granddad, the Senator? It's all marble floors and walls. The gigantic vault is right out of the movies."

"Sweet!"

"Yup. Dad inherited it from Grandpa Clinton. He was going to sell the property when he came up with this brainchild and built this pad up here instead." They had reached the upper level. The room was sizeable, with high ceilings that reminded Zach of a very posh private club. The billiards table, the old-fashioned saloon bar in the corner. Poker tables. The couches that made for intimate groupings. "Not bad, eh?" Jason had already beelined it to the liquor. He poured himself a scotch and offered his guest choices of bourbons. "Any preference?"

Zach indicated the Old Rip Van Winkle bottle. "If it worked for Rip …"

They toasted and went to sit by the couch that had a clear view from the industrial-sized window that overlooked a park. They sipped, with country music playing in the background. "So, you never moved out on your own?" Zach asked.

"Yeah."

"When? After college?"

"I only did two years at university."

"Where?"

"Where *didn't* I go!"

"What? I thought you said you went to the University of Toronto."

"I went to three universities in two years. That should give you an idea of my …" Jason debated how best to describe his academic fiascoes. "I started at U. of T. Fantastic time." He rolled the scotch around in his glass. "Grades, not so great." He kicked back the scotch and poured himself another from the bottle he had carried with him. "Dad, or was it Mom? Someone suggested I move out here to get away from the negative influence of the Toronto nightlife. Get my bearings. So, I transferred to the University of Alberta."

"Is that in Calgary?"

"No. Up in Edmonton. I failed there too. So, it was on to plan C. Which should have never occurred. I didn't want to study anymore. I was bored."

"Where did you go next?"

"A small school in Rhode Island."

"Rhode Island?"

"My dad had a connection. A big mistake."

"And …?"

"I got laid a lot." He began to draw lines in the air, crossing them out in increments of five like they were bragging rights.

"That's not so bad."

"Well, yeah. It wasn't … *bad*."

The emphasis, the wavering on bad, had Zach curious enough to ask, "What happened next?"

"I was asked to leave."

"Leave. They kicked you out?"

"It was never actually spelled out on paper. Dad's people handled it." He could tell Zach was not going to stop asking. "There was an incident."

"An incident?"

"Jesus, you're going to have to let it go, Beauregard." Jason leaned in and spilled his scotch on Zach's chinos. "Shit. Sorry." He put the glass down to wipe off the liquid and then, without thinking, he went for Zach's lips. He had managed contact when Zach pushed him away.

"Whoa. Dude."

"Oopsie. My bad. The liquor takes over." Jason fell back against the arm of the couch and laughed. "I'm not *that* ugly, am I?"

"No. But you have a dick. I'm not into those."

"Why not?" He gave him a clever look as though to entice. "You ever tried?"

Zach wanted to get up, but Jason's legs had managed to toggle onto his lap and he felt pinned to the spot. "No."

"Then how do you know …?"

"Jason. Are you gay?"

"Me? No. Not really."

"What? You just tried to kiss me. I don't understand."

"To tell you the truth. Neither do I. I'm just always too horny for my own good. I'm like my mother that way." He thought for a second. "Maybe like my dad too …?"

"Are you saying your parents go both ways?"

"I don't think Father. No. But Mother …? Yeah. She's

munched on a few carpets. Now and again. That Natalie woman from last night. I'm sure she and my mom …"

"No! She seemed to be coming on pretty strong to Gary."

"Gay Gary?"

"Gay Gary." Zach laughed at the alliteration. "Yeah. How did you know he was gay?"

"Didn't you say so?"

"No. I don't think so," Zach answered, mulling the possibility.

Jason reached for the bottle, drank straight from it. "I do love my scotch." He took one foot, then the other, to kick off his shoes. With stockinged feet nestled on Zachary's lap, the compulsion to nudge the man's crotch came like lightning. Before he had time to consider any of his proclivities, Jason moved in on Zach and began to manhandle him. The Calgarian was stronger than he appeared. Muscles that came into action when he wanted, when liquor made him crave. There was a moment there when Jason was convinced he could make a conquest of Zach. That once their mouths could lock together, once saliva flowed freely and the heat between their bodies claimed some chemistry, that sparks would have Zach caving in. He had seen it happen dozens of times even if he had rued the days when it hadn't—on those occasions when his advances backfired.

Zach found himself lodged in Jason's arms and briefly weighed all the choices before him. He had never let any man get this far though he had defended against a number of flirtations. The taste of scotch on Jason's tongue, the smell of his aftershave, this whole Calgary tour was too much for the college grad. He shoved Jason away in one fell swoop. "Come on, dude. You're drunk." He got up and realized he had an erection. His disappointment was nothing compared to his confusion. He liked this Jason but was at sixes and sevens on what to do.

"You're absolutely right. Drunk. Lonely …" Jason jumped up and rushed towards the French doors that opened onto the expansive deck.

"What are you doing?" Zach asked and ran after him. He sprang to Jason's side as the man veered towards the edge of the parapet like a sail about to luff. "What the fuck!" Zachary held Jason by the waist and the man began to laugh before it turned into sobs. Oy, Zach thought, *what* did he have here?! With little recourse, he stayed by his side, grasping the mixed messages he, his body, and hands were giving. "Come on. I'm sure I'm not the first guy to reject you." The remark got them smiling.

"The handsomest … for damn sure."

"I'll take the compliment." Zach walked him back inside and closed the doors, which had no deadbolt. The coolness from the winds out on the deck combined with the residue of adrenaline had cleared the air; he felt safer. "Let's brew up some coffee."

He and Jason took the stairs and went to the kitchen. "Are you always this much of a mess?" They were at the counter sitting on stools.

"Maybe." Jason was craving scotch. He went to the cupboard and took out liqueur. "Want some?"

"You don't think you've had enough?"

Jason wavered but chose liquor in the end. "It helps me sleep," he said in a pitiful voice.

"And who's going to drive me back to the hotel? Are there cabs?"

"Are there cabs!" Jason laughed so hard, tears came out of him.

Zachary joined in, his Podunk remark laid bare. He took the liqueur and poured some into his own coffee.

"More like it." Jason clinked his cup with his. "You can crash here, you know."

"No, I'm not."

"I'll behave. Promise."

"Why don't I believe you?"

Jason gave him a saucy look. "I don't want to be alone."

The tenuousness of the phrase felt manipulative. "Don't do that," Zach said.

"Don't do what?"

"You're not going to lead me to believe you're going to hurt yourself."

"No. No!"

But Zachary couldn't be sure. Could he live with himself if misfortune ensued? "Is there a guest room?"

"Yes. There are two. But I have a king-size bed. I'll behave. Scout's honor." He did a finger gesture that did suggest the real deal.

"I was never in Boy Scouts," Zach confided. "You could just as easily have promised to fuck me just now. Some secret cowboy and Indian signal crap."

Jason giggled. He gulped down the rest of his coffee combo and got up. "I'll show you to your side of the bed."

TWENTY-FOUR

Bernie was standing at the end of the bed, partially hidden in the semidarkness, when Zachary awoke just past dawn. "Fuck," he blurted and accidentally banged his head against the headboard as he moved. The fright had his heart pumping. "Who …?" he muttered when the figure went toward the curtains and drew them open.

"Good morning, boys. Sorry," he said to Zachary. "I wasn't aware that my son was entertaining."

"Nothing happened," Zachary said, offended at the implication of carnal knowledge between him and Jason.

"I don't care if my boy sleeps with boys. Just as long as they're the *right* boys." Bernard Burnshaw was spry for his age. It showed in his step and the manner in his dress which was all bespoke. Even after an evening of philandering with a woman barely old enough to be his granddaughter, he held sway over the room. "Are you the right sort of boy?"

He held the pitch so that Zachary understood an introduction needed to be made. A glance at Jason proved useless, he was comatose. "I'm ... Zachary Beauregard."

"Beauregard? From?"

"From Beverly Hills. Originally from Louisiana. A few generations back."

"Louisiana Beauregards?" Bernie toyed with the idea of a connection. "I may have done business with some Beauregards from there. Years ago."

"Might be family. My grandfather's parents relocated to Santa Monica back in the thirties. Right before the war."

"A good war, that one," Bernie said, as if he had partaken in the fighting. He was still standing by the window when he looked appalled at his own progeny. "I hope your company pleased you."

"Umm ... Mr. Burnshaw. Nothing happened. I can assure you. I'm as straight as they come. I ... We ..."

"My son says that all the time." Bernie walked over to the door. "Got drunk, is that it?"

Zach could tell none of his protestations would bear fruit. "*He* did." The emphasis on the body next to him, blacked-out, was proof of that pudding. The change in the man's disposition from pleasant to disparaging made Zach get out of bed—proud that he had on his boxers and a T-shirt, that he wasn't naked.

"I have a busy day," said Jason's father. "Tell my son not to bother me. I'll be in the den. I don't want to be disturbed." The door was shut loudly enough to anger Zachary, as though he had been dismissed after committing a crime. He had done nothing but be obliging here. Helped the son, met the mother, and now he was being blamed for *what*! He jumped onto the bed and rolled Jason over.

"Wha …?"

"Your dad was just here."

"Yeah …?"

"He thought we fucked!"

"Did we?" Jason pulled the sheet away and Zach saw that he was naked.

"When did you take your clothes off? You had on boxers last night."

"You tell me." Jason was coming out of his torpid state. "Did I take out my contacts last night?" He blinked to fix his vision that was skewed.

"How would I know? I didn't watch you in the can."

Jason rolled his eyes to get a feel for what he had under his lids. "Shit." He stood, naked as a jaybird, and went to the ensuite.

Zach could hear him peeing. "So, did you take them out?"

Jason returned, still naked. "I think so. Yeah. But my vision's blurry."

"You might want to put on clothes."

"That won't fix my vision."

"No, but it might convince your dad we didn't screw."

"You worry too much. Anyone ever tell you that? My dad doesn't give a shit."

"Well, I do. I give a shit. I don't want him spreading rumors." Zach gave Jason an onerous scowl, like that might well be the outcome.

"No, Zach. My mother might dish to everybody in this

town if she found us in bed. My father? He couldn't care less."

"He did say that."

"What else did he say?"

Zach began to search for his clothes and saw them on the back of the chair at the desk. "He asked me if I was the 'right' sort of boy."

Jason laughed. He had pulled a robe from a hook at the back of the walk-in closet door and covered himself. "Sounds like Father. And what did you tell him?" Jason went to the window and opened it for fresh air. "*Are* you the right sort of boy for me?"

Zach was tired of the gay games. "I'm straight. I come from money. You decide." He had slipped into his socks, his pants, and shirt and was looking for his shoes. "Any idea where I left my shoes?"

"You're kidding, right?"

They went to the kitchen and saw the mess. "Did we eat?"

"Your dad. He must have made himself something. I need to go, Jason." He went to the foyer and found his shoes and put them on. "Can you call me a cab?"

"Dad's driver is downstairs. I'll call him."

"No. I don't want to be indebted to him. As it is, he's convinced we fucked. How will I ever fix that?"

"I have some suggestions."

"I bet you do."

Outside on the curb, waiting for his taxi, Zach had the weight of the world on his shoulders. When he arrived at the Palliser, he showered and ordered room service. He was eating his eggs and bacon, digesting all of the evening's antics, when Gary walked in with Jeremy and Lionel in tow.

"You had us worried," Jeremy said, like he might have been counseling one of his students.

"Why?"

"Where the hell were you all night?" Gary asked.

Zach had had enough drama for a lifetime. How many gays before you had a gaggle, he thought. "I was 'stuck' with Jason." The three men all looked perplexed. "You heard me. Stuck."

"How?" Jeremy was the first to pull up a chair next to the table. "Were you coerced?"

Zach flirted with the term in his head. "Yeah. Maybe. Maybe, yeah …" He swallowed the last of the bacon and took a bite of his toast. He spread a dollop of marmalade to finish the piece of bread. "*What* a family! They're nuts."

Gary and Lionel sat on the sofa like they were dating. "So … Tell us how it all went down."

Zach spent the next five minutes familiarizing them with much of the day and night's components.

"You could have been raped, Zach." Jeremy said it so severely, Zach felt a need to defend Jason.

"I really don't think so."

"You've heard of the apple not falling far from the tree, right?" asked Lionel, who generally kept his cards closer to the vest than most. "The Burnshaws … They have a reputation around town."

"I'm sure the father does. And the grandfather probably did too in his day. But Jason … I'm telling you, guys. He's just pretty messed up. Even if he'd wanted to rape me …" Zach had never perceived Gary in any feminine way, but the three men before him presented as a triad of nervous Nellies and he had to bite his tongue not to find them comical. "He couldn't have. That's all I'm going to say." In the synopsis of the evening, he had kept to himself that Jason had been naked next to him all night. Kept mum about the aggressive pass so that all the sexual material was turned into palatable psychobabble for his listeners. He reported to them that they had argued over politics. About sports. Painted Jason as a competitive alcoholic who had never successfully launched from his parents. If the LA scene had taught Zach anything, it was how to spin a yarn without much substance.

"So, do you think he'll want to invest?" Jeremy asked, wanting them to refocus on the prize.

"I think he will. I didn't go there very much. It was all just about getting acquainted. Laying the foundation. But he'll bite."

Something was amiss for Jeremy, an intuition from his days with Justin. "You're not leaving stuff out, are you?"

Zach was insulted more than worried. "What do you mean?" He saw Gary's defenses go up too.

"Yeah, Jeremy." Gary was feeling paternalistic towards Zach. "What gives?"

A moment of circumspection came over him. "I don't feel good about all of this. Maybe none of this is worth it."

"It's too late now," Gary proclaimed. "I didn't drive all the way up here ... We had a plan. It's going to work."

Lionel got up and poured himself a coffee. "It's not as if we're breaking any laws." There was no more cream, so he opted for sugar. "It's just to get access to the old man. Get him talking. See what he knows. For that to happen, there has to be some kind of business dealing. Money has to be exchanged, or close to being exchanged, so that he gets involved. Feels like there's some skin in the game for him and his son."

Zach felt sorry for Jeremy's father. In all of this convoluted business of theirs, *that* was the piece of the puzzle that fit the least for the young man. He had no ties with the beginning of this ancient imbroglio. What he had been told by his grandmother was just enough to bring him onboard.

"Your grandfather and I, Zach—we were fond of Rafael," she had confided with him back in LA. "He swept through our lives without our realizing how important he was. Gary wouldn't be asking if it didn't mean a lot. To all of us."

Zach could still see his bubbe's eyes that remarked on something special. Their personal history from long before he was born.

Gary stood. "Any more coffee in that pot?" Zach poured him the last of what remained into a travel cup he had next to the bed. "We're not doing too badly, Jeremy. We've met the son, the dad. The mother. And the mother's friend. I think Natalie can help us out."

"How?" Jeremy asked, not having met any of these people yet.

"She gave me her number. Told me to call."

"You're going to have to sleep with her," Zach warned. "She was all over you."

"I can handle the Natalies of the world. Especially if she wants to finance our project. That might persuade Jason. Even his mother? We'll get Bernie involved that way."

At the penthouse, Jason had gone back to bed to nurse his ego when his father marched in. "You didn't fuck him!"

Jason was roused out of his slumber. How he could *hate* his father's tantrums. He placed the pillow over his head.

Bernie pulled on Jason's shorts and pinched the skin by accident.

"Oww."

Bernie backed off but stayed by the side of the bed. "You had one task. Seduce him."

"He's straight. He doesn't bend that way."

"You make them bend."

Jason got up.

"Where are you going?"

"I have to pee. Do you mind?"

Bernie waited as his son finished and came back into the room. "What are the plans now?"

"We didn't make any."

"Did he ask for money?"

"No. He didn't ask for any money. He's loaded."

"That's what he told you?"

"Not in so many words. It's implied. He went to Groton. But you already knew all of that." The scion to the Burnshaw legacy slid into his jeans. "I think your sources are all wrong here." Jason tried to leave the room, but his father stopped him.

"You'll make a date. For tonight."

"I don't think that'll play. It's too soon."

"He can always refuse. What's he going to do? Hang around with that Jerome fella?"

The jitters gripped him. "He never mentioned anyone else but that guy, Gary, who's staying at the Palliser." Jason tried to move away again. "How do you know they haven't figured out that they're being tailed."

"People like that are dumb." Bernard's smirk was full of derision. "They're outfoxed before they even start."

Jason thought differently. Zach hung the moon; their night together had proved that. "I'll call. But don't hold your breath."

"Use the Burnshaw charm."

"Is that what we're calling it now?"

Bernard had a mind to smack his son. He hadn't in years, but his behavior was bordering on belligerent. "I know you'll do the right thing, Jason." The implication had everything to do with who paid the bills. Who kept whom in money and booze.

TWENTY-FIVE

Natalie had heard the door to the garage open, but her concentration was solely on the pills she was crushing in a ceramic pestle. "What are you doing here?" she asked.

"I *live* here?"

"Of course you do, darling." She sent an air kiss toward Jason, who paid no heed as he took a bottle of chardonnay from the refrigerator to pour himself a glass. "Your mom's upstairs resting." The euphemism for waiting for a fix was not lost on Jason. "Did you need anything, dear?" Jason toasted to her and gulped back the white wine. "A rough day?" She petted his cheek; he was so close.

"You and Mom made up pretty fast."

"Don't we always?"

"Who called who this time?"

"Does it matter? All that matters is that I'm here."

They accompanied each other up the stairs. "Why don't

you come in and give your mother a kiss?" They were at his bedroom door. "I'm sure she'd love that."

"I'm just picking up my lucky jeans and leaving. I'm in a crunch here."

"Your lucky jeans?" Natalie held the pestle with the powdered medications next to her chest; her smile intimating that she could guess who the jeans were for. "I love the sound of *that*. Is it …?"

"Don't, Natalie."

"Is that you, Jason?" Emily beckoned from her bedroom.

Jason and Natalie understood that the call of duty could not be ignored. "I can't stay long," he said, pleading for Natalie's cooperation.

The bedroom curtains were open but with no other light in the room, the air felt somber, as though the walls harbored more than a chronic addict. Emily, resting on the chaise longue, looked older than her years; the lines of fatigue and drug use unmasked without proper makeup. Jason approached for the obligatory kiss when his mother pulled him down to hug him. He lost his footing and fell beside her. "Why do you have to be *so* adorable?"

"I wish Dad felt the same." He rose and put himself together for a quick exit.

"What's he been up to now?" Emily sat up, wanting to show concern but more focused on the bowl in Natalie's hand. She signaled for the drugs.

"Nothing. Just Dad being Dad."

Natalie moved towards the chaise and deposited the pestle onto Emily's lap. The women were so pathetic, Jason thought. A sensible son would stay, fight the good fight, but those battles had been lost too often to matter much anymore.

"He doesn't approve of your date?" Coming from anyone but Natalie, the comment might have been boorish.

"I don't have a date."

"Your lucky jeans …?" Natalie teased. "Come on, Jason. Give us something to gossip about."

His mother's attention had not left the drugs and Jason knew, categorically, that she and Natalie wanted to snort. He could almost taste the high himself. "It's not a date. It's Dad's bidding. I'm on his payroll, last time I checked."

Emily put the muller down and stood, walked straight to her son by the door. "What's he plotting now?"

"Nothing. Nothing at all," Jason said, aware of how disastrous it would be if Bernie's intel was exposed.

"Does he know about that Gary and his movie business?" Natalie had taken out a silver straw from some pocket.

"Gary?" Emily asked.

"He's with that lovely boy you met the other night at dinner at the Palliser. I told you I wanted to invest …?" Emily's confusion was visible. "I thought Gary absolutely divine. Now that's a man …"

"He's gay, in case you didn't notice," Jason said, as if to dissuade her of any intentions on her part.

"*That's* why I shouldn't invest?" She giggled with mild tsking.

"No …" Jason felt rattled. "Did Gary talk to you about investing?"

"This is Calgary. I know when venture capital is on the table, Jason." Natalie sat down on the ottoman by the chaise.

Her impatience could be substantial at times, even when she didn't want to tip her hand. She recovered by saying, "Besides, everyone's a little gay sometime, Jason, right?"

Another allusion that was not lost on him. How much sex *did* these women have together? He was at a loss with that entire enterprise. "Not Bernard Burnshaw," he stated.

"Don't be so sure of that," Emily said in a murmur that made the women laugh. He thought he heard his father's private investigator's name, Gustav, spoken under her breath as she went to Natalie's side. The ladies each did a line from the stone bowl like Jason was no more than a ghost.

"What's that boy's name again? The one with Gary?" Natalie was contorting her nostrils so that she wouldn't sneeze away any remains of the bump.

"Zachary," Jason said. "Why?"

"I've loved that name ever since …" Her thoughts wandered as the buzz took over, leaving Jason with a wide-open field to make his departure.

The swim was refreshing after their late tennis match. "You have to excel at everything, don't you, Beauregard?" They had raced ten laps in the twenty-five-meter pool with Zach winning by just under a length. Yesterday's win at racquetball—just a memory for Jason.

"I'm competitive," the American admitted, out of breath.

"I am too," Jason replied, splashing his opponent in the face. "I'm famished."

In the showers, Zach didn't care anymore. He walked naked, knowing the score, disregarding or more to the point: he had taken measure of Jason's character and found a trustworthy adversary. All of the gay men's counsel did not fit with who he was hanging out. He had decided to play their game but give Jason an out at every turn if he could.

They were dressed, on their way to the SUV. "I should never have taken sleeping pills last night." They got into his Jeep Wrangler.

"Is that why you were so out of it? I thought the booze put you to sleep."

Jason backed out of their parking spot. "The booze helps but …"

"But …? What?" Zach's ambivalence carried over the long silence.

They were entering the elevator when Jason answered with, "Don't you ever take pills?"

"Prescription?"

"Yeah. Or otherwise."

"I have. I don't make a habit of it."

"No oxycontin?" Zach shook his head. "Adderall?"

"No. That's similar to Ritalin, right?"

"Yeah. Don't you do any drugs?"

"Of course. Lots of pot in high school. Did acid on occasion my first year at Stanford."

"No molly?"

"No," he said, thinking of his grandfather, how he had frowned on abusing the body he proclaimed as a temple. "Why?" They were back inside the penthouse, and Zach's nerves were fraught. "You're positive that your dad's going to be out?"

"He was royally pissed off at me today. He won't be back tonight. He's probably at some high-stakes poker game."

"We should have gone to your mother's." They were in the kitchen setting up plates and cutlery. "I'm not sure I'm comfortable here."

Jason took the takeout food from a pub and put the spread out on the table. "You saw her the other night. Between my dad this morning and her?" He did a balancing teeter-totter gesture.

"Your dad's pretty scary."

"You think?"

As the meal progressed, Zach commenced his pitch about setting up a studio and a film production company in town. "Could you see that happening up here?"

"Yeah. Canada's always looking to bring capital and talent from the States. The government has all these tax deals. That includes Alberta."

"Your dad, would he ever think of investing?" Zach could hear the premeditation in his spiel. "That came out wrong. I'm not hustling you."

"Hustle me. I don't care."

"Really?"

"People must hustle you to get to your grandmother all the time. No?"

"Yeah, that's true. The minute anyone finds out who my people are."

"People?"

"You know. My peeps."

Jason rose and went for a bottle of champagne stored on the upper level. He popped it open and poured the bubbly into flutes he had set on the table.

"Are we celebrating something?"

"Yeah." Jason produced two pills and swallowed one. "Here. To happy times."

"What is it?"

"Molly. Come on. We're celebrating you setting up shop up here."

"Whoa. First of all. It's my grandmother's business."

"Why isn't she up here herself?"

The question made Zach apprehensive, like Jason was on to him. To them. To their scheme. "She ... Because I'm a sucker for my bubbe." Without much thought behind it, he reached for the ecstasy and swallowed it.

"Bubbe?" Jason asked.

"That's Yiddish for grandmother. You never heard that word?"

"Yeah. I must have."

They drank the champagne over the next hour as they meandered about the place. "That's the man who made it all happen," Jason commented. The family tree tour had taken them from room to room at framed documents and photos.

"The Senator?"

"No. The Senator inherited all of *this* guy's wealth. Great-grandad, Chester Burnshaw."

"And the Senator didn't squander it?"

"Apparently, Clinton was a real wheeler-dealer. Mostly broke the law through government patronage."

"Doesn't sound kosher."

"The stories I've heard!"

"I'm all ears." Zach could not believe his luck. The ecstasy was like a truth serum, with everything being served to him on a plate.

"He had quite the reputation. Scary, from what I could tell."

They had been sitting out on the deck, enjoying the expanse of the night sky. Chilly though it was, the stars in the firmament along with the molly, mixed with the music coming from the billiards room in the background, made for a potent blend.

"Scary as in …?"

"He was into revenge. Natalie once told me a story she'd heard when she was a teen. They were at some country club function. Someone made a dig at our family's expense. And one of the men mentioned the Senator. Used the title as a verb, as in 'being Senatored.' What the hell kind of threat was that …! She said everyone went very quiet." Jason refilled his glass. "He didn't take kindly to people telling him no, I guess. Not the finest heritage, right?"

"Sounds like every Hollywood producer."

"Your grandmother?"

"She's tough, but not like that." Zach swilled the last of his champagne then twirled with his arms out like they could have been wings fastened to his body. "Wow, this feels *awe-some*."

"My dad takes after the Senator, I'm afraid."

The statement halted Zach almost on the spot. "He did seem to have that kind of an edge this morning. Must be tough for you."

"Sometimes." Jason stood. Without any effort, he put his palms on the back of Zach's shoulders and began to massage him. He kneaded the muscles, the trapezius then the deltoids, and waited for Zach to put a stop to his advances. When that didn't happen, Jason gently pivoted them into the billiards room as though their bodies had been attached. "I give great shiatsu."

"Never heard that one before." Zach's giggling became

contagious and Jason pulled him with him, down the stairs. In Jason's bedroom, Zach let himself get undressed to his boxers. "You're going to behave, right?"

"Scout's honor."

Bernie and Gustav, his PI, were in the securities firm on the first floor of his building. The hidden camera in his son's bedroom showed a clear view. "Jesus. Finally! I never thought we'd get this."

Gustav averted his gaze. He had been around Jason since the boy had played junior hockey with his son. The gay sex didn't bother him, but using Jason as honeypot for this footage did. "You going to interrupt this?"

"I haven't decided. If I go up now …" He looked at Gustav Larsen, less for his opinion than for gut instincts. "Which will work best? Interrupt now, or wait until after the fact. What do you think?"

"Do you really want Jason pulled into a rape case? Go up there now and scare the boy. That should do the trick."

What would Clinton do? Bernie was set on *some* type of payback, but no one had played all their cards yet to be certain of victory.

"You're going to run out of time here, sir. It's now … Later might make you lose everything."

Bernie went upstairs and marched into the bedroom as Zach was fucking Jason hard. He turned on the lights. Zach was disoriented momentarily—a hallucination he thought that came from the drug. All of his senses were heightened so he couldn't cease what he was doing. He orgasmed and fell onto Jason's back elated by his prowess.

"What are you doing?" Bernie yelled. He went to the side of the bed. "I heard screaming. Have you hurt my boy?"

Zach was so stoned; he was trying to make sense of the negative energy coming his way. All he owned was this comforting love that exuded from all of his pores. An experience he had never had before. He nudged Jason and said, "Your dad." Jason, who was out cold, did not respond. Zach nudged him again, stronger this time. "Jason. It's your father. You need to wake up."

"Did you drug him?" Bernie demanded. He pulled Zach who fell to the side of the bed, naked, his dick messy with bodily fluids.

"No. We both did drugs." He went to Jason who was unconscious. "Is something wrong here? I can't figure out what's happening."

"I'm calling the police."

"What?! No. Don't call the police. Maybe he needs coffee. Splash some water on him." Zachary, panic-stricken, ran to the ensuite and took a glass, filled it with water and came back in. He threw it over Jason's face, wetting Bernie's trousers in the process. "What's going on here?"

"It's obvious. You took advantage of my son."

"I need to call my friends."

"You'll do no such thing." Bernie strode up to him and insisted to his face, "What drugs did you take?"

"I ... We did molly. We drank champagne. He gave me a massage and then ..." Zachary only recalled foreplay. Jason liking what they did. He could have sworn Jason had asked to be taken. Bareback. His host had *said* the word *bareback*, hadn't he? But that would have sounded so guilty, Zach thought, stating it aloud for Bernie's consumption.

"Why are you awake and my son is out cold?"

"Jason takes sleeping pills. Maybe he took one before." He remembered Jason going to the bathroom now. "He took sleeping pills."

"How do you know that? Did you see him?"

"Yes," he lied. "I remember now." Zach saw his clothes on the floor and went for them.

"What do you think you're doing?"

"I'm getting dressed. I'm going home. I mean. To my hotel."

"No, you're not. Don't touch those clothes. They're evidence."

Zach froze midway, naked and confused.

"You're not leaving until Jason wakes up. For all I know you'll leave the country. I've met you Hollywood types before." He reached for a bathrobe and tossed it at Zach's feet.

A knock at the door scared Zach to his core. Gustav Larsen walked in. "Sir. I need to get going." He faked surveying the room like it was all new to him. "Everything all right here?"

"No, Gus," Bernie said, giving Zach a menacing stare. "This young rascal took advantage of Jason."

Gustav stepped towards Zach who flinched, convinced he was getting a beating. "Is that right?"

"No. Nothing could be further from the truth." Zach heard his voice come out as bombastic. Did molly give you that kind of freedom? To take on a whole different posture?

"Do you want to look at the security footage, sir?"

"What?" Zach was flabbergasted.

"That can wait till the morning. Can you call Dr. Savage?

Have him come over right away. We need some medical assistance. Get his opinion before we call the police."

"I can't stay out all night again. My friends will be worried."

Bernie nodded to Gustav.

"Come with me," said the PI. "You can use the phone in the office." Gustav escorted Zach out of the room.

TWENTY-SIX

The gay caucus at the Palliser Hotel was in full swing when the telephone rang. "Where are you?" Gary asked. When he heard Zach's story, he said, "Put that man on the phone." He cupped his hand over the microphone. "Shush," he told Jeremy and Lionel who were arguing. He waited for Bernie to finish. "If you want me to call the police, I will. You can't keep my nephew prisoner. This is Canada. Not Russia."

"Mr. Silverman, you don't want to be using that tone."

Had Zach told them his last name? "How do you know my name?"

"I know all there is to know about you. Your 'nephew' is in a lot of trouble."

The man was as formidable as Gary had expected. "Zach has done nothing wrong."

"I have footage that might discredit your claim."

The mention of footage turned everything upside down.

He listened as Burnshaw elucidated. When Gary asked, "As soon as Jason awakes?" the man assured him of his intention to release Zach, and, after a few more exchanges, he hung up.

"What's going on?" Jeremy's face had blanched at the prospect of a legal conflict.

"We've been played." Gary was in a tizzy as he relayed the particulars.

"I should have realized the Burnshaws would do this," Lionel said. "It's all my fault." Jeremy and Gary waited to be enlightened. "It was too good to be true." The man sat down on a side chair. He had been so sure of himself before, like he might have been on the same social strata as the Burnshaws. "I hadn't wanted to tell you this."

"Oh, Lionel," Jeremy was feeling nauseous, much like the night Gary had told him what had happened to his father. What was it that his aunt Thérèse had told him back in Ottawa? The Dussaults might not have been the most reliable of families. "What have you been hiding?"

"Not hiding. Just didn't think it was necessary to tell."

"Well, goddamn it, Lionel. Spill the beans. Now!" Gary was angrier than Jeremy had ever seen.

"Back in the mid-forties, my dad made a bit of a killing on some land deal." Lionel could still see his father from that day. He had come into the house smoking an expensive cigar—not an everyday occurrence. "I was in high school. The war had just ended, and everybody was going wild here. Land was being swept up for oil speculation." The image of his father drunk, picking up his mother into his arms was quite vivid. "My dad couldn't care less about oil. Hated all of that. He was a farmer to his bones."

"He didn't want to get rich?"

"He was pretty well-off farming by then. And cattle prices were picking up again."

"What's this got to do with Burnshaw?" Jeremy's focus was on his father's fate.

"The Senator had lost to dad."

"How?"

"It's still unclear … even to this day. I suppose Dad did something sneaky, used a connection he shouldn't have. How else to get one over on the Senator, right?"

"Are you saying my dad was set up by your brother *and* your father?"

"I didn't say that! If it was revenge on the Senator's part, Dad sure didn't know. Why do you think I went along with all of this, Jeremy? I've been wanting to find out my whole life. Ever since Rafael disappeared from our lives back in '49 … there was this cloud."

Jeremy had heard enough. A premonition from that first night when Lionel had taken out the albums—the clippings from as early as 1949—had been a clue he had purposely untethered. He went to the phone. "What are you doing?" Gary asked. Jeremy gave him the phone. "You need to call your friend."

"Who? Judy?"

"Yes. She needs to come up here. We can't outsmart the devil. You heard Lionel. The Senator preyed on my dad to get back at his father. We're in way over our heads."

"I didn't say that, Jeremy." Lionel stood up, caught between loyalties, and went to where the others were standing.

"He's framing Zach for rape," Jeremy iterated. "You think that man is bluffing? You think this will just go away? They're like assassins. They probably have a body count."

"He's not going to let his son get involved in some made-up scandal. Just to hurt …" Gary stopped. How had they gone from a sure thing to who was doing what to whom? For which crimes? "I'll call. But you all need to bring this down a notch. I can handle this Bernard Burnshaw motherfucker." He dialed, not thinking of the hour.

"This is pretty late," Judy said at the other end of the line. "I'm not a night owl anymore."

"It's two in the morning," Gary said. "You'll live."

The private jet landed flawlessly at the neighborhood airport just west of Calgary. Judy walked over to Gary who was standing by the Rolls. "You look beat," she told him.

"I am beat." They hugged. "Did you sleep on the plane?"

"Like a baby on Valium."

"Jeremy, Lionel. This is Zach's grandmama, Judy."

The four drove into downtown Calgary towards the penthouse address. "I can't believe they're holding Zach there. Is that even legal?"

"This is Calgary." Lionel had learned over the years that depending on law enforcement to do the right thing in that town could backfire. "The Burnshaws run this town. They'll make it legal, and it'll stick."

"You make it sound like this is the Wild West."

Lionel took his cowboy hat from his lap and tipped it against his forehead. "You should be here for the Stampede. Just think Deep South but with cowboy boots. You'll get the idea."

At the door on the street, Gustav was waiting for them. "I'm afraid, Mr. Burnshaw will insist on my patting you down. There are no ... weapons allowed in the penthouse."

"For Christ's sakes," Jeremy said.

"We're civilized," Gary began, then recalled how many guns shot people dead in the United States every day. "Fine. Frisk us all you want."

The foursome was allowed into the private vestibule and Gustav did his thorough search. "I'm sure you'll understand. Under the circumstances."

"I don't," Judy said. "But don't be fooled by civility. We have high-priced lawyers the same as Burnshaw."

Gustav acknowledged with a nod and took them up in the elevator.

On the landing, Jeremy saw a second security camera. How could Zach not have spotted the fortress-like atmosphere? His uneasiness made him veer sideways on purpose, damned if his likeness would be captured that easily. Inside the apartment, they were greeted by the blare of a video game in a far-off room.

"Where's my grandson? I demand to see him immediately."

Gustav escorted them down the hall into Bernie's office. The ostentatious wood paneling and the dark décor were reminiscent of the old guard Judy had fought against in Hollywood in her hotshot producer days. It fueled her ire.

Bernie, seated behind his desk, pointed to the chairs in front of the oak veneer. "Had a good flight?"

"I want to see my grandson. Now." She took a beat before adding, "Please."

"You'll see him. He's upstairs with Jason."

"They're still friends?" Gary asked, incapable of comprehending how all of this was going down.

"They're young. And very stupid."

"My grandson just graduated summa cum laude. From Stanford. He's no dummy."

Bernie pushed a button and a panel went up to show a screen. He clicked on the video footage of Zach screwing Jason. The camera zoomed into a close-up of Jason, who appeared unconscious; only the grunts of Zach, huffing and puffing, hell-bent and concentrated on coming, could be heard. He seemed in a trance, unaware or uncaring of his partner. The takeaway for the viewers was no better than a sullied waywardness, one that Judy couldn't abide.

"Turn that off," she commanded in a voice she had often used with studio executives who were trying to destroy her project of the day. She was not about to be sidelined here.

"Is that what they're teaching kids at university these days?" Bernie quipped.

"What does this prove?" Gary asked. "Your son's a delinquent. His reputation is mud."

"Says who?" Bernie asked as casually as if they were discussing lunch items on a menu.

"What's your game?" Judy asked. She was tired of men running the world.

"I might ask you the same. Mr. Jerome. Mr. Silverman. Mr. *Dussault*." There, he had placed his cards for all to see.

Lionel was the only one not devastated by the reveal. "You son of a bitch," he said.

Bernie tisk-tisked at the slur. "Still upset over land deals?"

"Upset? My daddy whooped your daddy's ass." Lionel

had a notion to get up but Gustav's presence at the door—gun in holster, was all the inducement he needed to stay put.

"You know how family folklore tends to get embroidered." Bernie had a glass of water next to him and he sipped it. "Your daddy was a patsy. Played into the Senator's hands."

Lionel would have none of it. He glanced at Jeremy who was trying to figure everything out. "Don't let him do this, Jeremy. This is how the Burnshaws always win. They twist things ... Play people against people."

Jeremy stood and Gustav stepped towards him when Bernie put his hand up. "That's okay. Everybody's free to move around. This isn't jail. Nobody's doing time here. Yet."

Jeremy gazed around, did a three-hundred-and-sixty-degree turn, imagining the number of security cameras throughout the penthouse. "How many?"

"What?" Gary asked, as though Jeremy had addressed him.

"Cameras. How many in this room?" He stared at Bernie for his showdown.

"Does it matter? Yes, you're all being recorded, if that makes any difference."

"So, you know then that Zach didn't rape your son."

"I know no such thing."

"Of course, you do." Jeremy approached the leather-top desk. "You know because we all know that Zach is straight. What happened on the film you just showed was contrived. I'm not saying Zach didn't fuck Jason. I don't think your technology is *that* advanced. But Jason won't admit to being raped by Zach."

"He won't?"

"No. Jason's a decent guy. He likes Zach."

"And you know that how?"

"Zach told us." Jeremy was feeling so much relief he wanted to scream and shout it out. "He's not like you. Not like the Senator at all."

"And what could *you* possibly know about him …?" Bernie asked, aware that he had lost the reins.

"You set this up. If you know my last name, then I suspect you know something about my dad."

"Your dad?"

"Rafael Jerome." Speaking the name aloud in front of the Senator's son had the freeing effect Jeremy had anticipated. "Never heard the name?"

Bernie pressed a button and the wooden panel closed silently so that the monitor disappeared. "Never heard it."

"Really? Never a whisper? An eighteen-year-old boy being raped out in a field? A shame your security system wasn't up in those days. Dad could have used that evidence."

"Are you insinuating that my father, Senator Clinton …"

"Your father was a rapist. He fucked my dad in a dark, lonely field back in '49 and left him there to rot."

Bernie gestured for Gustav to open the door. "Get your grandson and get out of here," Bernie yelled. The first sign of the man out of control.

"See how it feels?" Jeremy pushed to belabor the tragedy. "I think the boys need to be brought in here. Now. They need to hear all of this. They need to know how their journey really began."

"Gus," Bernie persevered. "Show these people to the door."

"I want to see my grandson. I'm not leaving this room …"

"Get the goddamn boy, Gus." Bernie demanded.

Gustav left and was in the hallway when the commotion caught all of them off-guard. Lionel was the first to get to the door when Zach ran in. He saw Judy and hugged her. "Bubbe, what are you doing here?"

"How else were you going to be rescued?"

"Rescued?" Zach saw how everyone was standing. He was about to speak when he heard Jason scream his name at the top of his lungs. The group ran and reached the stairs in the living room when they saw Gustav holding Jason captive. "What's going on?" Zach asked.

"They want me to say you raped me. They're going to make you pay …"

"Shut up," Bernie went to his son. "Take him upstairs."

Gustav had Jason by the crook of the elbow when Zach stopped them cold. "Maybe I did rape you."

"Honey," Judy said, "you don't mean that." She approached and tried to hold his arm when Zach pulled away.

"I was stoned. He was practically comatose."

"You didn't rape me," Jason whimpered. "He …" Jason said, indicating his father. "He set it all up." Jason's crying was turning into a pitiful moan. "Tell them. You prick."

"Shut up." Bernie came to hit Jason when Gustav intervened. The two men—employer, employee—vied for control, when Bernie gave in. "I'll have none of this." He pointed deliberately at Jason. "You're no son of mine."

He started up the stairs when Jeremy yelled, "Bernie. What is it about rape and the Burnshaws?" All eyes went to the elderly man who never looked back, continued up the stairs. A long silence ensued. "Come on, Jason. You can come with us. It's okay," Jeremy said. Jason glanced at Zach who shrugged. The newly assembled posse walked out the front door.

TWENTY-SEVEN

They had settled at Lionel's for dinner. Judy had Suzie on a leash and Rex and Troubadour were loose, running beside Jeremy as they walked along the open field down from the farmhouse.

"You seemed so sure of yourself back at the penthouse," Judy said. Suzie was determined to dig up something by a large boulder, and Judy was fighting to gain some control of the bulky animal.

"You want me to take her?"

Judy complied willingly. "She *is* a handful." She rubbed her arm where the muscle had tensed over. "You don't really know my grandson …"

"I feel like I do. Strange, huh?"

"Strange indeed." The footpath they were on stretched as far as the human eye could see. "How far does this trail go?" she asked.

"I did a few miles early on in my stay up here. I gave up when I got to this outcrop." He checked to see what hour it was. "We should head back. Food's being served at seven."

They turned around. "Do you think we can trust this Jason …?" She had almost placed the name in quotations as though he represented the *other*. The enemy. The crossing of a forbidden line in the sand. The puzzled expression from Jeremy made her clarify. "What are we going to do with him? He's a grown man. He's not a boy." What she was actually saying was: He was a Burnshaw. Why associate with the enemy?

"We'll figure it out. His mother will be there for him financially," though uttering that held no reassurance for Jeremy, given all that he had heard of Emily Clark. The broader question, what Judy had initially asked, had still not been attended to and Jeremy continued. "It's something Zach said the other morning. That he trusted Jason."

Judy could not fathom this compromise. "And that's enough for you?"

"You're his grandma. I'd think that that would be …"

"You don't understand." Judy turned and her face was eclipsed by the western sun, orange and red, brightly illuminating the landscape around them. "Zach is … related to you."

Rex and Troubadour, even Suzie, picked up on Jeremy's dismay. Dog and man appeared entranced as though waiting for the other shoe to drop. "What are you saying …?"

After supper, when all of the arguing over how best to discover more pertinent information on the Dussault and Burnshaw families had been exhausted, Judy signaled for Zach to come with her. Inside the upstairs room where Jeremy had stayed upon arriving at Lionel's the month before, Judy sat her grandson down.

"I know what you're going say."

Judy was taken aback. "I don't think so ... but shoot."

"I'm not gay. Honest. That video ..."

"Oh honey. I know you're not gay." She got teary-eyed; she felt so much love for her grandson's innocence in that flicker of a moment, before she would have to destroy so much of what he held dear to him. "I wish Jethro were here." Zach misunderstood and tried to interject with his own commiseration when she interrupted him. "The reason I'd like him to be here, Zach ..." She wanted to find words that did not exist. The untangling of life's quirky mysteries that were, in the end, inconsolable when confronted with the truth. "Your great-grandfather Mosley." Zach gave her a blank look. "Your dad's talked about Mervyn, right?" Zach nodded. "What did he say?"

"Not much. I can't recall. He was a big Hollywood *macher*."

"That he was. He was also a *momzer*."

"Ouch." Zach had never heard the man referred to that way. "Like a typical Hollywood bastard?"

"*And* some."

Judy had never contemplated divulging the nitty-gritty aspects of her background but there was a time for everything, and now was her point of no return. "In the old days," she heard her say it and laughed. As if! Old days. Modern days. What men did to women never changed. "Your grandfather used me."

"Used you? What do you mean?" Zach's stomach was in knots.

"He didn't sell me. Not exactly."

"Bubbe," Zach started to stand up.

"You'll need to sit for this. We'll both need to be sitting for this." Her wine was almost gone, and she wished she had brought a bottle upstairs. "When I was about fourteen … I developed young. You've seen pictures." He had. "Dad wasn't about to put me in the movies. Not that I ever wanted that. I never did. But he knew how much the guys at the studios loved to ogle me." Judy's entire sense of self was on display as she proceeded, holding on to what she grasped was a long life of self-imposed bravado. A front to survive. "He'd bring me to the lot. I'd sit around and watch them rehearsing and shooting. Now, *that*, I enjoyed. I was fascinated by the mechanics. How scenes were set up. The camera and the lighting. The sound guys. The way producers pushed people around." She was playing for time. Hated that she knew the end of her story and that Zach didn't as yet. "He'd let me walk around. Let me go off and do my own thing."

"Did something bad happen, Bubbe?"

Something bad! she thought. How did being promiscuous by design meet that criterion? "I had no supervision. Imagine, me, at fourteen, on a film set with wolves all around. I was pretty. I was the daughter of a bigshot producer. It was Hollywood. That's how I lost my virginity."

"Shit. Bubbe."

"I thought I was special. Knew all the ropes. I drank booze. I let men fall in love with me. I thought I was in total control."

Zachary's vision of his indomitable grandmother was being revised even as he sat there in silence.

"Fast-forward to 1949."

"1949? Isn't that the year you were married?"

"Good memory. You get points for that." She saw Zach pleased with himself. If only it were *that* simple. "It's also the year I got pregnant." She could see Zach doing the math. "You must have heard that I had to get married, right?"

Zach wavered, thinking he might have heard that at some point. "Maybe, yeah."

"I've been building up to this. I wanted you to understand how all of this came about."

"All of what?"

She could tell Zach's uneasiness coming to the forefront. "When I met Rafael …"

"Jeremy's dad?"

"Yes. It was August of 1949. I'd known Jethro a bit. Here and there at school. He was dating another girl who he was madly in love with. A Charlene Bennett. She was very pretty. A year younger than all of us. Very bright, she'd skipped a grade. Maybe that was why everything kind of went the way it did …"

"What do you mean?"

"We've told you how Rafael showed up. In Santa Monica?"

"Yeah, yeah," he said, wanting her to hurry, get to the point. "What about Rafael?"

"The last night he was in town. We had a party in a bungalow at the Miramar."

"At the Miramar?"

"Yeah. Back then it was quite swanky. Gary had rented a bungalow for our party." She could still see the bedspread pattern on the bed. The asparagus green of the curtains with the pearl lame thread design of vine leaves that went with the throw pillows. "The evening took a turn at some point. Too much booze, too many … secrets."

"What do you mean, secrets?"

Judy's face was flush, like a hot flash that couldn't be, these many years after menopause. "I want you to remember, Zach. We were eighteen. We had *no* clue about real consequences." She recalled the brief conversation with Jethro about getting an abortion. He had asked her if that was what she wanted. Her saying, "No, not really"—had she intuited *then* who the father of the child was?

Zach stood up and moved to the set of drawers. For no apparent reason, he opened and closed a few. He was agitated and wanted to leave. "I don't think I need to hear this stuff, Grandma." He used the moniker she hated and felt bad for being mean-spirited.

"Zach." Could he sense where this was going? She thought not. "If Jethro was here …"

"Why do you keep saying his name like that? Why aren't you calling him Grandpa …?"

He knew. All that was left was her saying it. "Because, honey. Jethro wasn't your grandpa."

Their tears began simultaneously. Admitting what would have been inconceivable months, days before, was as apocalyptic as the calamity she had endured in early September of '49 when her period hadn't come. The hero of the day had surely been Jethro.

Judy and Zach closed in and hugged each other. "Jethro *so* loved you. You were like a son to him, truly." In saying that, both grasped that his dad, Benjamin, had been betrayed, rejected possibly for the sins of the mother. Though, truth be told, Judy knew that Jethro blamed himself for everything. The contrivances of societal norms that had deceived everyone that long ago night. "I saw something broken in Rafael. It's what attracted me. I felt safe with him. It was a mitzvah that he fathered your dad, who fathered you. That's how I've always thought of it."

By the time they came downstairs to join the others, Jeremy had done Judy's bidding.

"How did you …?" Gary asked over the cheesecake Lionel had baked. They were at the kitchen table. "I mean when? When did you know for certain?"

"You won't believe this." All forks went down. "When you showed me pictures of Jeremy when you got back from Paris last summer. That shot of him in the church."

"In Notre Dame?"

"Yeah. I saw Benjamin in that face. A younger Bennie."

"Really?" Gary asked.

Zach studied Jeremy to see where the similarities might lie between him and his dad. "I don't see it." But as he spoke, the angularity and the position of the eyes, even the aquiline nose—less pronounced in Jeremy, began to gel. "Yeah …"

"It's not like I didn't always suspect."

"Did Jethro?"

"I think so. A part of him did. Maybe not at first."

"And you never spoke about it?" Jeremy asked.

"Never."

PART IV

SANTA BARBARA, WINTER 1998

TWENTY-EIGHT

Santa Barbara in December sparkled, weather patterns for the holidays that had sunny skies and no rain in the forecast. Zach and Jason walked into La Maison after an afternoon of surfing. "So, how were the waves?" Gary asked.

"The waves were solid."

"Did Jeremy manage to stay on his board?"

Jason made a more-or-less gesture with his hand.

"Come on, Jason," said Zach. "For a man his age, I think he did quite well."

"A man *his* age?" Gary was transferring a piece of brass to a better location. He carried it cautiously, cognizant of how easily he could throw out his back. "Shit, how do you refer to me when I'm not there?"

"As a youthful, distinguished gentleman," Zach sang back.

Gary came by and squeezed his suntanned cheek. "You can charm the pants off of me anytime." He caught Jason's grin and worried at this blossoming friendship before him. He had seen it before, long ago, through his own myopic view of life. The lamentation of unrequited love for Rafael that lived, to this day, in a corner of his heart.

"Don't fool yourself," he had told Jason when the transplanted Canadian had been accepted to UC Santa Barbara for the winter quarter. Gary had brought him a housewarming gift to the downtown condo his mother had purchased for him, mere blocks from his antique shop. "Zach is absolutely straight. He's never going to have sex with you again. Not even if you give him molly."

"I know. I get that."

But did he, Gary wondered. The albatross of the boy's family dynamics stated otherwise. "Do you even talk about it?"

"We did."

Gary doubted the veracity of his statement.

"Once. Okay?"

"And what did Zach say?"

"Just what you said. It's never going to happen again. But … he didn't say he didn't like it."

"Oh God, Jason. You need to move on."

"I am. I'm here, aren't I? I'm doing it right this time. I'm going to get my degree. Get my life in order. I'm drinking a lot less. You'll see. You'll be proud of me."

Gary had sworn an oath to be there for the boy whose grandfather had raped the man he had admired both from close and afar. The man who had sparked a vision for himself in the world, without ever laying claim to it. The catalyst that would forever remain at a juncture.

That evening, on the beach, after a quiet dinner without the boys, Gary and Jeremy strolled along at low tide, the rock formations rediscovered after being systematically underwater.

"Why do any of these things occur," Gary answered. They had been discussing rape. Ostensibly about Rafael, but Zach and Jason were on the periphery.

"For a reason, no?" Jeremy was thinking of his father, walking with Gary on a Malibu beach back in August of 1949 processing the exact same thing. Half a century of *what*? he thought.

"No. All happenstance," Gary declared. "A clusterfuck made of millions of uncontrollable atoms. You were in Paris searching for answers. *Thinking* you were running away from them. But you were seeking. No doubt about it. I was there because I've never recovered from my childhood loss of wonder from my brother's death at sea. Wanting to take photographs of Notre Dame as if *that* would do it."

"Not a bad substitute." The gurgle of the tide told them the shift was coming. "Weren't we standing at kilometer zero when we met in Paris?" Jeremy asked.

"We were."

"There's meaning in that."

ABOUT THE AUTHOR

Tobias Maxwell is the author of four novels, *2165 Hillside*, *The Month After September*, *The Sex and Dope Show Saga*, and *Thomas*; a novella, *And Baby Makes Two*; four memoirs, *Naked Ink, Diary of a Smalltown Boy*, Vols. 1 and 2, *1973—Early Applause*, *1977—The Year of Leaving Monsieur*, and *1983—The Unknown Season*; as well as a poetry collection, *Homogium*. You can find more by visiting his website and blog at:

www.tobiasmaxwell.com
bymax7@wordpress.com

ABOUT THE ILLUSTRATOR

Toronto-born Johnny Wales is an illustrator, animator, wood carver and Japanese puppeteer. He has illustrated seven children's books including: *The Toronto Story*, *Chung Lee Loves Lobsters* (winner of The Lucy Maud Montgomery Award) and *Gruntle Piggle Takes Off* (shortlisted for the 1996 Governor General's Award for children's illustration, and selected for the VII Premi International Catalonia D'Illustracio). He has published illustrations of Tokyo with Japanese commentary in the world's largest circulation newspaper *The Yomiuri Shimbun* once a week since 1996. He lives in an old farmhouse on Sado Island, Japan with his translator/craftswoman wife Chieko and their lovely dog Kyla.

www.johnny-wales.com